Lost Ohio

Lost Ohio

More Travels into
Haunted Landscapes,
Ghost Towns,
and Forgotten Lives

Randy McNutt

The Kent State University Press · Kent, Ohio

© 2006 by The Kent State University Press, Kent, Ohio 44242
ALL RIGHTS RESERVED
Library of Congress Catalog Card Number 2006000385
ISBN-10: 0-87338-872-0
ISBN-13: 978-0-87338-872-6
Manufactured in the United States of America

10 09 08 07 06   5 4 3 2 1

LIBRARY OF CONGRESS CATALOGING-IN-PUBLICATION DATA
McNutt, Randy.
    Lost Ohio : more travels into haunted landscapes, ghost towns, and forgotten
lives / Randy McNutt.
        p.   cm.
    Includes bibliographical references and index.
    ISBN-13: 978-0-87338-872-6 (pbk. : alk. paper) ∞
    ISBN-10: 0-87338-872-0 (pbk. : alk. paper) ∞
    1. Ohio—Guidebooks.   2. Ghost towns—Ohio.   3. Legends—Ohio.
    4. Ohio—History, Local.   I. Title.
    F489.3.M38 2006
    917.710444—dc22   2006000385

British Library Cataloging-in-Publication data are available.

For my nephews, Zane and Ian Bauer

People do not live in the present always, at one with it. They live at all kinds of and manners of distance from it, as difficult to measure as the course of planets. Fears and traumas make their journeys slanted, peripheral, uneven, evasive.

—*Anaïs Nin*

Contents

Introduction: Forgotten Ohio

While working in my mother's basement one snowy morning, I opened the top drawer of an old wooden chest and caught a glimpse of something red—a small box from my boyhood. It must have been hidden in there for thirty-five years, but I didn't rediscover it until 2000, when I was preparing to buy her yellow Cape Cod—the house where I grew up—in Hamilton, Ohio.

I sat down on the cold concrete floor, pulled off the lid, and peered in. I found mostly paper things from Ohio vacations in the early 1960s: three colorful state maps, five postcards of roadside scenes, a souvenir pen from LeSourdsville Lake Amusement Park, a faded brochure that read, "See Ohio Caverns, a Fairyland, West Liberty, Ohio," and a tiny black-and-white photograph of my father washing his finned Plymouth in front of a cabin at Indian Lake.

As I inspected each piece, early vacation memories ran through my mind as vividly as home movies. I could almost see my father driving the Plymouth and smoking his familiar brown King Edward cigar. A plume of white smoke blew out of his cozy wing like a ghostly interloper while my mother provided unsolicited directions. In the back seat, my younger sister, Robyn, sang the latest Top-40 hits, while I chanted, "When will we get there?"

Because of budget restrictions, our family vacations were short and regional in those days. (To us, an out-of-state vacation meant Santa Claus, Indiana.) We mostly stayed in Ohio in the early years. Even for those journeys, my father always packed his latest gasoline-company maps, just in case a route had been changed. Now, some people might ask, "What's so interesting about Ohio?" The attraction of the road and the family. The state was much more rural in the early 1960s, especially in the southwest, and we'd explore it during the summer. All winter, I'd go to sleep dreaming of pioneers and blue-coated soldiers and historic places. My father's road maps—and my imagination—could take me wherever I wanted to go. I'd spread them across the kitchen table for easy viewing, and in red ink I'd circle the towns and attractions that interested me. "Mom," I'd say, "what is a Wapakoneta?"

Finding my father's musty maps encouraged me to resume traveling in Ohio. I had stopped for a few years to write about other parts of the country, but even then I missed the back roads.

As an adult, I started my Ohio travels in 1981, the year I married, bought a house, and began writing for magazines. I set out on drives across my native state and as interesting a universe as any I have visited. (Marriage did not provoke my restlessness. Curiosity did.) I sought communities that thrived long before the interstate highways, MTV, computers, and inflated baseball statistics. On nearly every trip, I'd discover vanishing things: celebrations, motels, road art, drive-in theaters, traditions, inventions, folk tales, crusades, battlefields, forts, points of reference, geography, myths, attitudes, tall tales, gothic places. I much preferred to search for the metaphorical, the more abstract ghosts of the past, although along the way I heard folk tales about spirits in small towns. In my mind, they all blended into one big quilt of Ohio history.

By 1990, I noticed that we were losing rural places and quirky characters that were a direct link to the early 1900s and the time when Ohio was distinctly agrarian. Talking to these people was like talking to someone from a place far away. Now, watching our culture and history disappear under the juggernauts of time and development, I realize that we're losing an odd assortment of things—from legends to towns to the quintessential independent Buckeye. So I search for ghosts of many kinds: the supernatural, man-made specters, Ohio's past, and the mist of our vanishing culture. Sometimes I think I see my father's Plymouth passing me on the way to Ohio Caverns.

Today is simply a good time to look for ghosts. They walk among us.

My latest round of trips—I will never complete the mission, only the present sortie—ended in our bicentennial year, a significant time to wrap up things in a loose binding. On longer trips usually I traveled with my editor, Buckeye native, and wife, Cheryl, who helped me explore endangered places and rediscover Ohio and its back roads as an intrepid motorist might have found them in the 1930s. I took along a soft briefcase filled with a number of gasoline-company maps from the 1940s to the present; my tattered 1915 Rand McNally Ohio map and its counterpart from 2002; a 1937 Ohio map published by the Ohio Department of Transportation; and two little books, *Scenic and Historic Ohio* from 1925 and *Let's Explore Ohio* from 1961. The state map inside *Scenic and Historic Ohio* guided me to places that had existed when automobiles first arrived in the rugged countryside. It offered a stark comparison to modern maps. The other booklet, which sold for twenty-five cents, came out when I was in the eighth grade. Its color photographs remind me of an Ohio that no longer exists, but whose outline is still visible when the light is just right.

One bright September morning in 2003, a pivotal moment in my travels occurred only about fifteen miles from home, in the historic city of Montgomery. On that day, Ohio's past and present came clearly into focus when preservationists Diane "Dee" Eberhard and Mary O'Driscoll took me through the Universalist Church, built about 1837 at Montgomery and Remington Roads in what is now known as the Heritage District. In the cool air I pondered the colonial brick exterior's four big columns and small cupola. The simple architecture is reminiscent of the Christopher Wren and Williamsburg styles. Although it is not the oldest church in this Hamilton County city of ten thousand people, the Universalist is the most easily recognized, aesthetically, architecturally, and historically. It has touched everyone in town.

"Church members fired the bricks on site, including special wedge-shaped ones to make the pillars," O'Driscoll said as we walked between them. "Supposedly the workers left a bottle of whiskey inside one pillar."

Eberhard rubbed her fingers gently across the brick and said, "If you look closely you will see that the builders left impressions of their door keys on each pillar. I think that was their way of saying, 'I made this.'"

When church founders cast the bell, they dropped silver coins into the hot metal to foster a clear ring. The town still rings the bell on holidays, special occasions, and for weddings. The sound soothes O'Driscoll's mind.

"The church has been the heart of our city and my love, but in 1960 it was ready to be torn down by people who wanted to build a *gas station*," she said. "I can't imagine Montgomery without it. When Iran released the American embassy hostages in 1981, almost every person in town came over to help ring the bell in thanksgiving. It was a sacred moment."

Churches—especially the early Methodist, Presbyterian, and Universalist—hold an important status in Montgomery's history. In addition to their architectural and religious contributions, the churches provided a little local controversy. In the early nineteenth century, the more conservative Presbyterians decided that the Methodists had become too vocal and cocky for their own good. "The radical element among the Presbyterians waited until the Methodists were kneeling in prayer, then pricked them with pins attached to long poles," Eberhard said.

"Ouch," O'Driscoll said, and winced.

The two women looked at each other solemnly, as if ready to make a major pronouncement. Then at once they broke into laughter like schoolgirls. They know each other that well, for they have shared a love of history and community for decades. Eberhard, president of the Montgomery Historical Preservation Association, and O'Driscoll, vice president, live on the same street in an old part of town. A Cleveland native, O'Driscoll worked overseas for the Red Cross during World War II. She met her late husband at a Red Cross conference in Toledo, and eventually they married and moved to Montgomery, which felt like home. In 1970 she finally became involved in preservation, when the Presbyterian manse was to be torn down to make way for a large bicycle shop. "We took around petitions," she recalled. "We picketed. The events were shown on television. My husband was going to lunch with some men who complained about 'those hysterical ladies.' My husband said, 'One of them is my *wife.*'"

Though a generation younger, Eberhard is equally enthusiastic. She has channeled her affinity for preservation into pen-and-ink sketches of the city's historical landmarks, including the Universalist Church. She's also drawn her home, the elegant Crain-Eberhard House. The two-story brick house, built in 1882 by manufacturer George Crain, features elements of the Greek Revival style and a gable wing added in 1968. It is one of thirty-two buildings in Montgomery designated as city landmarks.

As we walked around the austere but elegant sanctuary, the women pointed proudly to an ornately carved pulpit, a pump organ that still works, a brass chandelier, a black Burnside heating stove, and three rows of white wooden pews. Originally, a board ran down the center of the middle pew, separating the men from the women. I can still remember what O'Driscoll said: "If you look carefully, you'll see where the board was taken out a few years ago and the hole was filled in. The outline is still visible at just the proper angle, when the light falls on it. In our trade, this faded image is called a ghost. To a preservationist, a ghost means evidence of something that used to be there."

Her definition struck me in a literary sense, for I'd already seen my share of ghosts all across Ohio. In 1996 I wrote about them in *Ghosts: Ohio's Haunted Landscapes, Lost Arts, and Forgotten Places*. O'Driscoll's comment gave my trips both meaning and metaphor. I'd been searching for many kinds of ghosts—missing pieces of our past that reflect a state of mind as well as a collection of landscapes. Suddenly I understood that vanishing Ohio is a place where rural America converges with small cities and fading history and disappearing culture. It is a place we're losing to burgeoning technology, global economy, technological immediacy, and, most of all, time.

One day in early summer, when the temperature and my sensibilities finally cooled, I wandered into the real Ohio. I didn't bother taking the interstates. Instead, I drove the back roads to search for forgotten small towns—those offbeat, indigenous places that once elected native-son presidents and enforced local dry laws long after Prohibition ended. (Some still do.)

I drove a used Jeep Wrangler, a Sahara with a tan cloth top that I never did pull down because the wind gave me a sinus headache. I bought the Jeep because it also provided four-wheel-drive in rough and muddy terrain. (More accurately, I bought it simply because I felt like it.)

Vanishing Ohio was not difficult to find. As rural horizons disappear, Ohio slowly transforms itself: farmland into subdivisions, meadows into shopping centers, old town characters into soccer moms. Sprawl knows no boundaries, no limits. It's all over the place—even in ghost towns like Rialto in Butler County. Recently, I noticed a big sign that had popped up in a field: "Coming . . . Rialto Place." Developers want to build a shopping strip near the site where a paper mill, the old canal town's only large employer, once operated. Meanwhile, more small towns decline or die across the state, victims of a changing economy and social fragmentation.

Like the pioneers of two centuries ago, modern suburbanites continue to push farther into the country, stripping the land and setting up far-flung outposts called subdivisions and shopping centers. Just when you think the process is slowing, it rises again. Rural Ohio is losing its cloistered innocence while being homogenized by Wal-Mart, McDonald's, and cyberspace. Old-fashioned, rural heritage, the kind on which Ohio was built, continues to disappear as the countryside gains more sophistication—or at least a higher level of communication. Development invades even the most unlikely of places, turning farms and historic battlefields into subdivisions, shopping centers, and ubiquitous fast-food pit stops.

A town can't change its location, yet location means the difference between death and survival. "I was hiking in Vinton County," rural sociologist Joseph Donnermeyer told me, "and walked by three places where towns used to be. A lot of rural towns like these die because what caused them to exist went away—railroad, iron-ore developments, and industry. Towns not linked to another destiny have been most vulnerable."

Old towns are disappearing around Columbus, Cleveland, Dayton, and other cities that are expanding like miniature galaxies. (Geauga County in suburban Cleveland has been identified as one of the top three examples of sprawl in the nation.) In my native Butler County in Greater Cincinnati, on land along Tylersville Road where farms once prospered, sprawl has edged into neighboring Liberty and Fairfield townships and is moving toward rural areas. Ignoring nearly two centuries of tradition, Union Township officials renamed their community West Chester Township. By encouraging development and erasing the township's original name, the community has created a totally new facade. Local officials sought to market their product, or township, to other suburban people. Somebody who was ready to move to the Cincinnati area from, say, suburban New York, could more easily identify with the name West Chester than the more common Union Township. I can identify with a headline I recently read: "Driving on Tylersville? Pack a lunch."

Three decades after the suburban invasion started in full, Union Township's small communities, including Tylersville and Gano, are ghost towns that have been replaced by subdivisions. I see the continuing losses as evolution, the end of an earlier lifestyle and heritage that dates to the founding of Ohio in 1803.

Ghost towns fascinate me because they represent lost dreams. They don't have to embody the ghost-town cliché: abandoned buildings, dusty floors, rotting joists. They can be any kind of town, even the inhabited. Ghost towns are scattered across the state and too numerous to count. Some came and went with the canals and railroads. Tornado, flood, fire, and disease killed others. Still others decreased in population when their people moved away. To qualify as a ghost town, a community must be declining, already gone, or taken over by a larger neighbor. Many are abbreviations of their former selves or buried beneath subdivisions. Most are forgotten or ignored. Some were planned but never developed. They remain towns only in name—ghostly places unknown to most people.

I saw it all across the land. While driving along busy U.S. Route 35 in the Greene County city of Beavercreek, I passed strip malls and apartments. I wondered if local people knew that they live near Pants Down, a notorious woods known in the late 1800s for its large number of robberies. On Dayton-Xenia Road, near a ghost town called Marsetta, groups of unsavory drifters routinely grabbed travelers and stole their wallets and pants, thus assuring themselves that no victims would go looking for the police until nightfall.

Such tales are disappearing now in a state in transition.

I go on the road for a few days, return home to write, file chapters in manila folders, and head out again to see more towns and people. In cold type, no one ever moves away. No one ages. No one dies. (But in reality, a number of kind people have passed). Sometimes I return to towns so many times that I have to compress my visits for the story to make sense.

Out there on black asphalt ribbons, deep in the heart of nowhere, I watch the images of towns and people grow smaller in my rearview mirror and finally fade to nothing. I feel at one with the speeding tires and the motion of the Jeep. In the cool rush of air on my sides, sometimes the movement seems strange yet vaguely familiar, as though it possesses a soul I once met but can't quite remember.

Back home in the solitude of my mother's house, I sit and watch the snow drift as high as the back fence and begin to understand. Those slowly disappearing images I saw in my car mirror and the blurry objects on the side of the highway were not solely optical events, after all. They were fragments of time rushing past me, quickly and almost imperceptibly.

I do not know where they went.

Drawing by Dan Chudzinski.

1

Big Dreams

Time is the longest distance between two places.
—*Tennessee Williams*, The Glass Menagerie

1

The Life and Times of Fizzleville

Those who travel on State Route 763 should have good brakes and new tires. The narrow road wiggles its way down steep hills between State Routes 41 and 125, passing a few farmhouses and privies and even fewer automobiles in rural Brown County. On the way, it's easy to overlook a little community named Hiett and mistakenly drive as far south as Slickaway, Stringtown, and Fishing Gut roads, or as far north as Suck Run or Stony Lonesome roads. From Route 125, visitors should go south on Route 763 to the Eagle Creek Covered Bridge and over some of the greenest water in southern Ohio. The road twists past Eagle Chapel, a wood-frame church built in 1876. The decaying building sits in a forest of weeds, where only the rushing water of the creek pierces the silence.

A few miles south, the road curves abruptly and a general store with two gasoline pumps appears on a rare piece of flat ground. The first thing I saw was nine pickup trucks parked in front of the rustic wooden building. A simple sign proclaimed:

HIETT GENERAL STORE
FIZZLEVILLE, OHIO.

For a moment, this visitor believed he had stepped into a Wellsian time machine and arrived in rural Ohio, 1920. Hiett, nicknamed Fizzleville, is that kind of town and a chunk of fading Americana. I only wish it could have been named something more colorful, more literal, as were such other faded burgs as Goosetown, Grange, and Sulphur Lick. But then, the visitor can't have everything his way.

Residents admit Hiett isn't much of a town anymore. Cartographers share that opinion. They usually omit Hiett from maps or misspell the name these days. This might bother some community-minded people in small towns, but it doesn't matter to the two hundred people living within ten miles of Hiett. In fact, they don't even call it Hiett much themselves. To them, it is just Fizzleville.

When Walter D. Grierson came to Hiett in 1866, after serving in the Civil War, he built a general store, where he sold dry goods, groceries, coffee, dry beans, and candy—anything the country town needed. By the 1880s, Hiett had a second general store, stock scales, a Grange lodge, six houses, a blacksmith's shop, a Presbyterian church, and a physician's office. After Grierson's death in 1926, the store remained in his family for generations—a total of 111 years, to be exact. Alma and John Lorenz, the last owners, operated it for forty years, until 1977. People called Alma the Queen of Fizzleville because she treated them royally. These days, however, only one house remains, Hiett is a ghost town, Mrs. Lorenz is dead, and her store has burned. Another store, built to look old, serves the people of surrounding Huntington Township.

A few years ago, a rumor started in Brown County that explained just how Hiett got its nickname. Some local farmers were sitting around the Hiett General Store one winter day, wondering why their community never grew. One farmer said it just fizzled, and soon the people living around the store were calling themselves Fizzlevillians. But that explanation is only a rumor, started, perhaps, by someone like Estil Earhart, the self-proclaimed mayor of neighboring Neals Corner, population four. Earhart claims Neals Corner is a suburb of Fizzleville. Others contend Earhart likes to tell the story to avenge himself against the Fizzlevillians, who have the larger of the two towns. To them, size matters most of all.

Days earlier, I had called the store to ask for directions.

"The stooooore," clerk Gerlinde "George" Shelton answered in a smooth Appalachian drawl.

"What town is your store in?"

"Fizzleville," she replied, slowly and confidently.

"Oh. Well then, where's Hiett?"

"Fizzleville."

"Thank you for clearing up that mystery."

When I finally walked in, five men dressed in coveralls and bib overalls rested on two old church pews that had been worn smooth by use.

The pews creaked every time another man shifted position. They stared at me silently, expectantly.

I spoke first, in jest: "So tell me, what is the population of Hiett?"

"With or without the horses?" Mitch Littleton answered.

"Without."

"Well, horses would bring it up pretty much if you count 'em. But then, if you're outside the city limits, you'd have to say ten or twelve families—not countin' the dogs."

"Of course," somebody grunted.

"Oh, sure," another said.

Just then, a customer entered the store.

"There's a councilman right now," Littleton said. "Let's ask him."

The man grabbed a loaf of bread and walked out without saying a word.

My questions about the naming of Fizzleville brought some snickers and guffaws, but all laughter stopped when Wilson Walton began to speak: "Well, there was five of us sittin' around the store one day and we decided to start a bowlin' team over at the alley in Aberdeen. When we got there, somebody said, 'Where you boys from?' Well, I don't know who said it, but somebody replied, 'We're from Fizzleville.' And the name stuck. That was more than forty years ago. I remember it because that's how long the bowling alley has been around."

Theo Jones shook his head knowingly and said, "No, no, no. That's not what happened. Here's how I remember it: a farmer and his wife were in a strippin' room—a *tobacco*-strippin' room. We were all strippin' tobacco back then. That was thirty-five, forty-five years ago. They saw that a town had once been here, but fizzled out, so as a joke they decided to name it Fizzleville. I was there when it happened. I can vouch for it. The bowling team came later."

"Huh?" Shelton said. "I always thought the name came from the bowlin' team."

"Oh, other versions of the story are still floatin' around," Jones said. "But mine is the correct one."

"Oh, boy," another man said. "Who *cares?*"

"This man does," Jones said, pointing to me. "He's taking down this town's history."

"What's left of it," somebody said.

They all grinned slyly, as if the whole thing were a joke.

"Has the date been set yet for the annual tractor pull?" asked John

Hardyman, a regular. "A lot of people come out to see it. They come from as far away as Cincinnati."

"Well, a few of them do," Jim Fite said.

"Now, let's don't start debating the size of the crowd," Phil Figgins said.

"Yeah, all those 'thousands' of people," Hardyman said.

"All right, boys," Shelton said. "Third week in June, I believe."

Although the general store resembles the one built in 1866, it has an electric cash register, a big freezer, and a kerosene heater. And, in typical small-town tradition, the store is still the favorite and only gathering place for people from a wide area. "The ladies used to get mad because their husbands would come up here to loaf," Jones said. "Those old boys would sit down next to the pot-bellied stove and stay for the whole afternoon."

Every inch of the building is used. The inside of the front door is filled with notices; owner Al Rhonemus calls it the community bulletin board. He said of Fizzlevillians, "How well do we know our neighbors? Well, we know one another's *dogs* by name."

The patch on his green baseball cap identifies him as a Fizzleville Booster. Four different styles of caps may be bought at the store, as well as reprints of a drawing showing how the store appeared years ago. Residents can also get the latest edition of a bimonthly newsletter, the *Fizzleville Times,* a one-sheet publication that informs people of the community about what the neighbors are doing. Rhonemus and his wife, Patty, editor of the *Times,* are retired teachers who bought the store in February 1981. "I taught thirty years, and after I quit I learned the store was up for sale," he said. "Alma Lorenz ran it for forty years, and when she died we were afraid it would be closed, or bought by somebody who wasn't interested in the community. So we bought it."

(Once, a big-city woman came into town with a friend, on their annual antiques excursion into the country. A local farmer met them by chance. During a conversation on some forgettable local subject, he happened to say, "Well, I do believe I read about it in the *Times.*" At that moment her jaw dropped and she said enthusiastically, "Oh, my, yes! Why, I also read the *Times!*")

Under the newsletter's hand-lettered masthead, these words appear in small type: "HIETT GENERAL STORE (In Downtown Fizzleville)." The publication speaks directly to the few people who live in the area. One April, Patty wrote:

And so, encouraged by the premise of a new and better growing season, we bring the *Times* once again to life. Sorry about the hibernation during the winter months, but sometimes when there is little good to say, it's better to say nothing at all. You know, it's human nature to complain about the weather. But lots of us praise God with thankful hearts that our homes have not been blown in upon us or washed out from under us. May God also help us learn from our past mistakes and also help us forgive and forget the mistakes of others.

Al and Patty believe the *Fizzleville Times* has brought a sense of identity to the rural Hiett area. The paper includes a sprinkling of Bible quotations, updates about families and who is visiting, birthday and anniversary congratulations, 4-H news, and consignment sales. Families send special notices to be published, and one anonymous resident, known only by his byline as the "old-timer," writes about farm life of a bygone era. "The farmers are waiting for signs of spring, the sun to shine, the temperature to rise," the editor wrote as spring approached. "It's a trying yet an expectant time. The spring and summer's work is being planned. All hope for a better and earlier start on the crop years."

Yet Patty also told readers that the time has come to start thinking about closing the store.

"We have to pay as much for gasoline as some stations in town sell it for," she wrote. "The utility bills keep rising. I can't imagine our community without the store. Yet it needs more going for it than it has now. New owner-managers might help. I'm too moody and Alfred is too busy to keep it going as it should. Be thinking and praying about it, will you? We're no longer able to pay the bills because many of our customers are having trouble paying theirs and we can't afford to keep going deeper and deeper in debt much longer. Something needs to be added to make the business profitable enough to keep the store in the community. Any ideas?"

The store generates a few additional dollars by selling bumper stickers that read: "Fizzleville U.S.A.; Where Is It? Follow Me!" and "I Followed And I Found . . . Fizzleville U.S.A." Red and blue ball caps come with "Fizzleville Booster" emblazoned across the front.

From his comfortable seat Wilson Walton looked over the cache of promotional items and said, "Bumper stickers, caps, pictures—seems *everything's* in Fizzleville. And did you know we usually get between forty-five thousand and fifty-thousand people in here for the famous Fizzleville Fair?" He paused and said, "Ain't that right, Gerlinde?"

"Oh, mercy, Wilson," she exclaimed. "Every year the cars line up for a mile down the road."

The summer fair (and other activities) are sponsored by Huntington Township's 4-H club, the Huntington Hot Shots. Rhonemus, who has also served as president of the Brown County fair board, organized the Fizzleville Fair with the Hot Shots. Walton and Figgins donated land across from the store for the Fizzleville Fairgrounds, and residents built a wooden fence and horse track. Other fair activities included horseshoe pitching, log sawing, square dancing, tractor pulling, and, of course, some impressive eating.

Hiett's main cultural event started small in 1966, and by the 1980s it was attracting people from all parts of Brown and Adams counties. "It's a time to get together with your neighbors and friends, a time to appreciate the little things," Al said. "School kids play 'The Star-Spangled Banner' at our fair, and we even have our own young gospel singers from the church. We have to set the date way in advance to be able to plan it all out. It's just good community fun."

"Please don't confuse this event with the tractor pull," Hardyman added. "It's the third weekend in August—usually. Folks are quite thrilled to stop here in Fizzleville."

"We started it as a joke," Littleton said. "We held a little 4-H fair here in Huntington Township—that's what Fizzleville really is—and some people came out to see it. That was in 1966. We usually have between, oh, forty-five and fifty thousand people show up."

"You mean between forty-five thousand and fifty thousand?" I said.

"No. What I mean is between forty-five people and fifty thousand people, usually on the lower end."

Everyone laughed at me.

"Oh, well," Walton finally confessed, "maybe it's more like one thousand people on a sunny weekend."

On those summer fair days, the town's population swells considerably. With or without the expanded population, no one really knows the town's exact number. After all, the U.S. Census Bureau doesn't even count Hiett. Nobody does.

Al Rhonemus savored the jokes, the population, the town, and the put-ons, and then he stepped out onto the porch of the general store.

He gave a raking glance south on State Route 763, and pointed toward the meager skyline.

"Well, now," he said, "let's see. That house, the one down the road, and the house after that one, they could all be considered a part of downtown Fizzleville."

As I drove out of town, leaving the little general store far behind, I thought of its precarious state and wondered how long it would survive in a world that is too expensive and too small these days. I felt the potential loss of something gentle and good. To me, the store is a symbol of an Ohio that is becoming increasingly forgotten, even lost, and we don't even have the time to notice its passing.

Death of the Patriarch

By eleven on that January morning in the late 1990s, an angry sky was spitting sleet and snow onto my windshield as I drove east on U.S. Route 50 in rural Highland County. The radio announcer was predicting a winter storm and by nightfall subzero temperatures. Even the cows were hiding.

When a green metal sign announced Rainsboro, I remembered the town as an oasis in a great swelter of August countryside: old grocery stores and general stores, places that sold soda bottles so cold they were covered in a sweaty frost, rescuing countless numbers of travelers who were only minutes from curling into charred parchment and blowing off the face of the overheated planet. Through the snow I recognized the general store operated by a man named Fred Barrett. He had been an octogenarian standing behind a wooden counter holding a stereoscope, one of those double-slide model viewers that offers the illusion of three dimensions, as though Mr. Barrett were conjuring up the Rainsboro he had once inhabited.

On my last visit in the 1980s, Mr. Barrett was already an icon in his own store. Even then, Rainsboro had become every small town on the cusp of decline; its history that of every town that once aspired to greatness and failed. Except for a small brick elementary school serving Paint Township, no public buildings remained open. Businesses had been abandoned. Although still open, Barrett's General Store had slipped into that gray divide of the past.

Once, a spot on Route 50 almost guaranteed any town immortality. The two-lane highway ran from St. Louis to Washington, D.C., passing through cities such as Cincinnati and Parkersburg, West Virginia.

Fred Barrett stands in front of his general store in Rainsboro. Author's photo.

Buses ran through regularly—until the federal government deregulated the industry in 1982 and bus companies dropped their less lucrative rural routes. For a few years after the buses stopped coming, a tiny residual customer base—wanderers sniffing their way to an uncertain waterhole—still found their way to Barrett's General Store.

By noon on this bleak winter day, however, cars and trucks sped through town, oblivious to the empty storefronts. Some of them stopped at the convenience store about a mile east of Rainsboro. I stopped to buy a Columbus newspaper and seek information.

"What happened to Fred Barrett?" I asked the clerk.

"Oh, he died a few years back," she said. "A woman who works near here took care of him at the end."

Considering his age, I wasn't surprised by the news, but her words still carried a hollow ring.

"So what's happened to Rainsboro?"

"People are burning it down," she said. "Five fires in the last month. They set fire to an old house again last night. I don't know what gets into people. When there's no work, I suppose they go berserk."

Returning to town, I parked and watched more cars shoot past, as though the town didn't exist. Then I walked around its two side streets, looking at two dozen older houses—a few well-maintained and newly painted, but too many abandoned or neglected. Several rusty mobile homes appeared so fragile that they might blow away in the coming winter storm and sail off into the void, along with Rainsboro's outhouses and unmet goals.

After warming myself for a few minutes in the car, I drew the courage to look into Fred Barrett's wide store window. I saw assorted merchandise and junk—oddities he collected by habit—stacked to the ceiling in disarray. Like the day, the store was dark and depressing—local history, missing in action.

The scene was ghostly. I sensed Fred Barrett all around the store. He knew a little of everything, people said. The farmers of Rainsboro knew that, so they towed their ailing machinery, automobiles, and tentative hopes into his garage. They always said he could repair any motor made in America, and if for some reason he could not, they were welcome to conversation made by the men who hung around the garage. With the village monopoly on lube jobs and good talk, Fred won a measure of prosperity for his work. Yet he was unhappy.

He had fretted and complained ever since Henry Ford abandoned the Model T in 1927. Nobody else in town grieved much over its passing, but Fred was inconsolable. He had built the garage to accommodate the Model T to the inch, not the Model A. To him, the old T was more than an automobile—it was a faith, a passion, a metaphorical machine on which the common man rode off to success. And now, it was gone. That hopeless conclusion struck him suddenly and finally one afternoon in the autumn of 1932. The next morning, he dragged rusty toolboxes into a back room, bought some staples to sell in front, and proudly reopened the shop as Barrett's General Store. "Don't remember havin' any feelin' about it," he said. "Just did it."

It was the only occupational transition he would ever make, or even consider. Fred believed a general store was a fitting place for a man who knew a little of everything. He could have gone broke those first six months and he would not have cared. He refused to quit, despite the Depression and competition from four other general stores. At times he ran so short of cash that he could not make change. So he sold hogs for three cents a pound and carved wooden toys to sell. Fred also taught himself to cut meat and cure bologna and to order bolts of cloth, fishing rods, cigarette holders—every ridiculous and conceivable thing. He never did learn to sell, though. Customers strolled in, heard his opinions, and left with something or another.

Friends and years passed. Faces changed. Farming changed. Everything turned askew, except for Fred Barrett and the cornfields that rolled gently over the seamless green hills of Highland County. Rainsboro itself remained a low place in the road, a momentary and disappointing premise among the fields—a school, a church, a few houses, and several stores. Rainsboro was just a crevice of a community to which the obsolete general store could cling.

Fred built his place of brick. It stands on Route 50, showing faded white letters on the sides that still read "Barrett's Garage." No matter. Nobody notices the subliminal message. For more than fifty years, people fixed their eyes only on Pap Barrett, the imperturbable and cantankerous man who seemingly toiled forever in a store as deep and dark as a cave.

Our meeting was by chance on that gray April day in 1984. Driving through town on my way to eastern Ohio, I suddenly felt hungry, so I stopped in Rainsboro. Fred's store caught my eye. I went inside and looked around, momentarily suspended between the present and the years when a teenage doppelganger was trapped in the back seat of his father's 1961 Plymouth Valiant. Fred sold me a candy bar and grunted. He didn't talk much. I asked if I could sit for a while and look at what he had in the store. "Yep" was all he replied.

Fred always moved slowly behind the counter. He was hard of hearing, hardheaded, hardpan. He was as stout as a grain bin. A century ago he would have been just another fellow trying to earn his way, but now his kind is revered. He would be considered an entrepreneur, a man of uncommon independence in an interdependent world. He could not understand the mystique. "An independent," he snorted, "is a fellow who ain't changed much and don't intend to." Such talk bewitched strangers. They stopped in the store for a candy bar or soft drink and believed they had discovered a shrine of American versatility. They spoke quietly of the past; Fred listened.

Bootjacks. Breast chains. Something called a horse fiddle. They were all stuffed inside the store like relics in a disarranged museum. Then Fred, the reluctant curator, would point to his trophy—a wooden plaque with a photograph of him holding two fourteen-pound catfish up on Brush Creek in the summer of '61. On holiday. The regulars thought Fred liked the picture because it was a documentation of his own real trip, in the manner that tourists bring back pictures of themselves standing next to the Parthenon while on once-in-a-lifetime vacations. The catfish, of course, were optional.

He did not leave the counter often. He and his wife, Elizabeth, worked behind it from eight in the morning until late at night, but after she died in the 1970s he could barely stay open until five. Business narrowed. Rainsboro was shrinking. A few old friends drifted in and out as always, while a few new customers came mainly for bread and soft drinks. Finally, the bread man said he couldn't stop any more; the route no longer paid for itself. Most people shrugged and drove off to a convenience store in Hillsboro, the county seat. Fred's older customers rebelled. They told the bread man that they depended on his loaves and on Fred's store. They threatened to write letters to the big-city newspapers, to the governor. In two days, bread reappeared on the dusty shelves. Customers claimed victory. Fred sighed and said it was a temporary one at best. He was just happy to still be able to swing open the old screen door in the summer and to sit around the black fuel-oil stove on cold days.

Looking into the back room, I saw Fred's garage as he intended it—dark and dirty. He flipped a switch and a single bulb illuminated the room in shadowy light. An old Ford sat there waiting for attention, tools scattered on the floor around it. A calendar still read 1932. Fred said nothing.

Behind us, in the store, Clarence Wogner was stacking cans on a shelf for Fred. A farmer and a feed man watched him from their familiar positions near the stove. "We come here because of Fred's sense of humor," Wogner said. "You've got to dig real hard to find it."

Ignoring them, Fred stood rigidly behind the scarred oak counter, staring at walls strung with fly swatters, fishing rods, nets, work gloves, ax handles, brooms, hammers. And a hand-lettered sign: "New fishing license on sale. By now, avoid the rush."

From their positions, the men watched carefully as a boy no older than thirteen walked into the store lugging on his shoulder a massive black radio—a boom box—with speakers as large as dinner plates. The boy slammed a carton of empty soft drink bottles upon the counter to receive his return deposit fee.

"Hiya, Fred!"

"Yep."

"Gimme Skoal. Put it on our bill."

Slowly, Fred pulled out an old, fat pencil and a tattered yellow account book, originally a child's tablet. He read the figures by flashlight on the dreary afternoon, holding the book four inches from his eyes. The boy watched. As the music played, he skillfully completed a spin, and faced Fred. The boy said, "Oh, yeah, I forgot somethin'. Gimme a Pepsi, too. And open it." He pointed to the returned bottles and added, "Now, mister, you owe *me* a dime!"

Wogner laughed and moved from the back of the store like a shadow. "Hey, Fred, we were trying to remember when Lou Hamilton got wired up outside. About '34, was it?"

"Huh?"

Wogner shook his head and yelled: "WHEN DID LOU HAMILTON GET WIRED UP?"

Fred cupped his ear and frowned. "Yep," he said.

Wogner turned to the farmer and the feed man and said, "Well, anyway, Lou had the irritating habit of coming over to the store after school to crank up Fred's car for a drive. Now, nobody touched Fred's car. It was a beauty. Always shined. So one day Lou came over for another spin. Fred was ready. He had hot-wired the car, and was looking out the window to watch. Lou grabbed ahold of the crank. WHAM! Got a shock on him he'll never forget. ISN'T THAT RIGHT, FRED?"

"Last time he ever drove my car, ain't it?"

A foghorn of a voice filled the store with laughter, and the farmer finally said, "Hot-wired! Kids always jumped up on the hood of my '38 Mercury when I'd go to the picture show up in Greenfield, so one day I wired it up and turned on the switch. Whoooo, those kids flew off the hood so fast that they lost their shoes."

"Nineteen hundred and thirty-eight," Fred said for no particular reason.

"I moved here in '30," Wogner said. "There ain't but a half dozen folks left in this town who came into the store then."

"Darn chain stores," Fred grumbled. "They're makin' it too hard for me to operate. I was ready to sell last year, you know, but the people who wanted to buy me out didn't even have the money for a down payment. I guess I ought to quit."

The men looked at the floor. Finally, the farmer said, "Where would we go?"

"What would we do?" echoed the feed man.

"Fellows," Wogner said, "there are no good answers to the eternal questions."

Fred did not respond. He had motioned for me to come to the counter, and he shoved a wooden puzzle into my hands. He said he carved it in 1924. After five minutes of trying to fit the parts together, I gave up. Fred laughed.

"That puzzle was invented long before that fellow Rubik came out with his cube a few years ago," Wogner said. "But Fred's is different because one piece is made not to fit. When strangers like you come into the store, he shoves the puzzle at them and watches them go crazy as they try to put it together. Then somebody distracts them while Fred slips a special piece—the right piece—into place. Then he always says, 'Well, what's so tough?'"

"When did the McCalls die and their daughter take over their store?" asked the feed man. "About '57?"

"No, no, no," Wogner said. "Time gets away from me. I can't remember . . ."

Fred stuck out a foot. "Bought these shoes from the McCalls fifty-five years ago. Good as they day I bought them." He adjusted his glasses, pushed back his black railroad cap, and looked out the big window toward the automobiles on Route 50. "I've seen history roll by here in my time. And change. But people don't change much. No, sir. They stay the same."

"Fred, they still need your kerosene lamps and chimneys. Remember that," the farmer said as he walked toward the door.

The men ambled along to their wives, hot suppers, and another Saturday night of television programs. Fred stayed behind, looking at old stereo slides in his viewer. An hour was left until closing time, but Fred said he might close early anyway. He had felt more tired and lonely lately. Not the aching kind of loneliness he once felt as a young man, but the nagging kind that crept into his room about ten at night, when he looked up and realized that Elizabeth wasn't there anymore. Yet the morning always returned, and Fred slipped on his old overalls and denim work shirt and hobbled over to the store to stand behind the counter once again. Surely that was the best place for a man who knew a little of everything.

. . .

Route 50—on which Rainsboro lies—is a horizontal line separating the county's two types of farm land: In the north, you can throw a handful of seed corn on the ground and it will grow in the rich soil. In the south, you need divine intervention to grow anything in the heavy, wet soil. The farms around Rainsboro have been growing smaller for fifty years. The root system withers, the organism dies.

Rainsboro could be any town; its problems are those of agricultural America. When small farmers retire or lose their land, they displace the communities around them. For every farmer who goes out of business, economists estimate the nearest town loses a worker and a store.

In 1830, George Rains founded Rainsboro with a healthy bank account and a prayer. The North Carolina abolitionist farmer had moved to Ohio, a Quaker stronghold, with his wife and eight children, when he was nearly sixty years old. He was a man who loved permanence. He had his children but he yearned for what he thought would be an even more durable legacy—a town. Such an endeavor would surely last. Before he died fifteen years later, he saw his town grow steadily, until it became a local trading center for farmers. Rainsboro's population reached 220 people, despite epidemics of small pox and spinal meningitis in 1876. It had a post office, a hotel, a woolen mill, a telephone company, and, over at the Woodmen's lodge, a brass band.

But a million cornet players couldn't change reality: Rainsboro was a country town and was therefore doomed to limitations. Take culture, for instance. Hillsboro, another town on Route 50 and the seat of Highland County government, always received the factories, the mansions, and what passed for culture in the rural county of the 1800s. About the time Rainsboro was getting excited about its brass band, Hillsboro had already formed its own women's group, the Friday Club, to discuss the important matters of the day—classical music, Shakespeare, flower gardens, and public speaking.

In Rainsboro, meanwhile, no one had the time for such frivolity. The town had become a mini depot for huckster wagons, which embarked at sunrise like little supply legions on missions into the hinterlands, carrying fresh eggs, dairy products, and vegetables. The wagons served farms and such small towns as Dallas, Turkey, Gall, Harriet, Winkle, and Fairfax. Today, these are mostly ghost towns with forgotten stories and similar histories.

Although George Rains's town has survived the better part of two centuries, it has lived without acclaim. In the daily realm of news, in fact, only one major local news event ever occurred—at least one that people can talk about—on Rainsboro's narrow streets: the apprehension of outlaw Robert "Little Reddy" McKimie, whom the locals once described as Horatio Alger in reverse. Born in Rainsboro in 1855, red-haired Bob must have been a charismatic character, for his story has been retold in town and in the county for more than a century.

McKimie grew up with an aunt in Rainsboro. A likeable boy, he claimed that he left to enlist in the army at fourteen. When he was twenty-two, in 1877, he returned to town a wealthy man. He told neighbors he had served in the army in the West and later earned a fortune in the cattle business. Now, he said, he wanted to settle in Rainsboro and start a family. At least he was serious about that part of his story. A few weeks later he married quiet Clara Ferguson, and they opened a dry-goods store. They hardly had time to enjoy their honeymoon when a U.S. marshal named Seth Bullock, a dapper man with a thick black mustache, arrived on their doorstep, asking the strangest questions about murders and robberies in Utah, Texas, and Wyoming. Clara was aghast.

Bullock had searched unsuccessfully for McKimie in four states, and then, acting on a tip, traveled to Rainsboro to see if this McKimie fellow was actually the killer called "Little Reddy from Texas." Indeed, they were the same, Bullock said, although McKimie denied the charge. He was wanted in Utah for killing a man and stealing his horse and in Wyoming as the most cold-blooded member of a gang of stagecoach-robbing outlaws. In their most profitable robbery in Wyoming, they stole $14,000 in gold—a lot of money in those days. Then, they disappeared into the dust.

After being charged, McKimie was taken to the Highland County Jail in Hillsboro to await extradition. But he soon escaped with the help of another prisoner (and, it is believed, with the cooperation of other townspeople who seemed to be under McKimie's spell). He easily tricked people into thinking he was the real victim. He was well liked in the countryside, where the farmers must have considered him some kind of Opie Taylor character who just happened to be in trouble.

For days, McKimie hid in the Seven Caves and in farmers' homes and barns, until he left to join his wife on the East Coast. They sailed all the way to Nassau but soon spent all his money. He could have stopped in a thousand places, but instead the bold young man returned to Rainsboro to form a gang, which robbed local stores, banks, and homes. In one year, the people of Rainsboro concocted the most fantastic tales of his exploits. He became Rainsboro's personal terror. Disguising himself with false mustaches and dyed hair, McKimie came and went as he pleased. After several reported McKimie sightings, the people were afraid to walk the streets after dark. Then one night, about one hundred local men surrounded him in a country cabin and brought him into town. This time, he didn't escape.

In 1879, he was sent to the Ohio Penitentiary in Columbus. After his release in 1890, he somehow avoided the charges pending against him in the West. Nobody knows exactly how he did it, and that adds to the mystery. Even today, Rainsboro still talks about Bob "Little Reddy" McKimie. Some people say he went back to the West after his prison term, changed his name to Ferguson, and went into business. Others say he joined the Rough Riders, was appointed territorial governor of Oklahoma, and died a millionaire.

There are many unsubstantiated stories, but nobody can say for certain exactly what became of Rainsboro's prodigal son. As far as the townspeople know, he is still hiding in the shadows, ready to fool another generation.

The cold wind roared at my back and the snow fell heavily on Route 50. I trudged to the car and sat warming my half-frozen fingers. Down the blurry street, I thought I saw history move before my eyes. It ran in a straight line from George Rains to Bob McKimie to Fred Barrett. I was in there, too, ignoring all of history for the moment, which was encapsulated perfectly in one of Pap Barrett's icy sodas.

The esteemed Mr. Rains could rest in peace for at least another day. His town—his long-sought permanence—was still alive, although gasping for breath in the cold January air.

3

Venice Times Two

On a chilly afternoon in early October, I crossed Pickerel Creek in the Blue Heron Wildlife Preserve on U.S. Route 6 near Lake Erie. On my right stood a light-green water tower marked EHCRWA in big black letters. I wondered: Is it a town or an eye test? (Later, I learned that it stands for Erie-Huron Counties Rural Water Authority.)

Mountainous gray clouds rolled across the sky like a scene in a fast-motion film. Autumn marched through the woods; its damp air felt more like late November. I fumbled with the radio and caught the latest weather forecast: rain, wind, and possibly an early—and colder than usual—winter. The wind whipped the canvas top of the Jeep so fiercely that I could hardly hear the announcer. With each big gust, the canvas popped loudly, like a gun firing. Beside me, brown fields of corn and soybeans lined the two-lane road. Its faded gray pavement matched the textured sky, and everything blended above and below. Signs with summer names such as Willow Point and White's Landing greeted me as I passed from Sandusky County into Erie County.

Out of curiosity, I searched for an Erie ghost town named Venice. It holds a slim connection to the old Venice that's near my hometown in Butler County, and a slim excuse was a good enough reason to head north. On the way, I thought about the two Venices and what they must have been like during the Civil War. Both played minor roles in Ohio's war days: looking the other way when escaped slaves came through town, sending their men into battle, and waiting out the fighting. All I knew about the northern Venice was that it was built on Cold Creek. The town is listed on only one new road atlas and on my deteriorating 1913 state map. Following their routes, I arrived at a crossroads on the edge of the city of Sandusky. I saw a few old houses, a bar, a restaurant called Margaritaville, a new retirement complex, a post of the Ohio Highway Patrol, and an abandoned winery.

When I drove through what I thought was left of old Venice (and this was only an assumption), I could almost see the present converging with the future. Time has roared through this little town like a tornado, blowing away families and shops and changing everything in its path. Suddenly, I was driving through a community and not noticing.

At Venice Road and State Route 6, across from the gray Cold Creek Trout Camp, I stopped to read a historical marker:

FORT SANDUSKY

Erected by the British near this junction in 1761; destroyed during Pontiac's Conspiracy of 1763. The fort was strategically located near Indian towns and trading posts on the Great Indian Trail between Detroit and Pittsburgh.

The place that would become Venice was a popular stopping point on the trail. A few miles to the north, on the Sandusky River, the French built the first fort in the Ohio country, Fort Sandoski, in 1751, and abandoned it three years later because of the British threat. French and British traders competed for furs in the area. The British built a blockhouse and palisade on the site of Venice during the French and Indian War. The area's Indians resented the new fort and British arrogance. In 1763, after the French defeat in North America, Ottawa chief Pontiac conspired to attack Sandusky and nine other British forts west of Fort Pitt (the site of modern Pittsburgh). On May 16, 1763, gatekeepers at Fort Sandusky allowed a group of Indians to enter. The garrison commander, Ensign H. C. Pauli, did not know that an Indian coalition of eighteen tribes was attacking Fort Detroit. After smoking a peace pipe, the Indians grabbed Pauli and quickly killed the fort's fifteen soldiers and a dozen traders. Warriors burned the fort and dragged Pauli to their village, where they threatened to kill him and forced him to run the gauntlet. When he had all but given up hope, an older widow intervened and asked to adopt Pauli. According to Indian custom, this was a proper way to replenish lost tribe members. He lived with the tribe until early July, when he escaped and met a group of British regulars who had just discovered the mutilated bodies of Pauli's soldiers at the burned fort. Soon, Pontiac's forces took nine British frontier forts, excluding Detroit.

After taking a picture of the Fort Sandusky marker, I stopped at the highway patrol office and asked a dispatcher for directions to Venice.

"It's the first road at the next light," she said.

"Not Venice Road. I mean Venice, the town."

She looked confused. "What town?"

"Venice."

"Never heard of it, sir."

"I think we might be standing in it. It should be here, according to my maps."

She turned to a fellow officer and said, "Hank, you ever hear of a town around here named Venice?"

"No," he said blankly.

Feeling defeated, I walked down the road and stopped at an old house where an American flag was hanging in front and a man was polishing a metallic blue pickup truck. He identified himself as Harold Schonhart, a truck driver, the former postmaster of Venice, and the retired postmaster of Sandusky. He had an impressive head of thick white hair, combed back in a distinguished wave, giving him a regal but rugged appearance. He wore jeans and a blue plaid flannel shirt over a red T-shirt. He was friendly.

"Where can I find downtown Venice?" I asked.

He looked at me as though he had met a fellow countryman in a foreign land, and said, "You're standing in the middle of what used to be Venice! I'm the oldest remaining resident, and I'm only sixty-five. Not many people, even around here, know that a town used to be right here where we're standing. It's too bad that the achievements of communities can't be remembered. I've heard that the town was named for its close location to the water—as in old Venice, Italy. Well, our Venice never quite lived up to that lofty reputation. When I was young, we had a regular town sign and all and a few businesses here. Even had a village hall. I can't remember if the sign said incorporated or unincorporated. I can't remember anything much about my town. I wasn't paying attention, and I let a little piece of history slip through the cracks. Now, nobody but me is left to wonder.

"But I can tell you this much: we had our own identity in the 1800s. Venice was supposed to be the next big town on the lake. We had the best port between Detroit and Cleveland in the days of the smaller wooden boats. Then in 1963, a few months after I became the Venice postmaster [Venice had seventy-two post office boxes], Sandusky annexed Venice.

That was the end of things for this town. The post office closed later that year, and I went to Sandusky to work. Venice went into hibernation."

Meanwhile, Sandusky has flourished. Its population has nearly doubled since the late 1800s, to about twenty-nine thousand people. Its landlocked port is still considered one of the better ones on Lake Erie, being only sixty miles east of Detroit and sixty miles west of Cleveland. Officially founded in 1846 (although settled earlier), the Erie County seat was on the doorstep of Venice. That was too close for two competitors in the shipping business, and the towns battled until Sandusky won.

Schonhart shook his head. He knows that Venice, on Sandusky Bay, once held so much promise that people considered it a potential metropolis. The town dates to 1817, but as early as 1811 Charles Butler had opened a leather tanning business near the Venice mills. The tannery provided settlers with much-needed leather goods. In 1823, Dr. L. B. Carpenter started a small distillery at the head of Cold Creek, but it was closed about 1830, perhaps because of competition from William P. Mason's distillery. Mason believed that he could more easily transport whiskey than corn to eastern markets, and he could use any surplus produce to make alcoholic beverages. The market for a stiff drink was big in those days, too. The new distilleries lead to the opening of barrel factories in Venice and neighboring Castalia.

With its five crude houses and noisy mills, Venice was a "major" community, only several miles west of Sandusky. Flour mills also flourished. By 1833, they established the first permanent cash market for wheat in the region. They could produce seventy-five thousand barrels of flour during the navigation season. Farmers brought in wheat by wagon until the Lake Erie Railroad opened to Tiffin in the second half of the nineteenth century. Soon, however, shipping became the major business in Venice. Community leaders extended the town pier out into the bay for a mile and a quarter. The first steamboat to dock was the *Major Jack Downing*. The townspeople predicted prosperity.

Behind the facade of trade, Venice had another life—a secret one. It was an important stop on the Underground Railroad, a loose coalition of white and black abolitionists, Native Americans, escaped slaves, Quakers, and other religious groups that helped slaves escape to Canada. In Underground Railroad code, Sandusky was called Hope. Venice was important, too, because its Cold Creek did not freeze.

Historians believe Venice is the place where the Reverend Josiah Henson escaped on his family's journey to Canada in 1830. Henson, a slave on a plantation in Maryland for thirty years, took his family through Ohio on the way north. He is considered the inspiration for a character in Harriet Beecher Stowe's *Uncle Tom's Cabin*. Henson never did reveal exactly where he crossed into Canada. Years after his arrival he wrote:

> One night more was passed in the woods, and, in the course of the next forenoon we came out upon the wide plain, without trees, which lies south and west of Sandusky city. The houses of the village were in plain sight. About a mile from the lake I hid my wife and children in the bushes, and pushed forward. I was attracted by a house on the left, between which [it] and a small coasting vessel a number of men were passing and repassing with great activity. Promptly deciding to approach them, I drew near, and scarcely had I come within hailing distance, when the captain of the schooner cried out, "Hollo there, man! You want to work?" "Yes, sir!" shouted I. "Come along, come along; I'll give you a shilling for an hour. Must get off with this wind." As I came near, he said, "O, you can't work; you're crippled." "Can't I?" said I; and in a minute I had hold of a bag of corn, and followed the gang in everything in emptying it into the hold.

The captain sailed with Henson and his family. When they landed in Canada on October 28, 1830, Henson said he threw himself on the ground with joy at being free.

In 1849, just as commerce began to flourish in Venice, a devastating cholera epidemic struck the Lake Erie coast, damaging the prospects of the new town and of others in the area. Gertrude M. Chapman, a young girl who grew up on her father's eighteen-hundred-acre marsh in Venice, was sent to Sandusky to live. She remembered those plague days even after she turned eighty-four years old. "A young woman came to my mother's house with cholera from Detroit, and she and five others died of cholera," Chapman told a local historian. "I knew many of the people buried in the old Sandusky Cemetery. They were many of them of the aristocracy of the town. They were buried in coffins made of rough boards. The people died like sheep. The coffins were piled up in the cemetery like cordwood. I have seen thirty or forty unburied at one time." The cemetery, named the Cholera Cemetery, still has a large gothic iron arch and gate with its name across its top.

A century after the epidemic, Venice still existed. Schonhart grew up in the Venice of the 1950s, the son of a grocery-store man who sold everything from salt to clotheslines. In the 1890s, the elder Schonhart and his brother delivered produce in a twenty-mile radius—even in winter. He worked in a 20 x 22–foot room with worn wooden floors, wide glass windows, decorative metal ceilings, and a potbellied stove. The men sold by bulk, right from the barrel. One of their more popular items was thread, which they kept in a big wooden cabinet made to hold the spools. The building also contained a large meat locker that was originally used to harvest lake ice. The Schonhart brothers wired it for electricity and used the room as their place to cut and store meat.

"The bar across the street was a grain mill," Schonhart said. "We had two bars, two groceries, two grain mills, and another mill down on Venice Road, besides a post office and a fishery. At one time, we had a big pier so the boats could stop and load grain. These things existed in the early 1900s. Then, slowly, they died out. I remember hearing people predict how Venice would grow someday and be bigger than Sandusky. They said it was an excellent port with a future. We were the biggest port between Cleveland and Detroit. Ships could load year-round here. Venice never lived up to its reputation, however, because the creek wasn't deep enough to accommodate larger boats. It was good for commercial shipping because the creek rushed so fast that it never froze, not even in the coldest of our winters. But it wasn't deep enough, and the bigger that the boats evolved, the more they went off to Sandusky and some other ports. They left Venice behind. The industry that stayed here for the longest was the fishery. Finally, it went out. Now, there is nothing left. People don't even know that Venice used to be a town, with its own history. I wish I had saved my father's old store signs and written down some of the stories about this place. Too late now."

We walked across the street to the former town hall, a two-story frame building with peeling white paint and boarded-up windows. Nobody uses it now. For a time, some people discussed the possibility of rehabilitating it, but it was too dilapidated. So it remains empty. "Even when I was a kid, the town hall was not functioning," Schonhart said. "But when this town was going good, my father told me, the hall had a jail with two or three cells. The building was used for our town's special meetings and functions, when Venice was a part of Margaretta Township."

In the mid-1800s, Venice also had its own school and a church. On June 3, 1867, the Right Reverend Bishop McIlvaine consecrated the new Church of Our Redeemer, which was built for twelve thousand dollars by Russell H. Heywood as a memorial to his deceased loved ones. Through 1879, Redeemer ministers confirmed fifty-six members and baptized sixty-four.

Today, the church is gone. The town's once second-busiest place, the old hotel, is a house. Schonhart said nobody remembers the name of the hotel, or who stayed there, but he has heard that some famous people did.

"It had a railing in front of the building for horses to be hitched," he said. "Later, the building was cut in half, and one half was moved across the street. The hotel had a huge bar—it must have been thirty feet long—in the lounge. The place had four fireplaces, two upstairs and two downstairs. When I was a kid, the mills stopped running, but railroad crews still came into town to stay a night or two. They were rowdy. We used to call them gandy dancers. The sad thing is, I can't tell you why. That's the story of Venice. There's nothing left anymore that you can relate to. It's a place with no name, and not much of a place."

I drove over to the Venice Cemetery and wandered around in the stiff wind. It was an attractive place with a bench and a slim-barreled cannon that appeared to be a World War II antiaircraft gun. Walking around the cemetery, I observed some names: Hooper, Matt, Sambow, Sessler, Hills, Scherz, Altvater, Addy, Leidorf, Becker. A large number of Germans rested there, under headstones obliterated by the weather.

Next door, the abandoned Steuk's Winery beckoned me with silence. I walked around the yard and tried to imagine the good times that people had in its three red buildings. In front, the main building was low and faded, adorned with big apples made of painted red plywood, all shabby and peeling. On the large glass window by the road, somebody had outlined in soap a picture of the cartoon character Goofy and with his finger had written, "No goofing, we've got chocolate by the lb., candy, and other goodies." Another sign offered honey, cheddar cheese, cider, wine, and baked goods. In back of the lot, a large red barn with a cupola included a date at the top, 1895. The once welcoming white front porch and wooden benches were overgrown with weeds and vines.

The lonely winery is a symbol of a town long dead.

. . .

The abandoned Steuk's winery in Venice, Ohio, on Lake Erie. Author's photo.

Every time I returned to the road, I noticed that things had changed in the countryside. Mostly I missed the rural characters and their unusual towns, places like Venice in Butler County. The unincorporated town—now a place where development creeps around—was known by two names, Venice and Ross, in the early 1900s. Ross prevailed in later years, though the split personality remains as subdivisions grow around the old town.

My memories of it are vivid. My older cousin used to take me swimming at Meadowbrook, a private park and pool on the edge of town. It was a grand place with green space surrounding it and a pool unlike the others I'd seen at the time. This one was oval shaped and concave, like a real lake. When I pass Meadowbrook these days, the old park is filled with cars for sale or in storage. It is no longer in the country.

Ross—older people still call it Venice—now lies between rural and suburban. It is losing its identity but not its purpose; several highways, including U.S. Route 128, intersect in the center of town. Not long ago, a local newspaper inexplicably described the town as "the Ross community of Ross." This identity crisis has been continuing for years.

In the late 1980s, I noticed that members of the Venice Fire Department wore uniforms with Ross Township on their jackets. On a recent trip, I saw a sign that read: "Venice, 12 miles." If this is not confusing enough, many of the churches still use Venice in their names while many local businesses use Ross. Once, a harried Cincinnati television reporter asked me how to get to Ross. He glanced at his fancy new maps, checked the highway numbers that I'd given to him, and said I must be wrong. "Ross doesn't exist," he said. "It's on none of my maps. Are you sure?" He looked at the map again. "Hey, wait—it's listed here as Venice," he said, totally confused.

One of my colleagues said, "Hey, is your map from 1898?"

Venice founder Jeremiah Butterfield arrived in the early 1800s, bought eight hundred acres at $1.25 per acre, and built a cabin. He found a pioneer's paradise filled with thousands of wild geese, turkey, deer, pheasants, quail, squirrels, and other game. The land was also filled with every kind of wood a man needed (and then some) to build a sturdy house: poplar, oak, buckeye, ash, walnut, sycamore, hickory, cherry, gum dogwood, and sugar-tree sassafras. The river was so thick with fish that hundreds could be caught in a large net. Butterfield was one of those larger-than-life frontiersmen whose exploits and hard work sound unbelievable today. At age twenty-one, he left his home in New York and traveled west. He found the Great Miami River and farmland that suited him and his young bride, Polly Campbell Butterfield. Once established, Butterfield worked relentlessly. Nothing could stop him. In the winter of 1819, he drove hogs from Venice to Detroit, more than 280 miles. There were few good roads then, and snowstorms hindered his travel. A nineteenth-century historian explained:

> Some of his men became disheartened & returned, but he pushed forward, breaking a path in the snow with his horse for his hogs to follow. After many days of hardship he arrived safely, sold out to a good advantage, & returned home with his saddlebags full of silver. Three times he shipped his hogs to Cuba, & in 1828 was shipwrecked. When the vessel neared the shore she struck a rock, & the captain and the crew took to the long boat. Mr. Butterfield would not leave until he had cut open the pens containing the hogs, which were on deck, & let them into the sea. They nearly all swam to the shore, so that he lost but a few . . . [and] made a profitable voyage.

On February 17, 1817, Butterfield and his neighbors received company when Benjamin Clark, a popular county physician, plotted a town named Venus, in honor of Venus de Milo, the ancient Roman goddess of beauty. Apparently the name was a little too sophisticated for the locals, who corrupted it as Venice. Yet the town grew steadily, boasting the first bridge across the Great Miami River in 1830, a new school, and businesses. For a time, people believed that Venice would grow into a large city.

Meanwhile, the other Venice continued to grow near Lake Erie. In the mid-1800s, Ohio's two Venices created a problem for the U.S. post office, which finally told the people of Ross Township to either change the name of their town or forget the mail. They borrowed the township's name, which honors U.S. senator James Ross, a lawyer, founder of Steubenville, supporter of Ohio statehood, and proponent of the free use of rivers as common highways.

As use of the Venice name gradually declined, so did local folktales and icons, including Elland, once the country home of Giles Richards. He grew up in and is buried in the countryside near Venice. His family's cemetery featured in its center an unusual monument—a great iron roller that had been drawn by eight yokes of oxen and used in the construction of the Colerain, Oxford & Brookville Turnpike (now U.S. Route 27). Mounted on a foundation of Dayton stone and topped by an iron urn, the roller looked like a rolling pin standing on end. Officials tell me they don't know what happened to the monument.

Forgotten, too, are many of the tales and memories of greater Venice, a nebulous area extending into Hamilton County's Colerain Township, near the old Venice Bridge. For generations local storytellers used to laugh at the exploits of teenage cousins George and Giles Richards (the same man who built the strange monument). They went out searching for raiding Confederates one afternoon in July 1863, and found them in a barnyard. The boys traveled in a buggy pulled by Zollicoffer, a young horse named after Confederate general Felix Zollicoffer, who fought in the Kentucky campaign.

Because their adventure went on to become a local folktale, a reporter for the *Venice Graphic* recounted the incident in a story on September 9, 1887:

The three Rebs fell in behind and the boys drove on. Giles knew they were in a scrape but George didn't realize the danger. Sure enough, they had not ridden very far before they ran into a body of at least a hundred of the Johnnies.

"Nice horse," remarked a big rawboned Kentuckian, as he thumped little Zollicoffer in the ribs. "Get out of here and help unhitch."

George got out and the Kentuckian rode away on Zollicoffer's back. Even then he did not appreciate that they were in a bad scrape, but he hunted up the officer in command and said: "Captain, we're in a pretty tough fix. We're pretty far from home to be without any horse. Haven't you got an old cripple you don't want that you can let us have?"

The audacity of the request startled the Reb, and for a moment he stared at his questioner closely. He saw nothing but innocence there, and with a queer sort of smile he said to one of his men: "Get this boy a horse!"

On another of my visits, big trucks rumbled past the Venice Castle restaurant while owner Lawrence Hyob rubbed his close-cropped head and puffed furiously on the stub of a foul-smelling black cigar. "The newcomers call it Ross, but they don't know any better," he said. "They never growed up around here. The old-timers will always call it Venice. I know that can be confusing at times. When the boys came home from Korea about '52, they told truck drivers to take something or another to Venice, and the stuff got lost for a month. A few years back, you knew just about everybody in Venice. You don't now. All the older ones used to sit around here and play cards. That's what they liked, and their wives always knew where they was at. But most of them are dead now. I'll keep this place like it is, though. If I ever change it, life in Venice won't be the same."

One winter day I walked into the Venice Pavilion, the town's most important piece of architecture, and saw an empty bar on a quiet afternoon. Paul Fiehrer was the owner then. He recalled the days when sweet big band music drifted from the large dance floor upstairs. "This place was built in 1917 for the Schradin family by George Sefton of Shandon, and it opened in April 1918," he said. "Then wouldn't you know it, old Stanley Schradin got himself drafted into World War I, leaving the place to be operated by his wife and family. It was a lot to manage. They ran a fried chicken restaurant with three bowling alleys in the basement. They bought vegetables from the farmers around

Venice. On the first floor, they kept oak candy and tobacco cases. The dance hall was upstairs. Its solid hardwood floors are so large that the Ross High School basketball team used to practice there. The family operated the Pavilion for twenty-six years. By the 1940s, this place was the best entertainment spot in Butler County. You could hear Cowboy Copas and other country-western stars on Saturday night. Everybody came here looking for a good time and they usually found it. We had four doctors in town then—a few lawyers, too. Now, time is sliding by and our lives have changed. Subdivisions are taking over."

Appreciating that life, women of the Venice Presbyterian Church documented their town's past on a quilt sewn in 1978 for the church's sesquicentennial. One quilter, Martha S. Reiner of Fairfield, said the women stitched for about a year and never complained. "It was hard work but it was a pleasure," she said. "We had lunch and a social affair. If we look thoughtfully at the events and the people and the places symbolized on the quilt, we can see the spiritual influences that served to enrich the lives of the people in our community. The homes must be seen as brave efforts of devoted fathers to provided shelter and comfort for the families. Consider some of their names: Isaac, Jeremiah, Nehemiah, Noah, and David. Can we doubt their devotion to the book from which their names came?" (As I write this in 2003, the church is celebrating its 175th anniversary with a special service, dinner, and a storytelling program about the old community and the church. Members will discuss the exploits of the Venice Cornet Band and dedicate a time capsule.) Church secretary Melanie Hanson said, "It gives me shivers to see the band pictured on the quilt. This is all about our community. But all this does make me wonder: Will we baby boomers leave our mark like the quilters did?"

The church now displays the quilt in a wood frame covered with glass. It is like a lost Egyptian artifact that was rediscovered and exhibited. Bordered with leaves, the quilt features squares with rustic designs of thirty local sites and people from the nineteenth century, including the Venice Pavilion—today, appropriately, an antiques mall—in the center of town. Other local scenes depicted on the quilt are the Venice ferry in 1884; the *Venice Graphic*, published and edited by Lewis Demoret from 1887 to 1912; and the Venice Cornet Bandwagon, operated by the Venice Cornet Band until the wagon and musical instruments burned in 1889. (Only a year earlier, proud townspeople had donated money to build a bandstand for the group.) The quilted squares also include the

Ross School, 1875–1939; the Log School, 1814–1824; the Venice Covered Bridge, 1853–1893; the Woolen Manufactory, 1822–1875; and the oddly named Cyrus Benton "Ditty" Haldeman, 1849–1937.

Ditty was a whittler known widely for his ability with arithmetic and one of those rural characters whose kind has faded from the countryside. Today, people like him are murky ghosts of the past, as much folk tale as flesh. Ditty never aspired to any important job; he never even left Venice. Ditty remained a bachelor, helped local kids with their algebra and geometry homework, kept many cats, hired his sister to keep house for him, read a lot of books, fished often, and left a mountain of books, newspapers, and magazines that grew organically all over his house. For a living, he repaired clocks and farm machinery. Supposedly he was a fellow of the Royal Society of Mathematicians in London and a member of the American Association for the Advancement of Science and the Mathematical Association of America. Once, a math professor from England came all the way to Venice to see him. As Ditty whittled that day, the man presented him with a complicated math problem. Ditty went over to his desk, grabbed a pencil, scratched his head, and in only a few minutes said, "Here's the solution to your problem." The truth is, nobody knows much about Ditty, but stories about his "figuring" prowess have been passed down like family heirlooms.

"Ditty, as he was familiarly known, was the only known genius to live in Venice," Martha Reiner said. "His only formal education beyond the three R's was received in the basement of the Presbyterian church. The minister, I. M. Hughes, conducted a school for higher branches of learning. He told Ditty's parents that he could teach Ditty nothing because Ditty already knew more than he, the teacher."

Sadly, tales of such quirky people are fading as the landscape evolves into suburbs and exurbs and a sport-utility world. Future communities will have to make their own legends, landmarks, and characters.

But for now, and for as long as the sesquicentennial quilt still hangs in the Presbyterian church, people will remember old Ditty and his town—Venice.

4

Footville Is Where the Worlds Meet

In Ashtabula County, in the northeast corner of Ohio, I pulled over to look at a panorama of wheat. On the radio Reba McEntire sang, "Is There Life Out There?"

I knew there was—somewhere. I just had to find it.

The afternoon steamed as I took State Route 46 into Ashtabula, a city of about twenty-five thousand people and the largest community in Ashtabula County. Despite its size, it is not the county seat. Jefferson is. It is a small town—no more than three thousand people—that happens to be centrally located, which is why it's the county seat. Ashtabula has a Lake Erie harbor reminiscent of a New England fishing village. At this harbor, conductors on the Underground Railroad helped escaped slaves board ships and head to Canada.

While in town to eat lunch, I glanced at the lead story in the daily newspaper: "Hot . . . Very Hot." By 1 P.M. the temperature had reached an uncharacteristic ninety-five degrees with humidity so high that it curled wallpaper. The restaurant, recommended to me by a service-station attendant, stood across the street from a white concrete flying saucer with a red stripe around its middle and a glass bubble on top. I asked a young waitress (these days, I consider thirty a young age) what the saucer used to be and she mumbled, "Gas station."

"When?"

She shrugged and said, "Long time ago."

"Oh," I said. "In the 1960s?"

She looked at me as though *I* had just emerged from a spaceship. "No. The '80s!"

No matter. To me, the saucer was fascinating—as large as a medium-sized airplane and mounted on top of a square box where the cashier once sat. Her estimate notwithstanding, the place is a perfect piece of 1960s pop-culture architecture.

After taking a picture of it, I got back on Route 46 and headed into the rural county. No particular reason. I just wanted to say I visited the extreme northeast corner of the state. According to my 1915 Rand McNally map, the county once was the home of now dead or dying towns such as Dick, Wick, Cork, Sweden, Denmark, and Padanararn. In Jefferson, I stopped at the Henderson Library and met director Susan Marirovits. She explained that many of Ashtabula County's small towns declined during the twentieth century. They lost their momentum. "I'm from Rock Creek, about seven hundred souls," she said. "It used to be twice that size when the railroad stopped in town. In fact, Rock Creek used to be larger than Jefferson, but Jefferson has started to grow a lot lately, attracting some industry. The mayor rubs his hands together and says, 'We could triple the population of this town in ten years.' I say, 'Well, maybe that's not so good.' You see, we're used to having a peaceful town. Naturally, this has caused some philosophical differences in Jefferson. I don't think we have to worry about that happening in Rock Creek."

Looking over the hot landscape, I tried to imagine it in the winter. I couldn't. I had heard many horror stories about snow in northeast Ohio. But they can't come close to the big snow of February 3, 1818, which struck the entire Mahoning Valley and areas to the north. At first the snow came down moderately, and pioneers thought it was going to be like any other snowstorm. Then it came faster, more furiously, until it coated everything but full-grown trees. "The earth was covered four feet deep," wrote the editor of the *Historical Collection of the Mahoning Valley* in 1876. "No stumps, no fences, no logs were to be seen on the newly cleared fields. All was smooth as the surface of a calm lake, and presented a most desolate appearance. I will not attempt to describe the labor of the days immediately succeeding the storm, in clearing away the snow, and opening such roads as were necessary for the convenience of the people. Deer were plenty at the time. They found it very difficult traveling through the snow. They could move only by leaps and bounds, and when they alighted were completely buried. The mercury soon went below zero, and continued frozen for many weeks."

In the late 1700s and early 1800s, New England settlers arrived in what is now Ashtabula County. The federal government owned much of the region then, and sold it to land companies to generate badly needed funds. Earlier, English monarchs had granted title to Virginia and Connecticut. The new government, fearing a major dispute, agreed to set aside tracts for the two states. Connecticut's land, most of it called the Western Reserve, was sold to the Connecticut Land Company. New arrivals to the Western Reserve brought their own Yankee concept of how a small town should look—greens, spires, frame houses, and brick streets. Pioneer Turhand Kirtland observed in his diary on June 3, 1798: "Arrived at Grand River, encamped, found . . . as fine large strawberries as ever I saw." The Western Reserve turned into a major agricultural area in a few years. By the mid-1800s, the area had so many dairy farms that the Western Reserve was called Cheesedom. Nearly every community had a cheese factory.

Pioneer towns included Eaglesville, Austinburg, Mechanicsville, Morgan (now Rock Creek), New Lyme, Ship, Gould, and Cherry Valley. Many towns died before the mid-1800s; they lost their main businesses, transportation routes, or other reasons for existing.

In 1799, Judge Eliphalet Austin was bitten by what was assumed to be a rabid dog near his home in Connecticut. When doctors thought he was developing signs of hydrophobia, they advised him to take a trip. (Obviously, the judge had a strong malpractice case.) Feeling better, he decided to go to land he owned in the Western Reserve. He founded Austinburg, which would become the home of the first church in the Reserve. In 1804, the area's first revival was held there, bringing forty-one souls to the Lord that night. But the church had neither building nor pastor. Determined to find a preacher at any cost, the judge's wife rode alone on horseback all the way to Connecticut—six hundred miles, one way. Impressed with her determination, the Reverend Giles H. Cowles agreed to return with her to Austinburg. The congregation's women, meanwhile, had been busy selling subscriptions, as they called them, to raise money to build the church. In 1812, it had the distinction of being the first building erected in the new land without the aid of whiskey as a refreshment. The men complained but were allowed to drink only beer.

Austinburg (originally spelled Austinburgh) became a premier pioneer town. It was the home of the Ashtabula School of Science and Industry, described as "a manual-labor school to educate the pious and worthy young? man for the gospel ministry." At its peak in 1850, the town had 1,285 people. It was one of the Western Reserve's earliest abolitionist centers, before West Andover, Cherry Valley, Hartsgrove, and Rome. Austinburg's pioneer Underground Railroad station keepers included Aaron C. Eliphalet and Joab and L. B. Austin. The road from Austinburg to Ashtabula was well protected by local abolitionists against slave bounty hunters. The abolitionists used to boast: "You might as well attempt to get a saint out of heaven as a slave out of Austinburgh."

By 1920, however, the town's population had declined to three hundred. Today, it is the home of only a few scattered houses.

Later that afternoon, I pushed reason aside and stepped into the summer sauna. Driving south on Route 46, I accidentally turned left on a gravel road and got lost among the fields. A sign in a field read: "Lenox Township—Zoned for Growth." A dairy barn was painted with a large mural of cows. Hawks circled above, and buzzards, with necks like B-29s, pecked on some roadkill. In this country, a stranger can get lost easily; tiny township roads intersect one another at seemingly a million points. In Ashtabula County, many local roads are made of gravel and road signs are wooden arrows painted white with black letters. As I headed east on one road, trying to find Eagleville, a cloud of dust rose before me like a funnel. A big 1980 Buick, moving at least fifty miles an hour, suddenly shot past me, leaving me sitting in dust as dense as morning fog.

I stopped at a farmhouse to ask for directions. An older man sat on the porch and looked at me skeptically.

"Not much in Eagleville."

"That doesn't matter."

"There ain't even a general store any longer."

"No problem."

"Bet you're lookin' for the cemetery. You one of them gemologists?"

"A genealogist? No, I'm not."

Looking disappointed, he turned toward the door.

Eagleville was not difficult to find, once I got back on a concrete road: a dozen older homes, well maintained, with a cemetery and the Eagleville Bible Church. I stopped in the parking lot and drank a Coke. I thought that Eagleville is the kind of town you pass on country roads and, mesmerized by the white lines on gray pavement, you ask yourself: Did I pass a town back there? Eagleville is also an obscure piece of history floating in time. Its name came from an eagle that perched on somebody's mill, according to local legend. The story might be true, for our ancestors generally took no great care in selecting names for their towns. If the community didn't bear the name of a rich pioneer or important official, like Austinburg, then the name selectors could get creative. The map of northeast Ohio illustrates the point: Novelty, Delight, Mecca, Freedom. Often, though, names like Eagleville simply stuck over the years because the town's official name—if there was one—didn't impress the people.

Nobody knows why Eagleville stopped growing. In the mid-1800s, it was a major business center, with a gristmill, cheese factory, hotel, hattery, tanneries, cabinet factory, shoe shop, millinery shop, saw mill, three blacksmith shops, several general stores, a school and a large Congregational church. Then, the place inexplicably vanished. "Like so many towns that once had some industry," Marilyn Aho of the county historical society told me, "Eagleville just petered out. It grew in the first place because the railroad came in. People from Jefferson came to town to catch the train to Warren. Of course, the train's long gone and so is Eagleville. When automobiles came in, people no longer had to stop. They just kept driving through town."

Eagleville did produce one shining story, however: Colonel Roswell Austin, who lived on a farm near town with his wife and son, Henry, was known for his understatement. "When Henry was a well-grown boy," local historian Laura Peck Dorman wrote in 1924, "his father sent him one afternoon to drive up the cows. He left the house and disappeared and was not seen again for years. Exactly seven years, to the hour and day, he was next seen there, driving up the cows from the Mill Creek flats. His father's only remark, as the boy came up to the house, was: 'Henry, you've been a long time getting those cows.'"

Footville was my last stop in Ashtabula County. No need to ask why I went there. The name was enough. I was disappointed to learn that it was named for a founding father by the name of Foot. I had hoped for something stranger, maybe a founder with a foot fetish. I continued into town anyway.

Marilyn Aho warned me: "We have a lot of little places that are no longer towns. I call them Ashtabula County's ghost towns. Places like Footville. It's defunct."

Defunct is a dirty word if it's used to describe your town. One older woman in Footville insisted that the community is bigger and better than ever. Of course, she's lived there only ten years. The remains of Footville do not support her claim. Gone are the lumber mills, a hotel, blacksmith shops, and a cheese factory (1871–1905). In the winter of 1842, the first classes were held in the new Footville School. Five years later, Lauren B. Foot built a new school, which still stands. Students attended it until 1935, when enrollment declined to twenty-five children. The next year, they were sent over to Trumbull Center for their education.

Since then, the old building has been used at times for meetings of the Ruritan Club, a group formed during Ohio's agrarian past to promote harmony between rural and urban people. At the turn of the last century, a distinct social gap existed between the two; city people commonly referred to their rural cousins as rubes, hicks, hayseeds, and bumpkins. Then came Sears, Roebuck and the mail-order companies, and suddenly any farmer from Ashtabula County could buy a white shirt and fancy collar band. Differences slowly melted.

These days, about one hundred people still live in the countryside around the intersection of Graham-Trask Road and State Route 166, near a park with a wooden church and former school that isn't used much these days. Downtown Footville is so small that it barely exists. (Its population reached all of sixty-nine people and a post office in the 1890 census.) The sign for the Footville Community Church is weather-beaten and you cannot read the times of the services. No matter. There are no services.

Footville and the Ruritan Club—its few elderly members were still getting together only a few years ago—find themselves out of sync with the times. There isn't much demand for small cheese factories and blacksmith shops anymore, and no one is seeking harmony between city and country people, who all too often are meeting each other on the road to home. So in this cockeyed modern world, Footville tries to make its place. On occasion, a big-city resident—the television camera operator from Cleveland comes to mind—will join the back-to-the-country movement and buy one of the few houses left in Footville. But he will be disappointed. The noise died a long time ago in this town; the softball diamond went back to grass. When I stopped at the house next door and asked a woman if the church ever conducts special services, she said, "Every so often, an old person will request to be buried out of there."

I wouldn't give Footville much chance of staying alive in the next few years, but then, who knows? If more people like John McMahan move into town, the population erosion could reverse itself. McMahan is not exactly a stranger to this place. The thirty-something pop musician grew up in Footville and for several years worked his ancestral farm. Then he heard the call of the road, which few musicians can ignore. He has traveled all over the world, living in New York, Europe, and, later, Cleveland, which was close enough to home that he and his wife moved back to Footville. He commutes the forty-five miles to Cleveland.

"There's something magical about the topography of this land that appeals to me," he said. "In this corner of the county, it's rolling and beautiful. The rest of Ashtabula County is flat. In the 1800s, my great-great-grandfather, Hiram Spafford, helped found this community, and now every day I pass the trees he planted along the road 160 years ago. I live in the house he built in 1830. My brothers and sisters live around here, too. So there was a lot for me to come back to."

McMahan said he knows, all too painfully, that few people are interested in Footville. When he tells people where he lives, they look at him with bewilderment. "It's the same old situation: the people left town to go where the money was, the city. The population of Footville was once much greater than it is today, but I believe all that will change in the coming years. People are going to get a taste of the city and find out they don't dig it. They'll want to come here. Back home."

5

Sodaville or Bust

Ohio is filled with tiny towns that blew off the map like specks of dust. Many of their names still remain in print. When I drive through these towns, I wonder: Who lived here? What did their people dream? How many families stayed on until the end? Often, no one is left to explain. Obscurity is the only ghost left.

On this trip, I sought to escape into the woods and forget the world and the terrorism that I'd been watching on television. But the news always managed to intrude. Finally, I crossed over the Adams County border and felt the world slowly recede.

The first thing I did was look up a native guide named Stephen Kelley. (When searching for ghost towns, the traveler should seek an expert who knows the history, the local topography, and, certainly, the temperament of the people.) Considering the rugged terrain and rural isolation, and considering that I've had shotguns pulled on me in such places before, I figured that a guide would be useful, even if he came unarmed.

I met the amateur archaeologist and preservationist at his Victorian house in Seaman, a village of several hundred people in northern Adams County, about sixty-five miles east of Cincinnati. You know you're in Seaman because it is the only town in the area with a hitching post on Main Street—and Amish horsemen using it. When I entered Kelley's white house, he was excited about having just acquired a grooved stone ax, one of the most recognizable prehistoric artifacts found in Adams County and Ohio. He ran his fingers across its smooth surface. "Unfortunately, when the pioneers started tilling the soil and discovering these relics, they called them tomahawks," he told me. "The settlers incorrectly assumed that these stone pieces were meant for warfare, because most of the contact between the pioneers and Indians had been in war up until then. The term tomahawk endures. So I always go around telling people, 'Please don't call them tomahawks!' Oh, I'm the life of the party."

The genteel, dry-witted man in his fifties looks like a modern pioneer: long sideburns, black boots, and a western string tie. When he finally has something to say, he talks in a logical, deadpan way, with a hint of sarcasm.

Adams County, population 27,330 in 2000, is his ancestral home and one of Ohio's most rural counties. Kelley retains a strong interest in its heritage, but he does not ignore the negative. "In 1900, our county had more than thirty thousand people and a lot of small towns," he explained. "By 1950, the population had decreased to twenty thousand, and some towns had declined. Why? No work. Our people left to help build the West." They left towns named Tulip, Lynx, Harmony, Unity, Sunshine, Harshaville, Jacksonville, Whippoorwill, Panhandle, Squirreltown, Tranquility, Scrub Ridge, Beaver Pond, Smoky Corners, Jaybird, Bacon Flat, and my all-time local favorite, Sodaville. I had to experience Sodaville, which I imagined as a place that once had Coca-Cola machines on every corner.

On the way, we drove through places of meager means that had almost faded until a few Amish farmers and tradesmen moved in from northeast Ohio in the 1970s. They bought farms and opened bakeries— even a pallet factory. Although the towns didn't grow much at their cores, the surrounding countryside grew and allowed the Unity General Store to remain open. It is a small, white frame building with a wooden floor and tight little aisles packed with loaves of bread and cans of groceries. We stopped to buy candy bars. A teenage Amish boy was standing at the worn wooden counter, contentedly eating a summer-sausage sandwich. The meat carried a distinctive aroma. The look on his face screamed contentment. "He may never go home again," proprietor Eugene Ryan said. Not far away, an Amish man was selling baked goods and weighing them on a battery-powered scale. He insisted that he will never compromise with high technology (or any worldly ways), but incidentally, credit cards are welcome.

Driving through the rugged countryside and its flinty hamlets, we experienced hallowed ground: land still untouched by smog and bulldozers. Near Burnt Cabin Road (another name from pioneer times), I saw a black buggy rolling along the south side of the road. The Amish have revived some local hamlets, preserving them like still lifes.

I remembered once seeing a photograph of an old Harshaville, population sixty-eight in 1890. The town had a post office, blacksmith shop, buggy repair shop, and other businesses; and now I was looking at the same kinds of businesses (minus the post office). As we drove through town we spoke of the miller Paul Harsha, who became wealthy living in this remote place in the 1840s when he opened a water mill on Cherry Fork Creek and built a brick house overlooking his new town. It is still occupied, as is his son's house by the creek. These two are among the only six homes remaining. The covered bridge still stands over the creek in Harshaville, as it did when General John Hunt Morgan's Confederate horsemen rode into town in 1863. Things have changed a little, however; Amish buggies now clatter along gray paved roads, and electric towers protrude like whiskers from the faces of charcoal hills.

Making a right turn on some country road I didn't recognize, we crossed Bundle Run Creek and stopped. Across the great bow of green soared a vulture, wings fully extended like a six-foot black fan. It circled, swooped, and landed in a field. Lacking the sharp claws of most birds of prey, vultures must make do with eating dead animals that they spot with telescopic eyesight. Adams County is filled with vultures, hawks, a few eagles, and other big birds. During one of my visits, sixty black vultures, birds protected by the state, died after eating meat poisoned by insecticides. To put the loss into perspective, consider that black vultures are known to live at least a half century. Perhaps a few of the sixty were around when Adams County's ghost towns were still active in the 1940s.

I hadn't stopped thinking of vultures when Kelley looked around the woods and announced that we were now sitting in the middle of another ghost town—Steam Furnace, home of the first steam-powered smelting furnace west of the Alleghenies in the early 1820s. Today, the only thing steaming in Steam Furnace is the fog burning off the creek. One house stands.

At one time, furnace towns boomed in southern Ohio. A neighboring Adams County town, Marble Furnace, employed six hundred workers. The town that grew up around the furnace took its name from the big smokestack that, from a distance, appeared to be made of marble. Hundreds of woodcutters chopped trees day and night and piled thousands of cords in mounds, set them on fire, and created much-needed charcoal. Their blazing glory lasted about a decade. By the 1830s, Adams County's furnace towns were losing business, being undercut and surpassed by the more efficient furnaces of southeast Ohio. Adams County supported four company towns—Steam Furnace, Marble Furnace, Brush Creek Furnace, and Brush Creek Forge Furnace.

"This place was busy at one time," Kelley said of Steam Furnace. "It developed into a company affair. The workers had to live out here in the woods. Giant mounds of cut wood and black hills of charcoal lay all around, in a wasteland of ashes. Then, all of a sudden, the fires went out. Steam Furnace and the other furnace towns had no reason to exist."

Kelley pulled out a brown paper bag and removed a crude gray metal object with a dish fashioned on the bottom. He said, "This is a slut lamp made in Marble Furnace. It belongs to the county historical society."

"A *what?*"

"A slut lamp. S-L-U-T. Now please don't call it a whore lamp, as a woman in the courthouse mistakenly does. In pioneer times, slut meant animal fat. It was often used with a wick for a lamp. This one's made of cast iron, and it's worth $350. I wish I could afford one."

Moving on down an unidentified country road, we arrived in another ghost town, Mineral Springs, an old health-resort town. The area reminds me of a moon base, isolated and self-contained. The town peaked about 1915, when the advancement of medical science and the automobile made the resort obsolete. Some people in the Mineral Springs area call it Tree Heaven. Conservationists can't stop talking about it. It is a scenic place to visit. Wandering the woods, I realized that this is one place that the developers won't touch—at least for a century. The terrain is too wild, too much trouble to tame. It is also an eerie place on the nights when General Electric, a major landowner, tests its jet engines a few miles away. The hills light up in white and roar ferociously, like a scene in a science fiction film. By day, the land is silent again.

White men first saw the springs about 1787, when the first surveyors entered the wooded county. Natives claimed the water had curative powers. Despite the presence of hostile Shawnee, surveyor Nathaniel Massie bought land in what is now northeast Adams County. He thought people would want to drink water that supposedly cleansed the kidneys and cured various ailments. The trouble was, a Shawnee camp sat only three miles away and the wilderness was filled with bears, cougars, and poisonous snakes. Massie finally gave up and sold the property, which included the mineral springs that fed Grassy Hill (also known as Peach Mountain).

Word of the spring's curative powers soon spread throughout the region, and in 1864 Hillis Rees bought the property and built a two-story log hotel just south of one of the springs. He also started a little resort town, Sodaville, to serve the increasing number of visitors who came to drink the water. By 1872, the town had a post office, two gothic hotels, cabins, and bridle and hiking trails. In 1881, the Cincinnati and Eastern Railroad extended its tracks to the area. Visitors got off the train at the Beaver Pond community, and traveled several miles by wagon to Sodaville.

Resort owners promoted the area's medicinal waters in an era before the development of the modern pharmaceutical industry. In the nineteenth century, such spas were popular across America, especially in rural Ohio, West Virginia, Kentucky, and Indiana. (Today, people don't need to visit such places; they can buy spring water in plastic bottles.)

Around the spring, pioneers observed large numbers of animals drinking the water. Soon they learned that the water contained large amounts of minerals. Speculators came in, built resort hotels, and with advertising lured people from the city and country. Doctors recommended that people drink twenty glasses of water a day. In southern Ohio and Kentucky, the water contained high concentrations of sulfur, which people often described as tasting like burnt gunpowder. Nevertheless, they drank it in volumes. An analysis of the water at Mineral Springs also revealed chloride of magnesia, sulfate of lime, chloride of calcium, chloride of sodium, oxide of iron, and iodine. Visitors often drank water filled with natural diuretics, cathartics, and sudoifics— namely, salt, various sulfurs, chalybeate, vitriol, alum, copperas, iodide, and Epsom salt.

As I traveled through the site where Sodaville once stood, I imagined visitors taking wagons and horses and, later, railroads up the big hill to a few small hotels and related buildings in the thick woods. Outdoors at night, Japanese lanterns provided warm light, and candles and gas lamps lighted the rooms. By 1900, hotel parlors echoed with music from wind-up spring phonographs and visitors debated the world's problems, laughed, and ate wild game. They also hunted, went fishing, received treatments on their aching limbs, and drank more water. Some people came here on vacation in summer, trying to escape the heat of Cincinnati and Portsmouth.

We drove around looking for Sodaville but found nothing left of the town. I wondered how it got its name. Kelley read my mind and said,

"There's always a residue when the water evaporates on leaves and on the ground. It fizzes and dries white—like soda." A few years after Sodaville's founding, other entrepreneurs bought land nearby and founded Mineral Springs, a resort and town named after the spring itself. Other than serving their guests, Sodaville and Mineral Springs had no purpose. Resort owners built a school and church with sharply pointed roofs. They named their church the Little Brown Church in the Vale.

"The area around the resort had an interesting mix of people—the native country folks and the city dwellers who came to the spa," Kelley said. "They had little in common and probably didn't have that much contact inside the town. For years a lot of local people have tried desperately to help this county live down its tough reputation. The truth is, it was a wild, rough county. One hill feud continued for twenty years. When the old man of a feuding hill clan died many years ago, he was buried with a loaded shotgun and a fiddle. In the early 1900s, a newspaper reporter wrote, 'All was quiet this week. Not one killing in Adams County.' During Prohibition, the county sheriff sold moonshine out of the basement of the courthouse. On the other hand, we've had some sheriffs who were champion still-busters."

Taking gravelly Peach Mountain Lane, we found the clearing where Mineral Springs once existed. Instead of towns, we saw an Ohio historical marker:

ADAMS COUNTY MINERAL SPRINGS
Medicinal value of springs promoted by Charles Matheny 1840. First Hotel built 1864 and resort named Sodaville. Under ownership of General Benjamin Coates 1888–91, Smith Grimes 1891–1908, and J. W. Rogers 1908–20. Mineral Springs Health Resort nationally known for its large hotel complex and recreational facilities. This hotel destroyed by fire 1924. Smaller hotel, built in 1904 a quarter mile north, continued operation through 1940.

Looking around, we saw the decaying red roof of a Mineral Springs hotel protruding from the woods. Although the sun burned my arms, the air was cool and pleasant on the "mountain."

"The second hotel stood over there in that forest," Kelley said. "It's frustrating because our old family homes and even this hotel are left to rot. But around here, people don't care. Down the road, a guy is selling a house that was built in 1805. What will happen to it? It will probably be torn down. It's always the same story. In the early 1940s, when the Mineral Springs resort was nearly out of business, my mother worked in the hotel. The war was on then, and nobody wanted to come out here. Hotel owners used to tell people that they could spend some time in Mineral Springs and not worry about getting dressed up and dealing with pretense. 'Social rivalry is unknown here,' they always said."

At the four remaining houses in Mineral Springs, two women worked in their gardens and hardly noticed us. With the exception of the school, which has been restored, no public buildings remain. Pieces of the church lay scattered in a pile. Through the window of one house we saw a dozen looms. Kelley said a Cincinnati woman, Jeanette Macmillan Pruiss, comes out to conduct classes in weaving. Her late husband, the respected surgeon Bruce Macmillan, spent parts of summers in Mineral Springs. "He bought hundreds of acres," Kelley said. "Fortunately for us, he bought and restored the old school and the cottage next door. He preserved our past. He was a world-class traveler. Doc always said, 'I just returned from Hong Kong. Recently, I went to Berlin.' I'd stand there and think I must be the world's greatest hick. I hadn't left Adams County."

When census takers arrived in Mineral Springs in 1890, they counted 108 permanent residents. The town had three ingredients for success: a post office, a train depot, and an express office. The resort included a bowling alley, a post office, a billiards parlor, hotels, and fancy gazebos. A brochure promised an idyllic summer retreat: "Hot and cold baths provided. Acetylene gas is in every room. The water is known to cure various diseases, including dyspepsia, indigestion, disordered liver, chronic irritation of the bowels, costiveness, hemorrhoids, chronic diarrhea, catarrh, diseases of the urinary organs, gravel and kidney diseases, female diseases, dropsy, ulcers, and all nervous and skin disorders."

Kelley laughed at the description and said, "When the owners ran out of diseases, I think they made up some more."

While Mineral Springs was attracting Cincinnati residents in the early 1900s, conservationist E. Lucy Braun discovered the woods around the town. Braun, who lived on the east side of Cincinnati in her own woods, loved the wilderness; to her, there was no better place to work than Mineral Springs. A pioneer of the modern environmental movement, Braun helped introduce the public to the word ecology and in the process became a nationally known botanist.

Emma Lucy Braun was born in Cincinnati in 1889. Her fascination with the woods of Mineral Springs would come naturally, for she and her older sister, Annette (a well-known entomologist who worked with her sister), grew up with schoolteacher parents who encouraged their children to respect and appreciate the woods. In 1914, Braun earned a Ph.D. at the University of Cincinnati, where she went on to teach until 1948. In 1917, she helped establish the Cincinnati Wild Flower Preservation Society. In 1931, her *Naturalist's Guide to the Americas* was the first book to inventory Ohio's natural areas. Even after she retired from the university, Braun continued to roam the woods of Adams County as well as the great forests in eastern Ohio and in Kentucky. She became the first female president of the Ecological Society of America.

"The Brauns are credited with discovering all the rare plant life here and publicizing it by writing about it," Kelley said. "It all started in the '20s and '30s, when E. Lucy and her sister came out here. They brought in other botanists to see their discovery. It has had a lasting impact."

She called the area the Edge of Appalachia, and she loved it. In 1928, she wrote *The Vegetation of the Mineral Springs Region of Adams County,* which is still in print. In 1967, the National Park Service opened the E. Lucy Braun–Lynx Prairie Preserve in Adams County.

The Mineral Springs resort peaked in the early 1900s when Alfred and Eugenia Bader bought the Mills Hotel, one of several hotels at the springs. The couple renamed the place Hotel Baderton and expanded the business. It operated from spring till late fall. The hotel featured a wide front porch with many rocking chairs, rooms furnished with brass beds, and a reading room. Log cabins—named Old Kentucky, Uncle Pat, Aunt Hannah, Blue Ridge, and Luke McLuke—surrounded the hotel on fifty-one acres, which included a long frame bowling alley, tennis courts, and riding trails. Visitors could stay there for twelve dollars a week, or twenty-one dollars for two people. (Special rates were offered for children and servants.)

Alfred Bader called the resort the Switzerland of America. In a 1915 booklet, he wrote: "Here in this joyous Pleasure Ground the old grow young and the young grow younger . . . leave all your cares behind. Plunge headlong into Magnificent Virgin Nature and be riotously, gloriously happy. Here in this joyous VACATION LAND, this HEAVENLY HAVEN, you may soothe jaded nerves, restore appetite, cure indigestion, add pounds to your weight, elasticity to your step, sparkle to your eye, color to your cheek, and set the rich, red blood of perfect health racing electrically through every vein of your body."

"Modesty was not one of Bader's most endearing traits," Kelley said. "He was a promoter who made a lot of money in the five years that he owned the place."

He pulled some old black-and-white photographs from a folder: Sprawling wooden hotels painted white in 1900; E. E. Richards presiding over his open-air fruit cannery on Peach Mountain in 1908, while guests look over his produce; two young women smile as they sit on a stone wall at a hotel in 1910; two boys sit on a massive wall overlooking the Big Spring in 1910; and ten carpenters, who built the Upper Hotel in 1904 for R. B. Mills, sit on a stone edifice at the Lower Spring.

When the Great Depression worsened in the 1930s, Mineral Springs nearly went out of business, a victim of hard times and changing lifestyles. The public had fallen in love with the automobile. The fortunate few with spending money wanted to travel and sightsee rather than spend a vacation at a rural health spa. The resort continued to decline and finally closed in the late 1940s. It could not survive postwar America's fascination with cars, music, and kids.

Nowadays, Mineral Springs lies near an eighty-eight-acre nature preserve, among an ocean of trees that cover the mountain. I walked with Kelley under the arms of ancient oaks that folded across the road like outstretched arms. At the old school, we stood on the porch and listened to the afternoon silence for a minute. I felt a rare serenity as I stared at a sky of deep blue. Slowly then, my ears tracked the screams of a distant blue jay. His melancholy lullaby plummeted, and we stood there looking at the houses and listening to the birds. Kelley shook his head as though perplexed by some minor mystery.

We walked around and found a wall that surrounded the original Big Spring. Visitors carved their names and initials all over the stone. Some were professionally inscribed. Among the dozens of names were "Wm. Schaefer, RIP. O. 1880. Lizzie M. Seiwert, 1901. Rosalia G. Smith, 1900. Wm. G. Popp Wil. Del. 1901. C.A. Liberman, Geo'town O. '04. O. J. Fetter, 1922. Harlan Walker, Dayton, O. 1904."

Behind the main spring basin, a larger, fancier inscription read: "TAKE A DRINK ON Wm. BRUCKMANN."

I said, "He must have been a politician or somebody important, because his name is prominently displayed. It's as if he owned the place. Apparently the owners wanted people to see his name."

Kelley said, "He was a Cincinnati brewery owner in the early 1900s. For a long time I wondered about him. I wondered about all these people. Did they enjoy themselves out here? Were any of them cured by the medicinal waters? What did they do for entertainment on hot summer nights? Mr. Bruckmann was one of the resort's wealthier patrons. Look at this inscription. It's so beautifully carved in the rock. He must have been a big tipper. One day I realized that I had missed his humor—the double meaning behind the words, 'Take a drink on . . .' It's safe to say he came out here to drink more than beer."

Bruckmann came from a long line of German American brewers in Cincinnati. His family's name was synonymous with beer in the Queen City. They distributed Dixie Beer, featuring a logo of a horse's head and a horseshoe. The Bruckmann brewery operated from 1856 to 1950 at Ludlow and Spring Grove avenues. William was a jolly man and one of three brothers who took over the brewery from their father in 1887. All the Bruckmanns had good senses of humor, particularly William. He belonged to a recreation club that on Sundays operated a little steamer—not much larger than a big canoe—on the Miami and Erie Canal. He'd take people to and from his brewery.

Probably Bruckmann inscribed his humorous line at Mineral Springs before December 1, 1918, when Congress prohibited the use of grain to brew beer, and thereby changed his and his company's fate. Bruckmann must have found the news unthinkable. No beer? Has Congress gone mad? That feeling was shared by tens of thousands of Cincinnatians who consumed large quantities of locally made alcoholic beverages. To call Cincinnati a "wet" city was an understatement. It produced almost one-third of the beer made in Ohio. In those days, drinking was more than a passion in Cincinnati; it was an all-consuming hobby. With its hundreds of German beer gardens, breweries, and neighborhood saloons, Cincinnati was a community nearly drowning in booze—until January 18, 1920, that is, when the Wheel Café received its last shipment of beer, two days before the Eighteenth Amendment, or Prohibition, took effect. In one day, Cincinnati breweries closed and familiar Bruckmann bottles disappeared—Bruck's Jubilee Beer and Big Ben Ale ("Always Right, Day or Night"). Other major names in Cincinnati's brewing industry, including Christian Moerlein, disappeared. But Bruckmann did not. The firm jumped on the no-beer wagon and produced nonalcoholic cereal beverages—called "near beer"—and malt tonic, which Cincinnati residents considered poor substitutes for the real thing. Yet that's all they had, unless they bought illegal brew from some three thousand speakeasies in the city limits.

When Congress finally repealed its Prohibition laws, Cincinnati's Bruckmann brothers, William and John C., were ready. On April 7, 1933, delivery trucks pulled out of Ludlow Avenue to deliver downtown Cincinnati's first legal beer in thirteen years.

Once again, the world was ready to take a drink on William Bruckmann.

II

Lost Legends

If there be a matter-of-fact people on the earth, look at Ohio
and you shall see them.

No visions here—no poetry here—all tabernacles of the
flesh—all stern realities.

—*Isaac Appleton Jewett,*
a Harvard graduate of 1831

6

Journey to the Center of Obscurity

My hometown, Hamilton, Ohio, is perched on the banks of the Great Miami and the river of time. It is at once old and new, bold and understated, gothic and neosuburban. I'm never surprised to learn something new about something old. In fact, I expect it to happen in Hamilton.

It is only fitting then that the tale of Captain John Cleves Symmes unfolds in Hamilton. Growing up, I heard the name Symmes mentioned nearly every day—Symmes Road, Symmes Township, the Symmes Tavern, and other area landmarks that bore the family name. Yet today few people realize that Symmes was once a controversial surname in the Ohio Country and the Northwest Territory. New Jersey native John Cleves Symmes, a former judge and a pioneer speculator, bought from Congress thousands of acres between the Little Miami and Great Miami Rivers, in what is now southern Ohio. In a transaction fiasco, however, the judge sold land he didn't own, causing financial turmoil among the pioneers and political battles with Governor Arthur St. Clair. Because the Symmes Purchase was the biggest real estate deal of all time in our area, the name Symmes echoes across the centuries.

Captain John Cleves Symmes was—and still is—mistaken for his irritating uncle. But the captain did not speculate on property. He speculated on ideas. He was more of a Don Quixote, tilting toward the polar caps and loving it. His theory of a hollow earth spawned a popular fantasy novel of the early 1800s, influenced the works of Edgar Allan Poe, and nearly convinced the United States to search for a strange race that supposedly lived inside the earth. (In 1863, French fantasy writer Jules Verne further promoted a hollow planet in *Journey to the Center of the Earth*.) Although the majority of Symmes's contemporaries ridiculed

Captain John Cleves Symmes as he looked during his tours to the East. Drawing by Dan Chudzinski.

him, his idea has continued to attract a small number of followers over the last two centuries.

Despite my familiarity with Hamilton's history, I didn't know that Symmes is buried beneath a hollow metal globe in old Ludlow Park, on North Third Street near downtown. In our Lane Public Library, the only resources available on him are a biographical paper in the local history room and a listing in a reference book called *Roadside Attractions*. Symmes's monument is listed neither in the Hamilton Chamber of Commerce's walking tour nor in any tourist brochures. No signs direct visitors its way. According to the chamber, only about a dozen people a year inquire about the monument.

For a century and a half, Captain Symmes remained an obscure figure in Hamilton's past—practically forgotten. Then in 1991, Historic Hamilton, Inc. hired sculptor Edgar Tafur to restore his monument, which had become scarred, covered by graffiti, and worn smooth by the weather. Tafur patched the damaged sandstone base, waterproofed it, and placed it on a new four-foot pedestal, increasing its stature to nine and a half feet. He also added bronze plaques with the original inscriptions that had been obliterated by time: "Captain John Cleves

Symmes was a philosopher, and the originator of Symmes Theory of Concentric Spheres and Polar Voids."

Tafur's work restored a measure of interest in the good captain. Reporters wrote news stories about his rejuvenated globe, and the city finally recognized the piece for what it is—sculpture. Then, within months, the captain quietly fell back into oblivion. The only Symmes who mattered was the judge. In early 2004, however, I was surprised to learn through the Internet that a group of Symmes's followers, the International Society for a Complete Earth, planned—ever so tentatively—its first Hollow Earth Convention. If and when the bash ever begins, it will be held in the only place on earth worthy of such a gathering—in Hamilton, Ohio. Founded in 1977, the society is operated by an anonymous German naval captain who claims to have visited the inner world. His followers say it is ruled by a "tall, blond, blue-eyed super race" called the Arianni, whose flying saucers patrol the world's skies to stay informed about what we surface creatures are doing. In a 1978 interview with Chicago newspaper columnist Bob Greene, Captain Ritter Von X said, "People will call us crackpots, will try to ridicule us and even stop us. But we are not crackpots. We are a small group [more than a thousand members] made up of physicians, engineers, and pilots."

Out of curiosity, I visited Symmes's grave in the park one gray winter day and pondered Ritter Von X's words. Other surface creatures walked past the monument without comment. Probably I was the only passerby who realized that a man and his dream lay beneath the globe. Other walkers never even glanced at it, as though it did not exist. I stood there wondering if the ghost of the captain ever returns to this forlorn spot to ponder his hollow ideas, or if he ever shoots off to the polar caps to see if they have ever opened. As I thought about it, I realized that his monument is such a solitary and final icon—burial without a headstone. Nearby, young men shot basketball and paid no attention to the black iron fence that surrounds the monument. A dark gray sky set a somber tone in the city park that's bordered on three sides by old houses. At least the place has a theme: On the north side of the park stands another nineteenth-century black iron fence; on the south, about eighty small pillars topped by round stone balls that resemble globes.

As I started to walk away, reporter's notebook in hand, a boy no older than twelve approached me.

"What are you doing with that notebook, mister? You the police?"

"No. I'm writing about this historic site."

"Hey, what's that ball [globe] on the top?"

As I attempted to explain Symmes's theory in five sentences, the boy grew bored and walked away. "Yeah," he said.

Over at the Butler County Historical Society (about four blocks north of the park), I asked curator Marjorie Brown if visitors ever stop at the museum to inquire about the captain. She said few people ever come, but just in case she keeps an old copy of his hollow-earth theory on file. "Definitely an eccentric," she said of the captain, "but a fascinating one."

His friend and supporter, businessman James McBride of Hamilton, once wrote a paper about the hollow earth's plausibility, adding a small measure of credibility to Symmes's idea. McBride was a prosperous and respected citizen, a trustee of Miami University, and the owner of six thousand books. In his paper he described Symmes as a slightly built man with bright blue eyes, a round head, and small, oval face. "His voice is somewhat nasal, and he speaks hesitatingly and with apparent labor," McBride said. "His manners are plain, and remarkable for native simplicity."

One night in 1824, Symmes told a Hamilton audience his theory: the earth is hollow, occupied by another people, and ready for exploration. Then he asked for volunteers to accompany him to the new world's polar entrance. All he would need, he told them, was two big ships and 250 tons of equipment. The proposal made them laugh. It was no way to impress his new neighbors. By then, the world's leading scientists and politicians had already dismissed the "Theory of Concentrick Spheres." Soon people started remarking about some long-absent friend, "Why, he must fallen down Symmes's Hole." Yet the Captain persisted. "When he had a poor audience at Hamilton, Ohio," *Harper's New Monthly* said in 1882, "he would think of neglected Columbus and trudge on to Gardiner, Maine; unnoticed there, he would console himself over the fate of badly used Galileo, and tramp away somewhere else."

He maintained that concentric spheres were the natural order of things: "Enquire the botanist, and he will tell you that the plants which spring up spontaneously agreeable to the established laws of nature, are hollow cylinders . . . even the minutest hairs of our heads are hollow. Go to the mineralist, and he will inform you that the stone called

Aerolites, and many other mineral bodies, are composed of hollow concentric circles."

Symmes believed that concentric circles existed with the planets. As they revolved, he said, they naturally created holes around their axis points, causing the oceans to enter one side and exit the other. His theory was ridiculed widely, and it was not even original. Mathematician Leonhardt Euler once considered it. In *Epitome astrononomiae* in 1618, early proponent Johannes Kepler claimed the earth was made of concentric shells. In 1692, astronomer Edmund Halley (famous for the comet that bears his name) suggested that the earth had three internal spheres that revolved at different speeds. He said the planet also had an interior sun. By 1716, he was convinced that a luminous atmosphere between the spheres might be the cause of the aurora borealis. Despite Halley's interest in the subject, the world did not embrace the notion of a hollow earth.

Probably Symmes didn't know any of these previous theories; he was not well educated, but he was curious and creative. That he could develop such an idea independently makes his work even more impressive. Yet scientists of the day rejected him. Cincinnati mathematician Thomas Matthews called Symmes's theory "a heap of learned rubbish." The more criticism he received, the more stubbornly Symmes refused to give up. In 1819 he wrote "Light between the Spheres," and managed to convince the *National Intelligencer* to publish the story. The exposure helped attract crowds to his lectures, but they were not always supportive.

In 1820, his ideas inspired a novel, *Symzonia: Voyage of Discovery* by the pseudonymous Captain Adam Seaborn, who wrote that on his adventures he discovered an island at the earth's end, where the people were five feet tall and far advanced intellectually. It was widely assumed that Symmes wrote the book, and he did not deny doing it. (When Arno Press of New York reprinted *Symzonia* in 1975, the company officially assigned authorship to Captain John Cleves Symmes.) Nevertheless, some scholars remain skeptical.

The thinly veiled world of Symzonia referred to the inner territory of the earth, which was inhabited by a race of fair-skinned and peaceful people. As the captain prepared to meet the subterranean people, he said: "I was about to secure to my name a conspicuous and imperishable place on the tablets of History, and a niche of the first order in the temple of fame." Of course, that also happened to be Symmes's opinion of himself, as architect of the Theory of Concentrick Spheres (or, as some less charitable people called it, the Theory of Symmes's Hole).

The author claimed the earth had a shell of about eight hundred miles thick, with openings at the poles that were fourteen hundred miles wide. The book, an early American Utopian novel, was excerpted in various publications. It explained Seaborn's polar adventures in what he called the Inner World, where he discovered Symzonia. Its inhabitants flew in airships, spoke in a musical language, defended themselves with huge flamethrowers, and lighted their dark world with a series of mirrors that refracted the light coming in through the polar openings. People living on the earth's surface were the descendants of Symzonia's exiles. *Symzonia* was one of the early fantasy books.

Bolstered by publicity from the novel, Symmes started touring Ohio's cities to seek converts. The book gave him a measure of notoriety, if not credibility. He took with him a polished wooden globe that came apart to reveal the internal spheres and the polar holes. It worked using iron filings, magnets, and sand, and today this rare piece of Americana can be found in the Philadelphia Academy of Sciences.

Despite his fascinating prop, "Captain Symmes met with the usual fate of projectors, in living and dying in great pecuniary embarrassment," historian Henry Howe wrote in 1898. "In person, he was of the medium stature and simple in his manners. He bore the character of an honest, exemplary man, and was much respected. He advanced many plausible and ingenious arguments, and won quite a number of converts among those who attended his lectures."

Unfortunately, Symmes lacked a public speaker's charisma. He was terrified of stepping before crowds. Even McBride admitted: "[There is] scarcely any thing in his exterior to characterize the secret operations of his mind. . . . Captain Symmes's want of a classical education, and philosophic attainments, perhaps, unfits him for the office of lecturer." Yet he began cultivating supporters (if not sufficient donations), and by 1820 he had become recognizable enough for John Audubon to sketch him in pencil for Cincinnati's Western Museum.

By coming west, Symmes was merely following the path of his uncle, John Cleves Symmes. The captain was born November 5, 1780, in Sussex County, New Jersey, where his uncle served as a state Supreme Court judge. (Their ancestors had come to North America in 1634.) The judge dreamed of going west to speculate on land and becoming rich, and in the process he founded the village of North Bend, near Cincinnati. Unlike his nephew, Judge John Cleves Symmes was a grumpy fellow who angered a number of business clients. Many pioneers—even people today—confused the captain with his uncle because they shared the same name. Actually, the captain was the son of the Reverend Timothy Symmes, a brother of John Cleves Symmes. The young man headed West and, once there, was promptly confused with his irritating uncle. So he joined the army and made sure people identified him as the captain.

At twenty-two years old, he fought bravely in frontier battles and served in New Orleans and at Fort Adams, near Natchez. He once said he joined the military "to merit and obtain distinction, and accumulate knowledge, which I had seldom tasted but in borrowed books." He wanted to be somebody. While in the army on Christmas Day in 1808, he married Mrs. Mary Anne Lockwood, widow of another captain at Fort Adams. She brought to the marriage five sons and one daughter, whom Symmes came to think of as his own. He fathered five of his own children with Mary Anne: daughters Louisiana (born 1810) and Elizabeth (1814) and sons Americus Vespucius (1811), William Henry Harrison (1813), and John Cleves Jr. (1824). Adding to the confusion, Junior would become known as Captain John Cleves Symmes Jr., which his father was often mistakenly called.

Eleven children became a financial burden on John and Mary Anne Symmes. For years, John continued to pay the taxes on land once owned by his wife's first husband, and when the man's children left home as adults, Symmes gave them the property without charging interest.

During the War of 1812, he was promoted from lieutenant to captain. While in the army, Symmes fought a duel with a fellow officer. The captain suffered a bullet wound to his wrist, which bothered him for the rest of his life. His opponent, whom Symmes shot in the thigh, later became a good friend. Symmes retired from the military in 1816 and settled in St. Louis, then in the Missouri Territory, to sell supplies to soldiers and Indians. He spent his spare time reading about surveying, geography, and philosophy and developing his theory of the hollow earth. On April 10, 1818, he issued the theory's *Circular Number One,* which he sent to universities and political leaders across the United States and the world. (Anticipating rejection, he wisely included a certificate of sanity.) He wrote:

TO ALL THE WORLD!

I declare the earth is hollow and habitable within; contains a number of solid concentrick spheres, one within the other; and that it is open at the poles 12 or 16 degrees; I pledge my life in support of this truth, and am ready to explore the hollow, if the world will support and aid me in this undertaking.

Jno. Cleves Symmes
Of Ohio, late Captain of Infantry.

N.B.—I have ready for the press, a Treatise on the principles of matter, wherein I show proofs of the above positions, account for various phenomena. . . . I ask one hundred brave companions, well equipped, to start from Siberia in the fall season, with Reindeer and slays, on the ice of the frozen sea: I engage we find warm and rich land, stocked with thrifty vegetables and animals if not men, on reaching one degree northward of latitude 62; we will return in the succeeding spring.

Also in his document, which he sent to every city and village he could find, he claimed that people lived inside the earth in a lush environment, that animals migrated there, and that the new world could be reached through a six-thousand-foot opening at the North. His writings were part mumbo-jumbo, part science, part rambling rhetoric. His theory intrigued a few people, who formed the Hollow Earth Society. They saw logic in Symmes's idea that "the earth, as well as all the celestial orbicular bodies existing in the universe . . . are all constituted in a greater or less degree, of a collection of spheres, more or less solid, concentric with each other, and more or less open at the poles."

In 1819, he moved briefly to Newport, Kentucky, about thirty miles south of Hamilton, across the Ohio River from Cincinnati. Being unsuccessful there, he moved to Cincinnati later that year. A local book editor called Symmes "the most remarkable man who came to Cincinnati this year" and devoted more space to him than the city's rich and powerful men. He lived in a three-story brick row house on lower Market Street, between Broadway and Sycamore Streets. The dreamer became so obsessed with his theory that he could do nothing but talk and write about it. Newspaper writers enjoyed mocking him. The Academy of Science in Paris refused to discuss the theory. Nevertheless, the odd subject attracted large crowds when Symmes spoke all over the United States. He made good entertainment—sort of an unreality show of his day.

About 1821, he moved to a farm near Hamilton, but he rarely stayed at home. There's no evidence that Hamilton sincerely embraced him or his idea, although the council did issue a friendly proclamation: "Resolved, that we esteem Symmes's Theory of the Earth deserving of serious examination and worthy of the attention of the American people."

On March 29, 1824, an amateur acting group, the Newport Thespian Society, put on a play, *The Tragedy of Revenge,* to raise money for his proposed voyage to the North. They encouraged him. Also that year, Cincinnati poet Moses Brooks praised Symmes:

> Has not Columbia one aspiring Son
> By whom the unfading laurel may be won?
> Yes! History's pen may yet inscribe the name
> Of Symmes to grace her future scroll of fame.

Other communities proclaimed him crazy. Congress refused his financial requests; so did European monarchs. Even the Ohio General Assembly ignored his pleas for moral support and intervention with Congress. On the road, he suffered from dyspepsia and other illnesses. While on an extended lecture of the East Coast, he ran so low on money that he couldn't pay his forty-dollar rent, and a New York landlord had him thrown in jail. A Cincinnati resident, who happened to be in New York, heard about Symmes's plight and paid his bail.

Although unable to launch his own expedition, Symmes did help stimulate interest in the mysterious polar areas. In 1828, several American groups prepared to go to Antarctica, including U.S. Navy officer Charles Wilkes. As a result of these explorers' findings, the American scientific community gained stature in Europe.

That year Symmes found a young believer in Jeremiah N. Reynolds, a graduate of Ohio University and the editor of the *Wilmington Spectator,* a newspaper in Clinton County. Reynolds convinced Symmes to embark on an exhausting tour of the East Coast in hopes of raising money for an expedition to the polar holes. While Symmes was not an engaging public speaker, people wanted to see him out of curiosity. As his health declined, he parted with Reynolds, who by this time had noticed a greater interest in the polar areas than in the hollow-earth theory. Symmes ended up in New Jersey, where he stayed with a friend while recovering from various illnesses. After returning to Hamilton, he continued to write. Reynolds and his contacts reportedly convinced

A monument to Captain John Cleves Symmes still stands in Hamilton's Ludlow Park. He is buried beneath it.

President John Quincy Adams to launch an expedition to the poles, but Andrew Jackson canceled the plan after he took office.

Symmes did not live to see any polar exploration. He died in Hamilton on May 29, 1829, at age forty-nine years and six months. To glorify his father, Americus Vespucius Symmes erected the city's most unusual monument: a five-and-a-half–foot stone marker topped by a twenty-inch globe weighing eighty pounds. (For the next forty-five years, Americus would promote his father's ideas in vain.)

Later in 1829, Reynolds convinced a New Yorker named Dr. Watson to pay for an expedition to the South Pole. While on the way, the crew mutinied and left Reynolds and Watson in South America. After spending time in Chile, Reynolds served as a U.S. frigate's secretary, and traveled around the world. In the late 1830s he returned to America and started lecturing on the polar caps and Symmes's theory. Even then, the polar areas were like other planets today—mysteries waiting to be seen up close. (When in the 1840s a wooly mammoth was found buried in the snow in Siberia, supporters of the hollow-earth theory shook their heads knowingly and said, "Ah-ha!")

Reynolds found eager audiences when he returned to the lecture circuit. An admirer, Henry Allan, heard Reynolds speak and relayed the ideas to his writer brother, Edgar Allan Poe, who became fascinated. Poe used them in his story "MS Found in a Bottle" and later in his only novel, *The Narrative of Arthur Gordon Pym*. As he lay dying in 1849, Poe reportedly cried, "Reynolds! Reynolds! Oh, Reynolds!"

The erroneous hollow-earth idea did not die with Poe. It lingered, reviving at times like a scientific plague. Important polar expeditions began in the 1850s and continued regularly for a century. By the 1890s, such trips were attracting major public attention, as explorers pushed their way farther into the snowy polar areas.

After several attempts, American Robert E. Peary finally reached the North Pole on April 6, 1909. He found no hole at the top of the world. No flame throwing little people and no lush gardens. He did find ice jams and cold temperatures, and he lost eight toes to frostbite. On December 14, 1911, Roald Amundsen of Norway reached the South Pole and discovered Queen Maud Land and conducted oceanographic research. He found no hole in the earth, either. From 1914 to 1916, England's Ernest Shackleton attempted the first crossing of Antarctica. On May 9, 1926, Richard E. Byrd explored the northern arctic region by airplane. On November 29, 1929, he took an extensive nineteen-hour flight over the South Pole, and established America Base on the Ross Ice Shelf.

Of the dozens of important polar explorers through two centuries, only Byrd came close to living out Captain Adam Seaborn's dream. America gave a returning Byrd a ticker-tape parade and honored him for his achievements, even when the world's critics questioned his findings. In those happy years before the Great Depression, before so many technological advancements had jaded America's attitudes, Byrd was the nation's adventurer and hero.

Although he did not discover any strange race of people, he did reach the top and bottom of the world and became the kind of national hero that Captain John Cleves Symmes always wanted to be—the man who saw the poles.

In the years following Symmes's death, two of his sons continued their own far-out quests. (Only William Henry Harrison Symmes, a physician, seemed unaffected by his father's legacy.) They must have inherited their father's passion for lonely stands, promoting the absurd, and inviting public ridicule. In the 1860s, John Cleves Symmes Jr.—military inventor, former assistant professor of ethics at West Point, and recent émigré to Prussia—designed a flying machine named the Simzee, a contraption that looked like an umbrella mounted atop two flapping wings. (To further add to the confusion, he named his son John Haven Cleves Symmes.) By then an influential friend had finally convinced Symmes Jr. to reject the hollow-earth idea, but he turned around and embraced his own improbable notion of the rickety flying machine. He envisioned sailing the machine to the polar caps to disprove his father's theory (as if by then it needed disproving) and then flying to Mexico and the United States, where he would surely be elected the next president. In letters to someone named John, he expressed his mounting frustrations and continued confidence against impossible odds. "Oh! For this day have I sought, & prayed, & striven, & fought—fought for patience or success—for 8 long years," he wrote on May 16, 1869. "For this alone. For this, I rejected your advice to 'turn my hand to something' that would help fill purse. For this have I lived so 'subdued' . . . and now I find the greatest place in my land opening its arms to clutch me; and the greatest place in all History—I see it—preparing for me."

Americus, meanwhile, remained equally busy. He farmed and lived in Hamilton until the 1830s, when he moved to Covington, Kentucky. He spent the rest of his life trying to vindicate his father's theory, an impossible mission. For his trouble he received his share of condemnation and laughter. He did manage to revive some interest in the theory, until polar expeditions in the 1850s helped end hollow-earth discussions for several decades. But ridicule did not take a holiday. The term "Symmes's Hole," fashionable in Ohio and other areas in the 1820s, had slipped into the public lexicon. It meant anything worthless. Unperturbed by the public's view of his family, Americus moved to a farm near Louisville (he named it Symzonia) and wrote hundreds of letters to editors to promote his father's theory, until it became an even worse joke. After gathering additional information, in 1878 he wrote a new booklet on the subject. He thought he had proved the idea conclusively. But by then, the world was too distracted, too modern, to care about concentric spheres.

When Americus sued a Louisville turnpike company for allowing potholes to form in a road, the defense attorney added insult to argument: "Mr. Symmes could see a hole where nobody else could, like his father before him."

Perhaps out of sympathy, the jury awarded Americus Vespucius Symmes fifteen hundred dollars for his trouble. He *did* find a hole, after all.

7

Separate Spirits

A couple of hours before dusk, I pulled into Zoar in northeast Ohio. Dense fog covered the trees and cupolas like bed sheets. At first, I thought I was driving into heavy smoke, but then I realized that the light rain and high humidity had created a wall of haze that stood along the Ohio and Erie Canal. On the town's narrow streets, yellow lights glowed dimly, invitingly, from back porches and gardens buried deep within the fog.

I came to stay the night in one of Ohio's historic communities: a German Separatist village that flourished in the early 1800s. I wanted to experience Zoar for what it was—a communal enclave in Buckeye farm country. I wasn't disappointed in the surroundings, for they reminded me of a set for one of those horror films about an old village coping with its demons. The place looked downright eerie in the thick fog. As I drove past log houses and the big, unused hotel, I felt a little uneasy, and then I remembered that this town also sponsors such benign events as a Christmas walk and a Civil War camp reenactment.

The old canal still has water in it—as well as too many big mosquitoes that attacked me through my open car window. As I carried my suitcase into the Cowger House Bed and Breakfast (known in Zoar as the Number Nine House), I paused to read a large, framed rectangular poster from the 1890s that was affixed to a wall in the dark rear hall:

PUBLIC SALE.
The trustees of Separatists of Zoar will sell at public sale . . . 100 houses! 100 milk cows! 200 young cattle! 300 sheep! 100 hogs!

At that moment I understood: the commune of Zoar didn't survive the new century of capitalism. At random I chose a room on the second floor. When the light shower stopped about thirty minutes later, from my window I watched the wooden town unfold like a flower. Everything brightened up. I walked down to the Zoar Store, built in 1833 and now operated by the Ohio Historical Society. It also operates eleven other buildings in town, including the Number One House, sewing shop, magazine complex, garden and greenhouse, dairy, and hotel.

Nowadays, residents live in the Zoarites' original houses. They call Zoar a living village. Because the old architecture is still intact, Zoar is one of the few towns that can live in both the past and present. In one way, its past version is a ghost town. The Zoarites are gone; in their place live modern families who are not members of the founding sect. The Zoar Community Association, a group of residents and business people formed in 1967 to preserve the history and heritage of Zoar, operates a museum in the town hall. Anyone can rent the Zoar Schoolhouse for meetings, weddings, and special events. It is as if the modern residents are simply caretakers for a dead race.

The community is no longer self-sufficient; modern Zoar is a commuter and tourist town. Larger events include the Harvest Festival, Apfelfest, Christmas in Zoar, and the Spring Garden and Backyard Tour.

The village is still undeniably German, settled by Separatists who fled Wurttemberg with their mystic leader in search of religious freedom in America. They called themselves Separatists because they often opposed the state's Lutheran Church for its formal doctrine. Originally, they were pietists, who believed in leading a purer life through individual rebirth and attaining a purer moral life through prayer meetings, Bible study, and attending Sunday school. When rationalism influenced church leaders in the 1700s, pietists separated from the Lutheran Church. Many of the Separatists were known as chiliasts, the believers in a doctrine of premillenialism (they thought Christ would return in 1836). Later, the sect drifted toward mysticism, and by 1791 it had grown larger, with dissenting pietists who opposed the new church hymnal as being too worldly. For breaking away, the Separatists were often harassed, imprisoned, and murdered by the state. Separatists did not accept sacraments such as confirmation, marriage, and baptism. They also opposed military service (a dangerous stance in the German

NO.1 HOUSE -- ZOAR VILLAGE

Many of Zoar's old buildings still stand, including the Number One House, built in 1835.

states of the period), and the more radical members refused to pay taxes. A few of them practiced vegetarianism and celibacy.

Zoar's founders arrived in Ohio in a century when communes, some of them religious, were operating in rural areas across the United States. They included the Perfectionists of Oneida, New York; the Shakers at various sites in Ohio, Kentucky, and the East; the Harmonists at Economy, Pennsylvania; the communal societies of Aurora and Bethel in Missouri and Oregon; and the Amana Society in Iowa. German immigrants with spiritual leaders also founded the Aurora, Amana, and Harmony groups. But each one espoused different principles.

The Separatists needed a new home and found one in America. Each member sold his possessions to help pay for the voyage. In August 1817, they arrived in Philadelphia. Assisted there by Quakers, the group arranged to borrow money to buy land. The Quakers suggested they settle in Ohio. In October, the members arrived in the Tuscarawas River Valley to build a village, which they named Zoar in honor of the place where Lot went after fleeing Sodom in biblical times. Over the next fifteen years, the Zoarites bought fifty-five hundred acres to farm. Their emblem became the seven-pointed star of Bethlehem; their symbol, the acorn.

The Zoarites lived as a commune after their early attempts at farming failed. Unlike other communal groups, which operated this way for political or religious reasons, the Zoarites did it for practical purposes; they knew no other way to survive. All property and earnings became common stock. On April 19, 1819, 53 men and 104 women established the Society of Separatists of Zoar, under the leadership of Joseph Baumeler (later spelled Bimeler), their agent and spiritual leader. He disliked ministers, saying they knew books but not God. He discouraged marriage (but in fact he was married with children). He and his followers did not use prayer books; they thought they were harmful and preachers deceitful. And members were ahead of their time in one way: Men and women held equal rights in making community decisions, and women worked in the fields alongside the men.

Despite having some success raising crops, the Zoarites needed more money to stay in business. In 1827, the group decided to contract with the state to dig the Ohio and Erie Canal, which would pass through their land. Most communities allowed the state to dig the canals, but the hardworking Zoarites recognized the coming of the canal as a means of getting out of debt. When members finished the difficult work in 1828, they earned $21,000—more than enough to pay the $16,500 mortgage that they owed the Quakers. Because the canal ran next to the town, the Zoarites knew they could make money from commerce. They operated four canal boats, provided services to canal travelers, and sold their surplus goods. In 1835, the society became practically self-sufficient and increasingly wealthy. Seventeen years later, its property was valued at more than one million dollars—a substantial sum in those days.

Unfortunately, the society had little time to enjoy its good fortune. Bimeler died in 1853, leaving the group without its leader. On top of that, canal traffic started to decline. But it took decades for Zoar to die as a communal society.

At its peak, Zoar was green and prosperous. Apple trees grew everywhere. Members loved flowers and planted them in large gardens in the center of town, where they grew vegetables, flowers, and small fruits. On an entire block, they built the Zoar Garden and Greenhouse in 1835. It symbolized the new Jerusalem described in the Revelation of John. In the center—called the Centrum—stood a Norway spruce, representing everlasting life; a surrounding arbor signified heaven. Around the spruce stood twelve juniper trees, representing the twelve apostles. A circular walk enclosed the Centrum, from which twelve other walks led farther into the four corners of the garden, denoting the various paths to heaven. From each of these paths led smaller ones, like the worldly paths that people take as they seek the Lord's salvation. Yet another, wider path went around the whole garden, to show the path of unredeemed souls.

The Zoarites grew flowers for their own enjoyment in the early years, but later they grew them commercially for markets in Cleveland and other places across the Midwest. Gradually, the society at Zoar branched into many different moneymaking operations. In the 1840s, at its peak of five hundred members, the community baked; made soap; grew grapes for wine; worked on the canal boats; brewed beer; raised and sold chickens and hogs (this was before they decided against eating pork); forged iron products; made pottery; milled flour; raised sheep for the wool; produced milk and butter; sewed clothing; and built stoves, tools, plows, and wagons. They also operated a general store and hotel that catered to outsiders.

Filled with their success, the Zoarites expanded. Dallas Bogan of the Warren County Historical Society in southwest Ohio told me he believes the Zoarites founded another town called Zoar in his county in the 1840s, although firm evidence linking the two towns is lacking.

Warren County's Zoar prospered immediately, keeping busy two blacksmith shops and two wagon makers' shops that employed eight to ten laborers. According to *History of Warren County, Ohio,* "Prosperity was destined only to be transitory. The streets of Zoar became long ago deserted and the sound of the hammer is no longer heard within her borders." Until now, that is. When I drove through the ghost town on U.S. Route 22 / State Route 3, I noticed development all around me. Now, suburban people are fleeing to Zoar because it is only about five miles from Interstate 71. The rest of Zoar consists mostly of a few small brick and wooden houses built from the 1930s to the 1960s, the Zoar United Methodist Church, St. Philip's Catholic Church, a storage building, and a body shop. Nothing remains of the old town.

Tuscarawas County was much better suited to a long-lasting town because it offered prime farmland, the canal, and the church elders. Yet visitors of the period must have considered the Zoarites an odd sect. After all, what Christian people disregarded baptism and the Lord's Supper? What kind of gentleman wanted no titles—not even mister? Kept his hat on in a public room? Called a sermon anything but a sermon? Because the Zoarites believed all men were equal, members neither tipped their hats nor bowed. They did not mark their graves. They worked on Christmas, Easter, Sundays, and holidays, which they barely considered. The Zoar women, who outnumbered the men three to one at one point, were largely responsible for digging out much of the canal. Residents' homes were numbered, but not in sequence; when people moved to another house, they took their number with them. (The Zoarites wanted to simplify everything, so they identified their buildings by numbers, not names.) Members were also obsessed with cleanliness. They scoured and scrubbed the village daily—even the trees. They removed and washed windows every day. They used two soaps—toilet soap for the face and a homemade soap for the body. Members caught using the more expensive toilet soap on their bodies received a reprimand. They drank beer—no, *savored* it. Never too happy with marriage, by the 1820s they embraced celibacy to give women more time to work on the canal. The Zoarites believed that God only tolerated marriage, and that it caused trouble in the community, but they did not forbid members from marrying. Celibate members divided themselves into houses of twenty each—for men, women, or both. They lived by the twelve Principles of the Separatists, including this one (number nine): "All intercourse of the sexes, except what is necessary to the perpetuation of the species, we hold to be sinful and contrary to the order and command of God. Complete virginity or entire cessation of sexual commerce is more commendable than marriage."

When children reached age three, they were placed in community nurseries until they turned fourteen. (In 1840, one of the town trustees refused to send his children to the nursery, so the town dropped the requirement. By 1860, the practice died out.) The idea was to free the women to work outside their homes. Mothers and fathers did not see their children too often in those days. Rearing the children was left to the nursery supervisors; some were harsh and cruel. They insisted that the children earn their room and board by performing household tasks. Children lived in quarters that were hot and humid in the summer and cold in the winter. The early Zoarites believed a kiss was sinful and didn't even believe in kissing their children.

While visiting the community in 1875 to write *The Communistic Societies of the United States,* reporter and author Charles Nordhoff couldn't reconcile many of the Zoarites' odd practices. He decided that he would not want to live in such a place. He wrote:

Yet, when I had left Zoar, and was compelled to wait for an hour at the railroad station, listening to men cursing in the presence of women and children; when I saw how much roughness there is in the life of the country people, I concluded that, rude and uninviting as the life in Zoar seemed to me, it was perhaps still a step higher, more decent, more free from disagreeables, and upon a higher moral scale, than the average life in the surrounding country. And if this is true, the community life has even here achieved moral results, as it certainly has material, worthy of the effort.

After visiting a dozen communal towns across America, Nordoff considered Zoar a town filled with dull and lethargic people:

Though founded fifty-six years ago, [it] remains without regularity of design; the houses are for the most part in need of paint; and there is about the place a general air of neglect and lack of order, a shabbiness, which I noticed also in the Aurora community in Oregon, and which shocks one who has but lately visited the Shakers and Rappists.

The Zoarites have achieved comfort—according to the German peasant's notion—and wealth. They are relieved from severe toil, and have driven the wolf permanently from their doors. Much more they have accomplished; but they have not been taught the need of more. They are sober, quiet, and orderly, very industrious, economical, and the amount of ingenuity and business skill which they have developed is quite remarkable.

In 1884, the town incorporated as a village, with an elected mayor, council, and secretary-treasurer. The religious society continued to function, without the commune. By 1898, when it was obvious that the boom times of the canal were never coming back, the members disbanded the society. Each received land, a house, and possessions.

Zoar became just another declining canal town with an unusual name.

I walked over to the Zoar Store and asked to go along on a group tour. A historical society guide named Steve Shonk, of Navarre, escorted us on a tour that he gives four days a week. He dressed in the style of Zoarite clothing that was typical in the 1850s, complete with broad-brimmed straw hat and white linen shirt and dark trousers.

While walking around town with him, for a moment I forgot that he was not a Zoarite. He was precise in his terms and explanations, and appreciative but not adoring of what the sect accomplished.

We walked along the damp blacktopped streets while Shonk talked. When he's not leading tours, he is writing the *Zoar Star,* a newsletter published quarterly by the Zoar Community Association.

The Zoar Store was built in 1833 at Main and Second Streets. The building served as the group's business headquarters, post office, and store. The early residents had so little money that they had to sell homemade utensils and other useful things to the farmers and hired men of the area.

"I don't know if there was any friction between the people of Zoar and the people of the county, but there was a healthy curiosity," Shonk said as we walked between the buildings. "They all did business together. They didn't have time for animosity. German immigrants were often sent straight to Zoar because they could find work there and speak the language. Newcomers would find out about the communal arrangement soon enough. Some didn't mind it. They'd stay on. Others would leave for Dover and Canton and other area towns.

"Zoar hired a lot of outside laborers. The town welcomed some of them, but some others were not received so well. This had more to do with practical matters than religious. In 1834, thirty-five to fifty villagers were claimed in a cholera epidemic. The town was left shorthanded. The Zoarites decided to hire outside laborers. Some of the elders were against the idea, fearing the effects of outside influences, but the group had no choice. They needed help. They decided to accept only Germans—poor ones who had less to leave behind in the world. The Germans were sought because of the cultural similarities. A man could join at age twenty-one, a woman at age eighteen. Of course, they could live in Zoar and not become a member of the religious sect. They simply received a wage and were not included in the ownership of the community. In 1847, a big wave of immigrants came over from Germany. They settled here. Some were not Separatists, but they ended up staying anyway. One of those families was Catholic. It didn't matter. Anyone could attend services in Zoar."

We passed the cobbler shop, a large wooden building where cobblers made and repaired all the shoes for the community. The frame building, constructed in 1828, is now the Cobbler Shop Bed and Breakfast. In back, owner Sandy Worley uses the original wash house (where all the laundry for the Zoar Hotel was done) for storage.

At Main and Second Streets, the hotel is the most gothic of all the buildings, with a large cupola, wide front porch, and dormer windows on the third floor. The building awaits renovation by the state historical society. Initially, it had forty sleeping rooms and a huge dining room. People of all income levels stayed there; many arrived by canal boat. Wealthy people from Cleveland came to town in the winter to observe how the Zoarites operated their greenhouses. (They heated them with coal.) All outsiders, whether multimillionaire, middle class, or poor, ate in the hotel dining room. No class distinctions were recognized; even a beggar ate here, and President William McKinley stayed more than one night. People used to walk up the winding stairway to the observatory or tower to meditate.

"The canal, the woolen mill, and the tin shop practically supported the town," Shonk said. "The people of Zoar mined the hills around the town and operated a foundry and two iron furnaces. After a slow start, they started making money and paid off their debts. They weren't afraid of hard work, and they knew how to invest. At one time, Zoar had one of Tuscarawas County's highest tax bills, because the commune owned so many acres. Back in Germany, the group got into trouble for refusing to pay taxes. They didn't want their money to support the army. In this country, they didn't have that problem. They had no problem paying their taxes."

As we passed the oddly shaped buildings, most of them built by the people of Zoar, I asked Shonk about the town's legacy. He thought for a moment and said, "Its legacy is in its buildings. Their houses still remain. Their furniture remains. They left us those things. It's fortunate that enough descendants were left to donate artifacts to the state when the community was being restored twenty years ago. We lost a few buildings to lack of use, but we still have a town and it looks much the way it did when the commune was running. It is living history to us."

Over night, the air turned cool. A misty rain fell across the fields. After a quiet, restful night at the Cowger House, I walked over to the log cabin that Mary and Ed Cowger also owned and operated as a smaller bed and breakfast. Although the couple, then in their fifties, enjoyed meeting people, they were also in a demanding business; taking care of two bed and breakfasts required a lot of time and energy. They had been in the business since they came to Zoar in 1984 and opened the

Cowger House. They later bought the cabin (built in 1817) and the first schoolhouse (1833).

As candles burned brightly on the rugged pine table, I talked in the cabin's main room, the dining room, and waited for the couple to serve a full breakfast. At 10 A.M., they walked in carrying poached eggs, sausage, biscuits, hash browns, hot tea, and orange juice.

Scanning the room, I noticed that every piece of furniture was original, at least a century old. I walked across the wood-plank floors to read a framed letter on the wall from a Civil War soldier who wrote that he could see hands and feet of dead comrades sticking out of burial grounds. The letter was just a small part of the walls' wealth of memorabilia: old photographs, the hides of two foxes, old proclamations, a horse collar, candles, a butter churn, a musket, and an ammunition horn. "It probably looks better than when the Zoarites were here," Ed said.

The retired history teacher and his wife sat directly across the table, watching expectantly while I ate at a tavern table made in 1850. Although this was June, the morning was gray and drizzly. The candle on the table provided a fretful light in the dim cabin. The couple seemed to be waiting for me to say something profound.

"Is it what you expected?" Mary asked.

All I could reply was, "Yes. Good." I felt a bit claustrophobic but managed to smile.

Ed said, "In the old days, innkeepers didn't have to be nice to you. They didn't even have to give you a bed. In Zoar, the first hotel opened in 1829. The building we are in was the brewmaster's home."

"To tell you how important he was," Mary added. "His was the second house built in town."

"The idea was, everyone had to work," Ed said. "They met at the assembly house every morning to find out where they had to work that day. They'd keep their children at the dormitory. The children didn't like the place, and didn't like the way they were treated. When one child died, the mother claimed he died of a broken heart."

The Cowgers spoke as if they personally knew the Zoarites, as if the German neighbors were still alive. The candles flickered lower. They saw the notebook at my side and asked if I wanted to write about the house. Mary was eager to talk.

"When we first came here twenty years ago, a woman who owned Number Thirteen welcomed us to the community," she said. "She asked me, 'Are you Christian?' We said, 'Yes.' She asked me three times. She said, 'Do you feel you were drawn here?' We said, 'Yes.' She said the town was different. We thought she was joking.

"Then one day we went to a meeting in the tavern and meeting hall. The building once had a huge horseshoe bar. We came down the steps to the tavern and I went to open my mouth and people surrounded us. I thought, Is this place possessed? They started talking about the ghosts of Zoar. A man said, 'Do you believe in ghosts?' I said, 'Not yet!' He said, 'Don't be too sure. If a ghost likes you, he will follow you all around from place to place.' Then they proceeded to all talk about their ghosts and how things were moved around their homes. It was like living in an episode of *The Twilight Zone.*"

The Cowgers wondered what to do. They had already spent their savings to buy the property. They talked with a neighbor who had also come to town looking for a relaxing and meaningful life; she had opened a bed and breakfast in the old dormitory building. She told them that the gothic dormitory was a magnet of negativity, as if all the frustration and hurt feelings of the Zoarites had built up inside its walls and were never released. "So many strange things happened there in the dorm," Mary said. "Another owner was walking up to the attic and passed his two boys. He turned around and saw a white mist following them down the stairs. The man was no kook; he was a former FBI agent. He was shaken up by it. We leased the boys' dorm for a time and stayed there, and our daughter claimed she heard a baby crying. There was no baby."

At this point, the Cowgers broke the news to me: a ghost lives in their inn—the one in which I had slept the night before. Sometimes he appears as a dark figure. The couple calls him George. He also appears in the annex cabin, where I was having breakfast. Visitors have reported seeing the man dressed in an old-fashioned, purple robe. That's not all. "A friend of ours told us he thought he saw something white drift by, and once somebody tapped him on the shoulder," Mary said. "Our friend was painting in the inn at the time. He left his paints and ran away. He was reluctant to tell the story, but I got it out of him finally. I asked him about it, and he said, 'This frightens me.'"

Ed said, "People say they hear parties, the clinking of German steins. I was skeptical, but one day I thought I heard the clinking and I yelled, 'Das ist gut!' I didn't hear them for a time."

By now, I was feeling uncomfortable. Mary went on: "One time, after a candlelight dinner, somebody asked about ghosts in our main house. A man said, 'My wife and I were on the top of the stairs and we saw a man this morning. He had long, white hair.' His wife added, 'The Quaker Oats ghost!' Then the man said, 'He was dressed in a purple coat and he went through the door but it didn't slam.' I told this to my friend Jenny, who lives across the street, and she said she had seen the man in the window, wearing purple. He must follow us from house to house.'"

A year later, the Cowgers learned a clue about the spirit's identity from a guest who stayed in the cabin. He said his father bought it in 1949 at a sheriff's sale and owned it for several years. The guest, a colonel in his sixties, explained to the couple that his father loved the cabin. He saw some meaning in the talk about the robe, saying his father once went to Japan and bought an unusual purple robe. He wore it in the log house frequently. Mary said, "That story gave me the chills."

Ed excused himself. I noticed that it was still dark inside the cabin, but outside the sun had started shining. Ed returned minutes later with a black-and-white photograph of a white-haired Cleveland physician who had also enjoyed the cabin years earlier. He loved it so much, in fact, that his family buried his ashes in the cabin's backyard. He is not the purple-robe ghost, but another spirit who can't let go. Ed said, "I suspect it is the doctor who we have seen around here, too. We have several guests who require no pampering whatsoever."

"Maybe the doctor makes house calls," I told him.

Someone does. About 1:30 A.M. several years ago, Mary was painting in an upstairs room in the cabin. Ed had already grown tired and left for the couple's main house. She remained to finish the room. "Fifteen minutes later, the front door opened," she said. "I know how that old thing sounds; it's loud and it sticks. I heard hard-soled shoes, heavy footsteps, coming up the steps. I could feel them getting closer. Then a man's voice yelled, 'Honey, I'm back.' Naturally, I thought it was Ed, so I said, 'OK. I'm finishing up.' Then suddenly I realized: Ed had been wearing tennis shoes. And Ed *never* calls me honey. Nervously, I called his name, and got no answer. Then I got shook. I grabbed the telephone and called Ed. When he answered, I said, 'Uh-oh.' He said, 'I'm on my way.' I was even more shook up when I remembered that I had locked the door when Ed left. No one could have entered that house from the outside."

Other strange occurrences have rattled the Cowgers over the years. Ed took a new roll of toilet paper to the guest room in the cabin. No guests were staying in the house that night, yet the next morning the paper had been removed from the roll and piled neatly down the stairs. A ghostly cat, perhaps?

Mary said, "I told him, 'Now, explain *that,* Mr. Logical.'"

"Of course, I couldn't," he admitted.

Mary said, "I was raised with Christian beliefs. I believe you go to heaven or hell. So I have a hard time believing in ghosts. The Bible talks of evil spirits. If you believe what the Bible says, you've got to believe those are evil spirits. Or maybe good. All I know is, I've seen these things and I don't like the experience. Leave me alone! I don't want ghosts playing with me."

"What if there are different dimensions, and for a few seconds they lock in and we can see each another as though we're staring through a screen door?" Ed said. He paused for a moment to reflect, and said, "Where do they end?"

I couldn't help but think of his theory as I shook his hand and walked down the creaky stairs, passing the hallway where the Cowgers had seen the shadow man. All I noticed there was warm air striking my face from a window, and the sun coming up over the canal.

_8_

The Song of Mount Nebo

Mount Nebo, an old ghost town in Athens County, lies on a remote
hill that most people will never see. It is on a peak called Mount Nebo,
reportedly rising more than a thousand feet above sea level. According
to legend, when the Shawnee arrived on the hill in the eighteenth century they found stone altars left by an earlier people. The tribe refused
to hunt in the area, saying the wooded hill was a mystical place better
left alone.

In the early nineteenth century, white settlers stood on the ridge and
looked down and thought they had discovered their own promised
land—Ohio. It spread out below them like a big green quilt, ready
to fulfill their every desire and provide food and shelter and enough
potential to meet their meager dreams. They named the hill Mount
Nebo, in reference to the mountain from which Moses saw the Promised Land. Its summit was named Pisgah.

But not every settler who came this way was looking to the earthly
plane for sustenance. Some were looking to the spiritual world. When
I first heard of Mount Nebo and its unusual history, I wanted to go
there. Its past is intertwined with the past of American spiritualism, the
belief that the dead live as spirits who can communicate with the living
through a medium.

I didn't need a medium to tell me how to get to Mount Nebo; I con-
sulted an Athens County map and, with my wife Cheryl as my guide,
set out to explore the ghost town around Halloween. (I didn't do this
on purpose; I happened to get a little free time then.)

Our first stop: Athens. At Ohio University, in this small city inside
Appalachian hill country, Halloween is an excuse for excess, especially

when the big night falls on a Friday. Book-weary students roam for some action, jack-o'-lanterns with silly grins perch atop black lampposts at brick fraternity houses, and young people's eyes reflect a little mischief.

I trudged toward the Alden Library on a mission while the university marching band practiced a rousing number on a crowded downtown street. Drummers rapped out a steady beat as I crunched the dry brown leaves on the brick sidewalk that leads up the hill to Alden.

I took the elevator to the fifth floor of the almost deserted building. A librarian in her thirties stared at me in boredom as I walked up to the counter.

"May I help you?"

"I'm interested in—"

"Spooks?"

"Close enough."

She handed me a large gray folder and said in a robotic monotone, "Sign here." She pushed a pen and tablet toward me. "We keep a record. Do you mind if I open the window to hear the band play? It's such a beautiful night."

Apparently the file is so popular that she keeps it on the counter for students and researchers. On its smooth cover a librarian had scrawled in pen the words "Spook Files," and stamped the official mark of Ohio University's library. Somehow, the university stamp gives the file—and its incredible stories—a little credibility. (Perhaps too much.) I spread about twenty photocopied stories across a large rectangular table. Among them I found newspaper and magazine stories written from the 1960s through the 1990s about ghostly happenings in Athens County—on the back roads, in the dorms, the cemeteries, the old buildings, the old towns. One writer claims Athens is the center of a pentagram that comprises area cemeteries and small towns. He said any community that falls inside that diagram is ripe for paranormal activity. Glancing at the headlines, I placed several of the more lurid stories into a pile: "Monster No Joke For Those Who Saw It," "Wilson Hall Has History of Paranormal Activity," "Watchman May Still Walk Rounds," "UFO Spotted Over Athens; Resembles Patrolman's Hat," and, my favorite, "Runaway Slave, Nicodemus, Haunts AOPI Sorority House."

But the story that impressed me most and prompted my trip to Athens County was the haunting of Mount Nebo. I had heard about this ghost town, on Peach Ridge in Dover Township, about ten miles north of Athens in Athens County. Fortunately, I had enough sense not to go there on the full-moon night when I arrived in town.

The next morning, I went to the Athens County Historical Society's museum to research Mount Nebo. The museum is a well-stocked place that also houses the genealogical group in a small building downtown.

Joanne Prisley, the staff director, took me to a research room where she keeps several histories of Athens County. She is a slim, gray-haired woman with a sharp wit and a keen researcher's eye. Unfortunately, Mount Nebo is one of Ohio's forgotten places. We couldn't determine much about the community's past. As she stood up to leave me with the books, she suddenly looked at me closely and said, "Now, I hope you don't believe all that gibberish about Mount Nebo and ghosts."

"Well—"

She sat down again and said, "Do you know that Athens County is supposed to be the most haunted place in the United States? Why, I have no idea. It's ridiculous! Supposedly some British psychic research group has made the claim. That reputation won't go away. Every Halloween, I am swamped with calls from television and print reporters who want to know about our ghosts. We've become their guinea pigs. Honestly, I never heard much about the subject when I was a student at Ohio University many years ago. It didn't start until after the late 1960s and 1970s, when *The Omen* and similar scary movies came out. I think they got people wondering about Athens. It is an isolated town and is therefore good for making up stories. A lot of radio and television students need something to write about, too. One girl talked about her sorority house being haunted by the ghost of a little girl. But the early family that lived in the house didn't even have children. Then there's the story of the ghost of a black man who was hidden in a building here in town during the Underground Railroad days. Why on earth would anyone bring a black man into the middle of an all-white town if they wanted to hide him? Besides, the building wasn't even built yet."

She finally walked away, muttering, "They get into how all of our old cemeteries and houses are haunted. If that's the case, then *all* old houses and cemeteries are haunted."

Two older women researchers who were sitting in the room with me looked up and wrinkled their noses. I smiled and closed my notebook. One said, "That Mount Nebo is trouble."

Totally intrigued, I decided to visit the Mount. I learned that the name refers to a ridge and a ghost town. The story began long ago, when ancient Indian tribes occupied the area and built burial mounds on the ridge. They considered Mount Nebo a sacred place and used it for funerals.

Today, the ridge is scattered with the remains of several small settlements: Liars Corner, Mount Nebo, Truetown, Sugar Creek, Millfield, and East Millfield. Little history remains of these towns, but I imagined all kinds of stories involving the naming of Liars Corner.

The story of Mount Nebo, the town, began in the early 1850s, when a Millfield farmer, fiddler, and mechanic named Jonathon Koons became interested in spiritualism. The movement had started in Hydesville, New York, near Rochester, when in 1847 sisters Katy Fox, eleven, and Maggie Fox, fifteen, claimed they "communicated" with ghosts, who rapped on walls to leave messages. Newspapers jumped on the story, and soon people everywhere wanted to talk to their dead relatives. The sisters' fame spread across the nation and the world. Two years later, one million Americans counted themselves as believers in the supernatural. Even many skeptics had to admit that it was great entertainment, although transcendentalist Ralph Waldo Emerson criticized spiritualism as "a rat revolution, the gospel that comes by taps in the wall and humps in the table." When reporters tagged the Fox sisters "the Rochester Rappers," they became even more famous. Spiritualism quickly arrived in Ohio, where George Wolcutt and George Rogers of Columbus painted portraits of dead people they hadn't known. Family members claimed they recognized the deceased relatives in the pictures. Meanwhile, spirit circles—support groups of spiritualists—sprang up in Cleveland, Boston, San Francisco, New York City, and Washington, D.C.

Back on Mount Nebo, Koons was skeptical at first. But he couldn't explain the happenings that surrounded a neighbor's daughter who was heavily into spiritualism. Her father warned her that she would bring shame on the family for practicing such activity, but she persisted. Koons attended one of her séances to learn more. "A rap ensued, which appeared somewhat about the table," he wrote in a letter to *Seraph's Telegraph* in March 1853. "I chose to present my own questions, many of which were asked mentally, which were all correctly answered."

When he went home, spirits visited him and apparently helped him quickly develop psychic powers, and he became a writing medium. According to Koons, all of the members of his family, including his eight (or possibly nine) children, also became mediums. Yet he needed even stronger evidence of life after death. This came when his oldest son,

Nahum, sixteen, received messages from spirits who instructed him to tell his father to build a table according to their instructions, and "place it in a private room for their own use, that then I should have incontrovertible evidence of the existence of spirits." So Koons built a room, twelve by sixteen feet with a seven-foot ceiling, and equipped it with the various requested items, including pencils and paper. It could accommodate about twenty-five people, but as many as fifty could squeeze into the room. "Then the spirits commenced writing without any medium agency whatsoever . . . which fact removed every lingering doubt from my mind, for the room was kept constantly closed against the entrance of my own family or any other person during the time the writing was performed," Koons told the newspaper's readers.

It was not long, however, until the spirits wrote out a bill for other implements and instruments of music, amongst which were found two accordions, bass and tenor drums, tambourine, guitar, banjo, harps, and bells, on which the spirits perform, and toys which are sometimes placed in the hands of the audience. A number of pistols were also requested, which were charged and fired by the spirits themselves in rapid succession. Trumpets are also blown by the spirits, and through which they articulate our language, deliver lectures, and sing and pray. Faints and pencils are also used by them, without any medium agency, with which they draw representations of celestial orbs and scenery.

By 1853, the Koons family had become well known in national spiritualism circles. Word of spirit gatherings in Mount Nebo spread throughout Ohio and attracted Dr. J. Everett, a Columbus physician who was fascinated with spiritualism. He attended spirit sessions at the Koonses' farm and became convinced that they were legitimate. J. Everett wrote a book about his experiences that was published by Osgood & Blake of Columbus, titled *A Book for Skeptics*. Its long subtitle more fully explained: *Being Communication from Angels Written with Their Own Hands; Also Oral Communication Spoken Through a Trumpet and Written Down in the Presence of Many Witnesses; Also a Representation and Explanation of the Celestial Spheres, As Given by the Spirits, at J. Koons' Spirit Room in Dover, Athens County, Ohio.*

The book attracted even more attention, and soon the family started hosting intrigued guests from across the country. Traveling by stagecoach from Columbus, visitors came to the farm to hear and see the spirits. They were not disappointed. Before each séance, Koons blew out the lamps and in the dark played his fiddle. Soon, patches of light flew around the room, and so did instruments—while being played by unseen hands.

Koons and his wife, Abigail, and their children often allowed the strangers to stay overnight at the farmhouse. Their lodging options were slim; Athens County was a rugged countryside. Koons liked it that way. He chose Mount Nebo because of its Indian mounds and its height; in this high, spiritual place, he believed his followers were closer to God.

Meanwhile, other mediums in other towns were starting their own shows. Those old spiritualists believed that the dead could talk to the living through tappings, séances, writings, and mediums. As spiritualism became more wildly popular in the mid-1800s, regional and local spiritualism societies popped up across the country. In parlors across the country, Victorian Americans gathered to discuss spirits and attempt to summon them through "home circles." Family and friends sat at dining room tables and sought to communicate with dead loved ones. From these meetings rose professional mediums, who, for a fee, of course, would contact spirits in the afterlife. In several cities across Ohio, spiritualism newspapers provided the latest news in the field.

At the direction of so-called ancient spirits, Koons built a new spiritual headquarters with a special séance room (he called it the spirit room) equipped with musical instruments. He invited neighbors to hear ghostly symphonies in the new log room next to the farmhouse. The neighbors noted that on the walls were mounted instruments, bells, and copper plates shaped like birds. Spirits told Koons to place certain instruments on two tables: tambourines, tenor and bass drums, a tin horn, a guitar, an accordion, a trumpet, a triangle, and a bell. Koons had trouble finding the instruments in the backwoods country, but he finally managed to buy and borrow them all. He asked his neighbors to sit down and stay quiet. When he blew out the lights, they saw hands with no arms and strange lights floating around the room. They later told of instruments being played by disembodied hands, tambourines flying around the room, and luminous pieces of paper floating around their heads. In this remote region, other neighbors reported hearing big orchestral sounds at late hours—the musically active spirits, perhaps. Stories still circulate about psychic activities at the Koons farm.

The family enjoyed company. They conducted spiritual readings for local people as well as people from other towns. Spirits wrote messages on a blackboard or on the backs of visitors' hands and on their foreheads. One spirit wrote so slowly on a man's hand that he said, "What's a matter, can't you write?" In a moment, the spirit wrote one and a half pages on paper, including complex drawings. Then the spirit quickly folded the paper three times and dropped it into the man's lap. Another time, it is said, a group of scientists came to the farm to conduct experiments. When a phosphorous hand materialized, the men passed it around for inspection.

Who were these spirits? Koons called them the ghosts of 165 long-dead people, including a John King, who called himself the first man on earth. The spirits described themselves as "pre-Adamite men," and they seemed at home with the Koons family. (Even more interesting, the spirit of King continued to appear for years through other mediums. They believed he was the spirit of the Welsh pirate Henry Morgan, who died in 1688.)

But Koons's neighbors were less than enthusiastic about the goings-on. They burned his barns, attacked his children, set fire to the crops, and threatened the family. Perhaps because of such violence, the family left for Illinois in 1858. (Some accounts say 1855.) For a time, the family conducted spiritualism missionary work on the road, and later they disappeared into history.

But Jonathon Koons didn't exactly vanish; his reputation followed him all the way to Illinois. A century and a half later, in fact, he is a cult figure among spiritualists as well as the target of skeptics. Even the famous medium-buster Harry Houdini knew of Koons. Houdini had a theory: Koons was a skillful inventor who managed to develop a crude and early version of a transmitter to project "spirit" voices. "To the best of my knowledge," the magician wrote in a story in 1922, "the first application of the principles of radio to spiritualistic manifestations was in 1852, when Jonathan Koons . . . installed a 'spirit machine'—described as a crude structure of zinc and copper for localizing and collecting the magnetic (sounds). This radio-telephone trick is performed in many ways. Statues of Buddha are popular bits of property employed by mediums; they are made to answer questions as glibly as hollow balls and trumpets."

Yet Jonathon Koons's reputation continues to live. Was he a faker or a believer? On the Internet alone, he is the subject of several stories written in English, German, French, and other languages. But apparently he was not a rube farmer from Athens County. Facts about him are scarce and contradictory, although in 1927 his paternal grandson wrote that Koons was born September 28, 1801, in Germany, where he was well educated in history, astronomy, and philosophy. In the old country he worked as a shipbuilder. After immigrating, he helped build ships in Philadelphia before settling in Athens with his growing family. By most accounts, the couple had ten children from 1837 to 1854. (Only eight are usually noted in public records.) But Koons also made time for lofty pursuits, such as writing articles for newspapers and magazines, and promoting spiritualism.

Although he didn't continue practicing as a medium in public, he stayed in the spiritualism faith until his death in 1893 in Northern Township, Franklin County, Illinois, where he had resided for many years. His marker in Middle Fork Cemetery reads: "Jonathon Koons. A pioneer and liberalist passed to Spirit on 26 day of Jan. 1893, age 91 Y 3M 29D."

Today, when darkness falls on Mount Nebo, people say you can sometimes hear a band of spirit musicians playing their old songs. Is that a fiddle melody coming from the hills?

After Koons left Athens County, a group of spiritualists tried to build a town on Mount Nebo, claiming that it was receptive to psychic happenings. In 1870, spiritualist Eli Curtis bought 5.15 acres for $250 and dedicated it to spiritual purposes. On this land he planned to build a city named New Jerusalem.

He worked with other members of the spiritualistic Morning Star Community but paid for the land mostly from his own pocket. According to Curtis, the community's main partners included William D. Hall and Chauncey Barnes, "having been appointed the Executive Committee of arrangement by a Spirit purporting to be Jesus of Nazareth, assumed, with 'Mother Hanaman,' to carry out the work of our community in & by organizing the Morning Star Community."

Barnes was the most active participant. On November 2, 1871, the *Athens Herald* reported: "We last week had a visit from Dr. Chauncey Barnes, who is now engaged in building up the new city of Mt. Nebo. The Doctor informs us that his church edifice is nearly completed, and will probably be ready for dedication by Christmas."

An unnamed newspaper reporter called Barnes "the Great High Priest of Spiritualism in this part of the country" and asked him about photographs of local people that also showed background faces—"dim, shadowy, and weird-like, but still perfect and distinct." (This trick was used sometimes by traveling photographers during the spiritualism craze of the late nineteenth century.)

"But Doctor," the reporter wrote, "by what process of reasoning do you account for these shadowy specters on your photographs?"

"By those unseen spiritual agencies which will in time flood the whole world with light," he replied.

"Of course," the reporter continued, "we had no reply to make to this, not being versed in spiritualistic lore, but at the same time the thought did strike us that instead of 'enlightening' the world at the present time, the fantastic tricks of the 'spirits' were just now rather obfuscating the understanding of the people. If an invitation were extended to him, Dr. Barnes would lecture in our village and, as he observed, 'give ocular demonstration to the truth of Spiritualism.'"

The group hired workers to erect the walls of a sixty-foot-wide tabernacle, called King Solomon Temple, which was octagonal with a door or window on each side and a cupola. A lack of money stopped the community from finishing the interior.

Five years later, Morning Star disbanded, and Barnes left the country. Curtis and his wife and Hall remained and later were buried nearby. The temple wasn't torn down until 1893.

Today, every trace of the spiritualists has disappeared from the hill. It is the home of Mount Nebo Trail, which runs from Athens, along Peach and Sand Ridges in Dover Township and others. Peach Ridge is also the home of five small, old cemeteries, including Hanning Cemetery, also known as Peach Ridge Cemetery. Some people claim the cemeteries are used by local witches for ceremonies, and writer Sandy Speidel mentioned that the cemeteries, when shown on a map, represent a pentagram. "There are numerous stories of strange happenings within the perimeter of the five cemeteries, some of which have been reported by people with no previous belief in such things," Speidel observed in 1973. "One of the cemeteries contains a natural rock formation in the form of a circle. People who have stood in the middle of the circle have reported extraordinary sensations, such as communing with the dead."

Driving up on Peach Ridge, no more than ten miles northwest of Athens, is like going back into pioneer times. The ridge (it looks like a mountain to me) is a wild place where nature rules. Autumn trees flash a spectrum of gold and scarlet leaves, joined by strikingly purple weeds. Even the ragweed looks pretty. In contrast, the gray drabness of poverty covers the Appalachian hillsides. Scattered along the narrow road—blacktopped but covered with loose gravel—are dilapidated, old mobile homes. A number of them sit abandoned not far from attractive homes that appear around the next bend, proving there is no distinction between the poor and the middle class on Mount Nebo.

Up on the mountain, you can drive yourself mad—and lost—by looking at tiny dirt roads and other minor ones that shoot off like arteries. You'll see Kerns Road, Sand Ridge Road, Swett Hollow Road, and others that lead over to Scatter Ridge and Tick Ridge. The thought of a Tick Ridge made me squirm.

With Cheryl at my side, I asked a man who was getting his mail: "How do you get to Liars Corner?" He said, "You've already passed the lane that leads over to it, and you missed it. Don't bother goin' back there. Ain't nothin' left." When I asked about Mount Nebo, he said, "Ain't nothin' there, either, 'cept two trailers owned by old man Rutter."

After asking more directions from two road workers, I went back three times until I finally saw the place with two mobile homes. On this land the Morning Star Community practiced its spiritualism. In front, a milk can supported an old-fashioned rural mailbox. In the yard hung three beer cans on a metal chain, with the hand-lettered title "Redneck Wind Chime" beneath it. Leaves floated in through the air like bats fluttering to roosting places. Nobody came to the door. Thankfully.

In the middle of the remote countryside, this idea struck me: Even up here, you see electric lines and candidate signs for the November election. You just can't escape politicians and power.

Winding back down Mill Creek Road and others, we saw homes decorated for Halloween with orange twinkle lights, pumpkins, and inflatable ghosts. A sign said: "Speed Limit . . . None." One house had a little greenhouse attached, and a ramshackle barn featured one of those old advertising thermometers, all rusted and bent. Nearby we saw a house with a dog-training grounds and another with a nursery business and mums in full bloom and a "no hunting" sign posted. At the Brown-Ford Cemetery, we found a gate hung between two brick posts. A bronze plaque read: "This gateway has been erected by members of the Brown-Ford Cemetery Association in memory of their pioneer ancestors resting here. 1970." Glancing around, I saw a guy in a red flannel shirt staring at us. He looked angry, so I started the car and left fast.

The last time we stopped on lonely Mill Creek Road, we heard no noise. Total silence. Surely no trumpets and fiddles played a song. Not even a bird or an insect chirped that day. As I started the car, it sputtered for the first time since we bought it. Cheryl turned to me with a frightful look and said deeply, "Spooky."

We laughed all the way back to Athens.

9

A View from the Tower

The first time I saw it, my eyes quickly refocused and I blinked hard and thought I'd glimpsed a set for Dracula's castle—just over a hill in, of all places, Richland County. Then I realized that the building with huge towers and thick walls and a long metal fence was not a castle at all. It was the Ohio State Reformatory, a musty monument to man's dark side and a de facto Scared Straight program for any child or adult who tours it these days.

The prison is also Ohio's largest—and toughest—ghost town. Although circumscribed by barbed wire and steel bars, the prison was a self-contained community that grew its own food and operated its own restaurant, post office, printing business, carpentry shop, cemetery, and other essential daily-life functions. At its peak, the population numbered thirty-two hundred. Unfortunately, its residents didn't live in this "town" by choice. The population turned over every few years, though some residents never left.

Today, few visitors can walk through the steel and stone corridors without reacting on some level. Many feel an overwhelming fear; others, only pity. Some wonder if ghosts stalk the old cellblocks. Based on the gothic appearance alone, writers for national cable television shows have dubbed it one of the scariest places on earth.

Most visitors feel exactly the way the prison's architect, Levi T. Scofield of Cleveland, intended young prisoners to feel—momentarily helpless and cut off from the world. Regardless of visitors' reactions, one thing is certain: the former maximum-security prison can suffocate you with dust, peeling lead paint, and degradation.

Long before the prison held Ohio's errant young people, a federal Civil War camp trained them to fight and kill at Camp Bartley (later named Camp Mansfield), which turned out 4,000 Union troops from 1861 to 1865. They included 750 members of Ohio's 32nd Regiment, which fought in various bloody battles throughout the South. Casualties were heavy; only about thirty-five of the original members survived the war.

The camp and the dark war days had long passed when the Ohio State Reformatory opened on the site on September 15, 1896, about sixty-five miles northeast of Columbus. It was touted as the state's newest intermediate penitentiary, designed for young offenders who weren't bad enough for the state pen but were too bad for the boys' industrial school. Initially, 593 cells held 1,200 young prisoners, who during the day helped build the rest of the sprawling prison—two hundred thousand square feet in the only building that still remains on the grounds. In its ninety-four years as a state prison, the reformatory housed an estimated 154,000 prisoners who ranged at different times from youthful offenders to hardened adult convicts.

From the start, Mansfield's prison was different. Usually, the Victorian prison system simply *housed* criminals. No more, no less. That's why the Ohio State Reformatory was considered so progressive. It sought to "rehabilitate young male offenders through hard work and education." Even its appearance, something like a big church in the front, sought to remind inmates of a higher purpose. Every prisoner worked in the shops or on a prison farm, and, with any luck, left the reformatory with a skill—or at least his life. By the time the state closed the prison on December 31, 1990, however, prison officials had become "enlightened." Their prisons came equipped with basketball courts, sometimes a campus atmosphere, and law libraries.

Unfortunately, some prisoners and visitors did not leave Mansfield, not even in death. Volunteers who lead tours talk of seeing ghostly forms and unusual balls of light flying through the corridors. Some say they are routinely touched by unseen hands and spoken to through unseen mouths. Other claim they smell the lilac perfume worn by the warden's wife on the night she was fatally shot in her bathroom.

The Mansfield Reformatory Preservation Society, an independent group, bought the prison from the state for one dollar in 1994 and now operates it as a historical museum. The group has a Web site on which former prisoners can share their memories. Using the pen name "an old-timer," one former resident wrote (with skull and crossbones beneath his name): "Your thoughts are locked in O.S.R. forever!"

Visitors are invited to check in for haunted house tours and weekend "ghost hunts" around Halloween (pizza is included, if guests can manage to eat anything in that environment). For less hardy visitors like my wife and me, the group offers weekend tours of the reformatory's inner sanctum.

We drove into the parking lot on a cloudy Sunday afternoon in June. Dark rain clouds stalked the horizon. I could feel moisture in the air and in my aching shoulder. When I first pulled off the main road and looked down the hill and saw the clouds rolling toward the prison, my jaw dropped. I tried to take a photograph, but the building was so long that I couldn't squeeze it into the 35mm frame. The Victorian Gothic and Romanesque architecture looked imposing in sandstone.

At the front gate, we chose the dungeon tour from among several options. A sign assured us that we would visit "the hole" and see much of the prison. I had already heard of its gruesome reputation. One inmate hung himself in the hole. In the tailor shop, an inmate mistakenly slit the shop supervisor's throat, thinking he was another prisoner. One inmate killed himself by dousing his clothes with lighter fluid and paint thinner. Another inmate committed suicide by drinking a batch of silage alcohol. Then there was another warden's wife: In the 1950s, she died when her pistol (or so the official story goes) fell out of a closet and discharged. Later, her husband died of a heart attack in the west wing's offices.

I didn't mention these things to Cheryl, who by this time was joking about our trip.

"Some husbands take their wives to the islands on vacation," she said. "We go to a prison."

We walked up several steps to what was once a central processing area for prisoners. At this point Ohio's young convicts once sat and waited. And waited. Looking at the high ceilings and wide lobby area, the prisoners had time to reflect on what they had done and how long they would be incarcerated. When a prisoner was first admitted, he sat on what was called a mourning bench, because he could mourn for being in prison. He could sit for a few minutes or a few hours. Later, he was admitted to a seven-by-nine-foot cell that housed two prisoners.

As we pushed farther into the gloom, our guide explained: "The prison cost $1.3 million to build. Now, we need $360,000 just to replace the roof. The place is listed on the National Register of Historic Places and for all practical purposes on the register of spooky places. If it looks bad, it is. The state just picked up and left it as it was—in rough shape. When they built this place, prison officials wanted it to look something like a cathedral, to help reform young lawbreakers through appearance. The prison once was a fancy place, with beautiful woodwork and attractive stone from a local quarry. Its first residents, 150 young convicts admitted to the west cellblock, were tough kids from across Ohio. Since then, tens of thousands of prisoners have done time here. They're in a dubious fraternity. Many former convicts go through on these tours. They clue us in on things we don't know—and things we'd rather not know. We get forty thousand visitors a year who take the historic tour, the Hollywood tour, the dungeon tour, and the tower tour. By the way, lead-based paint is peeling throughout the place. Estimated removal cost is $5 million. So it isn't going anywhere. Just don't touch anything."

One part of the main building has fifty-seven rooms. These days, the main building is all that remains of the original complex of several buildings. The state razed the others after it closed the prison in 1990. (The heat hasn't been turned on since then, so the place is closed to tourists in winter.) Just as state prison officials were ready to tear down the main prison, the Mansfield volunteers formed their group and asked to buy the building. The group will seek government grants to pay for renovation, which in 1998 was estimated to cost $16 million. In today's dollars—well, the cost is completely out of the question.

Hollywood discovered the prison in the 1970s and 1980s, when film companies shot *Tango and Cash* and *Harry and Walter Go to New York* at the then-occupied reformatory. In the 1990s, after the prison had closed, film crews arrived to shoot *Air Force One* with Harrison Ford and *The Shawshank Redemption* with Tim Robbins. Large paintings of Lenin and Stalin, leftovers from *Air Force One,* still adorn the main room of the prison. I thought I had entered a Soviet relocation camp. A plastic and plaster stone wall from *Shawshank* and other props, including a cardboard sewer line, are available for public inspection.

As we trudged along, we saw cellblock east—six stories high, steel, and built mostly by prisoners. It remains the largest freestanding cellblock in the world, our guide told us; two thousand prisoners once lived in the two cellblocks. "Prisoners washed the floors and windows daily," he said. "With two thousand people living in here, disease could go through the men in a hurry. Another five hundred prisoners toiled on an honor farm around the prison. Prisoners wore blue uniforms. If they misbehaved, they were issued gray ones. If they were caught having sex, the warden added one year to the offenders' sentences and sent letters of explanation to their wives, fathers, and mothers."

Prisoners learned trades in the school, carpenter shop, broom shop, print shop, lock shop, and other shops. "A *locksmith?*" a tourist asked. "Doesn't that seem like an odd trade to teach a convict?" Our guide laughed and said, "Yeah, well, the prison also had a barber school. But I wouldn't want to sit in a barber chair if the barber was living here. One time, a prisoner came in for a shave. He was unlucky because he owed his barber several packs of cigarettes and refused to pay up. So the barber sat him down, spun the chair around, and put a straight razor to the fellow's neck."

We walked down two flights of stairs to the dungeon. At the bottom, tour members stood aghast.

"This is it—the hole, solitary, whatever you want to call it," the guide said. "Solitary. When the prison was first occupied, the hole had double doors. One curved out, one curved in. Prisoners did the eight and eight. They laid on the floor—naked, with no beds—for eight hours, then they stood up for another eight hours. For the first two days, they had nothing but bread and water, then after that they had full meals that were slipped under a hole in the door. That's where they got their light—with one exception. If a prisoner gave a guard a hard time, the guard would stand in front of the slot to block the light. The temperature in this area was ninety-three to ninety-six degrees. The high temperature was a way of maintaining control. In the 1950s, there was a riot at the prison. All 120 rioters were rounded up and put down here—six guys to a cell, for thirty days. You can imagine what the temperature was like. None of them died, though."

The hole terrified prisoners who had any sense. They had heard horror stories about practically existing on tomato soup. "When you hear the door to the hole slam shut behind you," one former prisoner wrote on the group's Web site, "that's when you realize: goodbye, freedom, you have hit the lowest of the low."

"Oh, yes, people have died down here," the guide explained. "One time, they had to put a couple of guys to a cell. When the guards opened one cell, a guy walked out and his cellmate didn't. They found him dead, under a bunk. The prisoner who walked out didn't like his roomy. Maybe he snored. Another time, a prisoner escaped from these cells—nobody knows how—and he bludgeoned to death a guard. Those are the only two circumstances that I know of where people died down here, but there probably were other deaths. This is no motel."

We stopped in a big, empty room where the prisoners once lined up to take meals—the commissary. "There was no talking, no smoking, no laughing," the guide said. "The prison maintained strict discipline while feeding two thousand men in an hour. They can't do that in modern prisons."

What amazed me was the control that authorities exercised over the inmates. Assistant superintendents lived in the prison with their families. Generations of children grew up inside the Ohio State Reformatory, probably none the worse for their environment.

In 1950, warden Arthur Glattke and his family lived in the prison. One day his wife, Helen, was rummaging through a closet when she knocked a loaded pistol onto the floor. It discharged. The bullet struck her in the chest and killed her. Rumors flew through the prison that she was murdered, but the coroner ruled her death an accident. Monica Reed of the preservation society claimed she visited the warden's quarters and found it "off the wall with paranormal activity. I got about forty-five minutes of orbs flying right at the camera."

As we walked past grimy, dark cells, our guide pointed out where a prisoner once scratched the word "welcome" in the cement. "I have no idea what he used to do it with or how he got away with it," he said. "Right over there, a group of prisoners were moving scaffolding that they used to wash windows with when suddenly something fell and a couple of prisoners were killed and several hurt. This place has known some tragedy. You're welcome to step inside any of the cells at any time to take a picture, but please don't close the doors. You might become a part of our display. We have no idea how to unlock them."

As we stood on a lofty ledge looking down into the black steel canyon, the prison opened before us like a dragon's mouth. It appeared to go on forever. Nothing stirred—no rats, no mice, no air currents. Somebody said he saw a few pigeons. I tried to imagine being held inside this place on Halloween night, on a ghost hunt about midnight, and seeing nothing but dozens of tiny white beams shooting around from visitors' flashlights and wondering what else might be out there in the darkness.

On entering the southern end of the building, our guide announced, "Prepare to enter the car wash." It was a light-colored tile shower room—so long that it resembled a bus station. Sunlight from a rear window illuminated millions of specks of dust. The air was so thick that it reminded me of standing in a snowstorm. I hesitated to breathe; fifteen seconds later, I gave up the idea and inhaled. "The prisoners called this place the car wash because they had five minutes for a shower," he said. "The guards had too many prisoners, so they ran them through all at one time. They came in the door, hung their clothes on wires, got soaked down fast, and left—on Saturdays only. The rest of the week, they'd stink. If you took a shower only once a week, a bar of soap would last you a year. By Friday, the prisoners were pretty ripe. That's because they worked all week. When a former prisoner came through here on a tour, he told me that the shower was segregated with blacks on one side, whites on the other. He said it was not unusual to see blood running on this tile floor. Somebody else had been stabbed."

None of the prison guards carried guns. They had only nightsticks. The guards who did carry weapons worked in six towers that surrounded the prison yard. They reached the towers by climbing metal spiral staircases. Up there, they carried pistols, shotguns, Tommy guns, and rifles. They worked eight-hour shifts, alone. The towers came with their own restrooms, eighty-five feet in the air.

Moving on into the mailroom, we stood where Hollywood actors had worked. Of course, prisoners also had worked there in another time. They sorted mail. About nineteen thousand pieces came into the prison each month; about nine thousand pieces went out. A prisoner could lose his mail privileges for disobeying the rules.

In the basement, the walls looked like corridors in a medieval castle. "Sometime before the prison closed," the guide said, "somebody brought a seven-foot plastic statue of Jesus and stored it down here in the tunnels. I don't know why. One night a new guard came down here to work and was wandering around with only a flashlight. You can imagine how dark this place gets. He turned a corner and came face-to-face with Jesus. He got religion real quick."

No matter how hard they schemed, prisoners could not run away from their destiny. Once they were inside, they rarely left the place on their own.

"The prison used to have a shoe factory," the guide said. "It shipped shoes all over. Well, one of the prisoners decided he had stayed here long enough; he wanted out. He asked a couple of buddies to help him. He hid inside a crate and his friends placed shoes on top of him and nailed

The Ohio State Reformatory in Mansfield as it appeared in the mid–twentieth century, before most of the buildings were demolished.

the lid shut. It was moved out of here and onto the shipping dock. Pretty soon it was put on a truck and moved out of the prison. The prisoner didn't care where he was headed, just so he was leaving. The truck continued and was finally unloaded. The prisoner waited until he heard nothing, then kicked open the top of the crate and sat up. That's when he got the shock of his life. He was inside the Ohio Penitentiary in Columbus! The warden said that since the guy liked it so much there, he would transfer him and add some time onto his sentence."

Not every incident ended so humorously. On a steamy July night in Columbus in 1948, former Mansfield prisoners Robert M. Daniels, twenty-four, and John C. West, twenty-two, met over drinks and relived their unhappy days in captivity. Daniels was cocky; West was unafraid and ready to kill. The men sought revenge for the way a guard had treated them in Mansfield. They only recently had been paroled: Daniels served three years and two months at the reformatory farm for car theft, and West served a little more than one year for the theft of auto parts. They had been friends in prison. Daniels was a handsome and intelligent young man who held a powerful influence over West, whom the prison psychiatrists had labeled a moron. West enjoyed killing. He tried to imitate Daniels in every way, going so far as to buy the same kind of suits that Daniels wore. Daniels used West the way a puppeteer uses his puppets. Reporters would call them the Mad Dog Killers, and their story could make a modern gangster movie.

After drinking heavily on the night of July 23 in Columbus, the men decided they needed a little cash. They walked into Earl Ambrose's tavern with guns drawn and demanded money. Ambrose had the audacity or stupidity to stand up to the two thugs. West shot him dead and laughed. He and Daniels took four hundred dollars from the cash register but missed the twenty thousand that Ambrose had hidden in a safe.

They took Ambrose's car and drove to Mansfield to find a guard who they had hated during their incarceration. A newspaper reporter reconstructed their conversation:

"I want to kill that guard," West said.

"We could kill him slow, and really settle the score," Daniels said.

But during the long drive that night, the two decided that an even better target would be John W. Niebel, the prison superintendent. He and his family lived in a large white house next to the fifteen-hundred-acre compound. "We didn't like the Mansfield superintendent and planned . . . to go up there and beat the hell out of him," Daniels said later.

Daniels and West arrived early the next morning and rang Niebel's doorbell. Niebel woke up and answered the door while his wife, Nolanda, and twenty-year-old daughter, Phyllis, slept upstairs. Daniels and West forced Niebel to take them upstairs, where Daniels raped Phyllis Niebel. After torturing the family, the two men took them outside into the darkness, ordered them to remove their clothes, and shot them with .25-caliber pistols.

Newspapers splashed the story across page one. They called Daniels the "glamour-boy killer" because he wore white shirts and ties and smoked cigarettes.

From Mansfield, Daniels and West headed toward Indiana. Police established roadblocks on all the major highways. Along the way, the two men stole another car in Tiffin, Ohio. West shot the car's owner when he refused to cooperate. The two abducted his wife and kept her temporarily. Four miles up the road, they decided to steal a truck. West shot the driver in the head and laughed about it. Not far from the Indiana border, they came to a roadblock set up by the Ohio State Patrol at State Routes 224 and 637 in Van Wert County. West wounded two deputy sheriffs but they continued to shoot and finally killed him.

Deputies captured Daniels without a struggle. He was tried and later executed in the electric chair on January 3, 1949. A reporter wrote: "One would scarcely have recognized him as the cocky youngster who wisecracked with newsmen on the rear steps of the Van Wert County Jail last July 23." A final headline read: "No Swagger Left as Daniels Pays for Crime Spree."

The Daniels-West killing spree and other negative incidents represent the prison's bad karma, which hangs in the air like stale smoke. Some people have tried to capture it with cameras. "One of the former guards came through here on a tour with a digital camcorder," the guide said. "She saw an orb—a little ball of light flying around. We have some weird stories. My son was up here one day taking pictures. He later found images on the field other than what he was shooting. We don't understand it. It just happens."

Quietly, we left the cellblocks and headed to the lobby to look around the museum and gift shop. The museum, in the former superintendent's office, is as stately as the cells are stark. Rich woodwork and spacious windows underscore the difference between the law enforcers and the lawbreakers.

The furniture collection includes some old oak teachers' desks that were crafted by prisoners. The walls are like big lineup cards, filled with pictures and words about young inmates who were incarcerated in the prison in the late 1800s. I was surprised that their sentences didn't run longer; some stayed only a year or two for serious crimes. The walls also held old black and white prison photographs from the early 1900s. They gave me a chilling sense of being there at that time.

As we walked around the gift shop, I noticed people buying postcards, T-shirts, old photographs, and even black plastic license plate holders that read, "GHOST HUNTER . . . Ohio State Reformatory Historic Site." All proceeds go to the preservation society to operate the prison.

We gladly walked out of the prison a couple of hours later. Even the dark, thickening air of an approaching thunderstorm felt fresher than the air in the cellblocks. Out front, under the big towers, we met Ike Webb, a seventy-five-year-old former captain of the guard who had worked in the prison from 1954 to 1965. He had stopped to visit on this Sunday, as he does about once a month. He enjoys watching the people and their reactions. "In our time, they knew the rules and they obeyed them," Webb said of the inmates. "They were starting this prisoner-reform stuff. I didn't like it, so I left. They were giving inmates too many privileges. We didn't treat them mean or nothing, but we had discipline. All that has disappeared. We believed in security first, then rehabilitation. Now, it's the reverse. You can't teach somebody something if he won't listen. We didn't have as many prisoners return as parole violators. A couple of years ago, they got as many as sixty percent coming back. We were lucky to have ten percent."

He said the prison operated with 175 guards; 42 worked on each of three shifts. They controlled as many as three thousand inmates on a few occasions.

"In '57, we had a riot that started with some juvenile delinquents who had been sentenced to 'one-to-age,' meaning when they turned twenty-one we had to turn 'em loose," Webb said. "They knew it, too. They started a riot for the fun of it. They had no complaints; they did it just to *do* it. Rioters intended to take over the dining room, so they'd have food, but we locked it up real quick. Eighty percent to 90 percent of the inmates wanted nothing to do with the riot, and they ran into their cells. About a hundred continued to roam the yard. We rounded them all up and put them in the hole. They stayed down there for ninety days—until we found who their ringleaders were. We had no more trouble with them after that. The hole cured 'em real good. See, when I worked here, the hole was different. We had only twenty cells. No bed. No light. Inmates slept on concrete floors. The temperature was kept at ninety-two degrees so they wouldn't catch cold. For breakfast, they'd get two slices of bread, and for lunch, a bowl of soup. On the third day, they'd get a full meal. Then the process would start over again. It was a good place to go if you wanted to lose weight."

Tour coordinator Jan Demyas, who oversees thirty volunteers, was selling tickets and trying to talk to us at the same time. She is among those people who are convinced that the prison is haunted.

"On the scale of one to ten, we're in the seven-to-eight range for paranormal activity," she explained. "The hole, the warden's quarters, the fourth tier of the east cellblock—these are the places where sightings occur more often. But they're not limited just to those places. Sightings extend over the entire building, and they're not always where people died. In fact, we have no idea how many people died here. That's state information, and we do not have access to it."

She said many people hear sounds in the prison and that one woman claims to hear a little girl singing every time she visits. But Demyas said no record exists of a young girl who died in the prison.

"I have no idea how these spirits got here, but they're definitely here," she said. "I don't dispute it. Too many people become affected when they enter here, even in the daytime. One young man who visited from Maryland took fifty-two pictures while on tours. When he had them developed, he had more than one image that he couldn't explain, including a small child in the background. He said he and his buddy were the only people standing in that area of the prison. A lot of times, the spirits are not even identifiable. They will be sounds. One year, a lot of people developed their film and it had flames in the background. So it's not defined images. It's different."

Many visitors echo her thoughts. A Portsmouth woman wrote to the preservationists that she and her friends went on a ghost hunt in 2002. Her letter was posted on the prison's Web site: "The first thing that happened is one of my friends and I saw a black figure at the end of the bottom of the west cellblock as we were walking past the scaffold . . . the figure disappeared soon after. It couldn't have been our shadows because the light source was in front of the three of us. The second thing that happened was when we were walking into the east cellblock on the bottom. First, we felt a cold blast of air, which was noticeable since it was so humid in there that night. As we reached the middle of the east cellblock, up above us we heard what we thought was the sound of the cells slamming. They continued to slam and get louder and closer to us. It really startled us because there were no lights above us anywhere. We also knew those cells are so hard to close that they couldn't possibly be slammed over and over by somebody."

John Toney, president of the prison preservation group, suggested to me that some spirits come from the Civil War, or even earlier. Of course, he said, the prison itself holds enough bad memories. "It can be scary," he said. "We've had a few people get so frightened that they've asked to leave. We have to be careful in there. You can get lost down in those catacombs. Last year, it took us two weeks to find a little kid."

He contorted his face in an exaggerated grimace and winked.

I think.

10

Louisa's Legacy

One day in 1861, a weary John Batterson Stetson arrived at his sister's little house in Waynesville in rural Warren County. The train trip had been arduous for the sick but hopeful man who wanted to earn a fortune and a reputation out West. But first, he knew he had to achieve the nearly impossible: conquer tuberculosis. He never doubted that he would win.

In those days, Ohio and Waynesville were technically no longer the West, except to Easterners like Louisa Stetson Larrick. Since 1803, when Ohio entered the Union, the borders of America's great western nether region had slowly expanded to include Missouri and beyond. That's where John Stetson was heading—toward the golden horizon. On the way, he wanted to see his sister Louisa and recuperate at her home.

Only months earlier, on the Larrick family farm outside of town, Louisa's world had finally crashed. She felt trapped and hopeless. Her marriage was crumbling. She felt stifled by Hiram Larrick, whom she had married in 1838, so she left him and moved into the little house in town. For that bold move she earned the contempt of many townspeople, who did not take separation or divorce lightly. To them, leaving a spouse was sinful and disrespectful.

Her move, as well as the impending visit from her brother, would change the direction of her life and those of millions of other people, but at the time she didn't realize it would mean anything to her. She only worried about her health and the health of her children. She prayed they wouldn't catch tuberculosis, and that her brother would miraculously recover. She did not consider turning him away.

Louisa and John were products of an Eastern upbringing and a large family. Born March 2, 1819, in Connecticut, Louisa was the daughter of a small-time hat manufacturer, Stephen Stetson III, and his wife, Marianne Batterson. Brother John was born May 5, 1830, in Orange, New Jersey. Being eleven years his senior, and one of an army of twelve children, Louisa was never extremely close to John, but her parents stressed togetherness and a strong family bond. They made it known that John, being a son, would one day enter the family business as a partner. Louisa, as were other girls of her era, was expected to marry her way into prosperity.

John didn't fare much better. Although he didn't receive a partnership in the family hat factory, he worked for his father long enough to learn the hat trade from the inside. His brothers earned all the money and left him struggling. So he decided to start his own factory.

But tuberculosis changed his plans. When doctors diagnosed the young man just before he turned thirty, his father assumed John would not live to see his thirty-fifth birthday. So Stephen Stetson had another reason not to invite John into the business. It was just as well, for a short time later his father lost all his money through a bad investment deal. He died soon after.

On the advice of his physicians, John Stetson left the cold, polluted Philadelphia for the West and its clean, warm air. He never thought much about dying, for he had too many dreams to fulfill. He wanted to be rich. The doctors said perhaps the clean air would help restore John's lungs, but they warned him that tuberculosis was a contagious, debilitating disease for which there was no cure.

In Warren County, John stayed with Louisa while he gathered his strength. The country air seemed to revive him. He felt stronger every day. From Waynesville, John left for St. Joseph, Missouri, where he found a job in a brickyard. Months later, he was promoted to manager. He saved his money and bought the business. He believed he would be healed and his material needs would be met; he didn't worry about the future.

On the verge of financial success a year later, he watched as the flooded Missouri River washed away his business and his dreams. Despondent, he attempted to enlist in the army at the start of the Civil War in 1861, but recruiters turned him down because of his disease. He felt even worse. They would take anyone, he told himself as he wandered.

On the trail he met a group of prospectors heading to Pikes Peak and other faraway places to search for gold. They accepted him. On long nights in camp he passed the time by experimenting with furs for hats. Others marveled as he took pieces of leather, shaved them, boiled them, loved them, and molded them into about any shape he desired. He preferred high crowns and wide brims to keep the sun out of his eyes.

John Stetson became an artist with leather.

Meanwhile, Louisa Larrick's town was suffocating her. It was too old-fashioned for her eastern tastes. People talked about her.

When I arrived in Waynesville, in search of her story, I envisioned the town as it was in 1860. I walked along its old-fashioned streets and imagined seeing Louisa walking to the general store. Superficially, at least, the town hasn't changed much since she lived. Most of the architecture is nineteenth century, and the town's antique shops sell the same kinds of utensils, tools, and other materials that the townspeople used back then.

These days, Waynesville, a Quaker community cut from the wilderness in 1797 and named for General Anthony Wayne, promotes itself as the antiques capital of the Midwest. Despite its old and Anglo pedigree, Waynesville's image is that of a German town. The annual Ohio Sauerkraut Festival assures that the taste and odor of old-fashioned sauerkraut drifts into people's consciousness and typecasts Waynesville as the home of sauerkraut and antiques. In that way, perhaps, the town has changed.

But there's more to Waynesville than musty rooms and cabbage. A few weeks after the annual October festival comes Halloween and a much closer approximation of Waynesville: the Most Haunted Town in Ohio. A writer applied the nickname in the 1990s, and nobody has bothered to dispute it. In fact, some townspeople have encouraged it by proclaiming Main Street as America's Most Haunted Street.

Ghost stories are the folklore of Waynesville, which lately has been promoting itself as haunted. Supposedly, haunted buildings line Main Street like tombstones in a country cemetery. Thirty years ago, town historian Dennis Dalton started collecting the old stories and interviewing people. So I asked the conductor of the "Not So Dearly Departed Tour" himself to show me around town and introduce me to Louisa Larrick—or, more exactly, to her reputation.

Dalton is the perfect neighbor for the job; he grew up in Waynesville in the 1950s, and he knows every house and legend. He is one of those vanishing characters, bigger than his reputation and perpetually in a good mood. He is the last of an indispensable breed, the small-town storyteller, historian, and folklorist. Physically, he reminds me of a Dickens character—ruddy-faced, robust, talkative, and dressed in an early 1800s costume befitting his status as Warren County's official town crier.

As we walked down Main Street, Dalton explained the stories behind each old house. I realized that Waynesville is at once a living town and a ghost town. Its past is superimposed on top of its present, slightly off-kilter, the way those old 3-D pictures look before you put on cardboard glasses. "I make the tours historical," Dalton said. "I tell about the times, the buildings, and the town. These stories are a part of us—our own folk tales. They can't be separated from the history of the village because it is all one. As a result, the people who take my tour leave here with more than just tales of ghosts."

On the surface, the village looks benign enough. Frame buildings are painted light yellow, peach, light blue, green, tan, and white. The brick Wayne Township House, a "newer" structure built in 1878, is painted red. The downtown is meant for walking and greeting neighbors. White wooden porches spill over into green yards. Black iron streetlights give the feel of New England. Yet two Waynesvilles exist, each without the other knowing. In Dalton's world, Waynesville is a town of ghosts, inhabited by the living but still dominated by the dead. He has studied their every move until he feels that he knows them.

When Dalton was growing up in Waynesville, Main Street had a variety store, a department store, several supermarkets, a canning factory, a greenhouse, two barbershops, a theater, a hardware store, a luncheonette, and a weekly newspaper. Now, the town consists mainly of antiques shops; merchants sell the past. With little industry, Waynesville should be dead. Yet other small towns envy Waynesville's economic success.

More than seventy antiques and specialty shops operate in five blocks. In the late 1970s, the antiques business provided the failing, out-of-the-way town with a strategy to compete. To R. Kevin Harper, a former village administrator who later helped the town exploit its past, Waynesville achieved a nearly impossible goal—thriving in a regional economy that is based on the suburbs. "We've capitalized on our own history," he said.

In addition to sharp entrepreneurs, Waynesville has other spirited boosters. They lurk in parlors and old shops, waiting for the annual return of Dennis Dalton and company. It's a long wait, but they don't have a lot of options. They're ghosts.

"I started this tour in 1987, right after I did the Haunted Hot Dog Roast in Springboro," Dalton said. "It has grown every year. I have to turn visitors away. They're fascinated. I think maybe it's the intrigue of the unseen. But I don't want people thinking that I'm exploiting our folklore. People simply have unusual experiences in this town."

I told him that I am fascinated with one story: Louisa's. She always did consider herself an Easterner although she lived in Waynesville from the late 1830s till her death in 1879. After leaving her husband, she spent most of her time in the two-story frame house at 234 South Main Street. It became her refuge from an unhappy marriage and the eyes of a prying village. Today her old home is the Cranberry Bog, a specialty shop. I stepped inside and walked around the three rooms on the first floor. They were crammed with dozens of home décor items, including framed prints and artificial flowers and soaps. The shop smelled sweet.

Outside, Dalton and I surveyed the frame architecture: beige with green shutters, two stories, a small brick chimney, a white wooden picket fence on one side of the yard, an addition on the back, and a small wooden front porch filled with wicker chairs. The front steps were lined with purple petunias.

"The Larrick House was built in 1820," Dalton explained. "In 1861, it became the home of Louisa, a Yankee from the old Stetson family. She had met and married Hiram Larrick and came to live on his family homestead on the southeast side of Waynesville. She never did like the town much, though. I can understand why. This was still the West to her. There wasn't much beyond it but St. Louis. She found the life disagreeable. Women smoked pipes. Small children chewed tobacco and spat on the sidewalks. Swearing, public drunkenness—life was rough and uncouth here. She became disenchanted with her life and husband."

Perhaps that's because by 1860 Louisa had become a Victorian baby machine. A native of Rockingham County, Virginia, Hiram Larrick had come to Ohio years earlier. He sought financial security but ended up needing a fortune to pay for all his children. After marrying on August 26, 1838, the couple produced nine children together—six girls and three boys: Elizabeth, 1838; Sarah, 1842; Lucy, 1846; Mary, 1847; Martha, 1849; Susan, 1851; John, 1853; Hiram, 1856; Ada, 1858; and George, 1859.

Dalton explained: "In 1861, after rearing her oldest children, Louisa separated from her husband's bed and board and moved into this cottage in town. Imagine the audacity of that woman! Separation and divorce were not considered minor social offenses in Victorian Ohio. In this case the woman had initiated the separation, which was unthinkable.

"That summer, her brother visited her after being sent west by his doctor to recuperate from consumption. Few people in those days ever survived consumption, or tuberculosis. He also suffered from asthma and other respiratory problems. His doctor could think of only one strategy—go out into the sunshine and warm air—which is what Stetson finally did. Out in Missouri, he took up with some wildcat gold miners. Another gold rush was going on then. He went the distance with them, more than seven hundred miles. He didn't get rich. When his strength returned, he started back to Philadelphia."

One night on the trail, on his way to the boomtown Central City, Colorado, Stetson told a cowboy that he could make a fur hat without tanning the leather. Using the hides of rabbits, Stetson felted a strange-looking hat that protected its wearer against the rain and the sun—exactly what one of the cowboys had requested that night and bet Stetson that he could not make. When he arrived in Central City, Stetson sold the hat to a Mexican cowboy for a five-dollar gold piece. It was the first Stetson cowboy hat. With it came an idea: manufacture the hats.

"On the way home, John stopped in Waynesville to see his sister, the only person he could think of who might help him," Dalton said. "He needed money. He had failed in the gold rush. He told her he wanted to start a one-man hat factory in Philadelphia. Louisa listened to his dreams and schemes, and grubstaked him with sixty dollars to help open the John Stetson hat factory. Sixty dollars was a lot of money to Louisa, probably her whole savings. John returned to Philadelphia and in 1865 opened a small factory with only a hundred dollars. He bought ten dollars worth of fur, went to work, and created the hat of the West, which he later named the Boss of the Plains."

With its six-inch crown and seven-inch brim, the hat looked like a sombrero. It could carry a half-gallon of water but received the nickname the ten-gallon hat. At first, Stetson sold his hats to shops in Philadelphia. When customers had little interest, he sent free hats to clothing distributors across the southwest. Soon, a few orders trickled in, then more, and within a year many western residents were wearing the Stetson. It became synonymous with cowboys; they used it to shade their eyes, beat out campfires, carry grain, drink water from, sleep on as a pillow, and whip their horses. In 1885, as sales continued to increase,

Stetson opened a large factory in North Philadelphia and hired four thousand workers. In the 1890s, the Canadian Northwest Mounted Police started wearing a Stetson hat, as did Canadian soldiers who served in battle in South Africa. The hat became a North America icon.

"He built the business into a multi-million-dollar operation," Dalton said. "He also manufactured dress top hats for gentlemen and, of course, his biggest seller, what we call the cowboy hat. Had he not come to Waynesville, and had his sister not listened to his dream, the American cowboy could have gone hatless—or, at least, not as well prepared to deal with his environment."

Dalton walked up onto the veranda of the Larrick cottage and peeked inside. The shop was now closed for the day. He started talking slowly: "We believe it is the ghost of Louisa who haunts this place; she lived out the rest of her life here and had little contact with her brother. She led a rather sad life. In 1887, the Larrick family contacted John Stetson and asked him for $250, the final payoff on a $5,000 loan that was the family farm mortgage, and John refused. By then, $5,000 was a paltry amount to Stetson. He was a multimillionaire. Somehow, the Larrick family managed to scrape the money together, though, without Uncle John's help. This happened two years before Hiram Larrick died. Not that John excluded his sister completely. Every Christmas, John sent hats back to the men in the Larrick family, but he was a terrible skinflint who sent them ordinary hats and the women common clothing. Yet in 1889 he paid $16 million for a broke Florida college, Deland, and put it back on its feet. Now it's the Stetson law school in St. Petersburg. I went there and could feel Stetson's personality all over the place.

"Well, Louisa, I'm sure, felt slighted. After all, she's the one who built his fortune with her grubstake. He did leave her one legacy, though. As I tell everyone, it wasn't stock in the business, a million dollars, or even a special hat named in her honor. It was tuberculosis. It struck her down in 1879, when she died poor. Meanwhile, John B. lived on—until 1906, when his company was selling two million hats a year."

John Stetson did repay his sister the sixty dollars. He built his business and fulfilled his destiny—live a long life and prosper. He once said, "There is no advertisement equal to a well-pleased customer." He had millions of them. He left a fortune of more than $10 million. But after World War II, tastes changed. Men stopped wearing hats all the time, even in the southwest. By 1960, his firm was still making 4.5 million hats annually. In 1971 the John B. Stetson Co. main plant in Philadelphia closed, after making hats for 105 years. That year the Stevens Hat Manufacturing Co. of St. Joseph purchased the firm's remaining inventory and equipment to continue making the famous Stetson hat.

"Poor Louisa couldn't help but feel left out of her brother's success," Dalton said. "I imagine she shed some tears in this house. But who's to say? She died in this very place and was carried across the Little Miami River to the Miami Cemetery, where everybody assumes she has been sleeping peacefully. But other people who have owned this building over the years would disagree. Every so often, some unusual things happen. One owner, an antiques dealer, told me she was reading in the back when she heard a commotion in the shop. She walked out there and saw something she will never forget. On the walls hung graduated iron ladles, used to dip lard during hog butchering. They were heavy. All of a sudden, they started swinging together, right on the wall, as if on cue and in time. No breeze could move those big things. The woman just stood there, totally aghast. Another time, a visitor to the shop asked her who was baking gingerbread in the kitchen. (This happened in the early 1970s, when they still had a kitchen in here. Of course, no one was baking anything at the time.)

"On another occasion, a young policeman saw a figure in the north window as he made his rounds at two A.M. It was on a moonlit night. He felt a sense of wanting to turn around and look over his shoulder. He saw something, a pale figure. When he got the nerve to take a better look, the figure dissolved before his eyes. We do know that Louisa has been seen in the last fifteen years. A neighbor across the street glanced over and saw a woman in the doorway. He described her as small with dark hair. He thought it was the shop owner, but his wife reminded him that the owner was away for the weekend. When he looked back, the figure dissolved into the wall behind her. He said she wore a print dress with a high collar. A Larrick descendant once told me that the figure fit the description of Louisa—right down to the dark hair and small frame.

"Only a few summers ago, a young sales clerk was working alone in the antiques shop when she heard a loud pounding on the front door, just before closing time at five P.M. She looked and saw nothing. She heard it again, and looked and saw a gloved hand—an old-fashioned woman's glove. The woman kept pulling on the doorknob. The clerk yelled, 'I'm sorry, but we're closed. Come back tomorrow.' The sound continued and the clerk rushed to the door and opened it, expecting to find an old woman. But again, she saw nothing. She closed up for the day and went out front, where her father waited to drive her home. She asked him who the old woman was at the door a few minutes ago. He said, 'I've been sitting out in front for fifteen minutes, and nobody has come up to the door.'"

Dennis Dalton looked at me and didn't say a word. He finished his tour and we stepped off the porch and headed briskly down Main Street. If I had been wearing a hat that afternoon, I would have tipped it generously to Louisa Stetson Larrick.

11

Travels in the Great Black Swamp

Nature took twenty-five thousand years to create the Great Black Swamp and man fifty years to strip it. The glacier did the heaviest work, grinding the earth like a bowling ball on an anthill. At Cleveland, the ice was eight thousand feet thick. Retreating fourteen thousand years ago, it dammed a poorly drained area on the eastern end of the Lake Erie basin to form one of nine ancient lakes, which eventually dried and left sand ridges in the clay soil the way ridges form on a beach. Along the newer Lake Erie, the lake plains evolved into a larger pear-shaped region in northwest Ohio, where black organic matter piled on glacial soil to nurture swampy forests for ten thousand years. It was the ultimate compost heap.

Swamp chestnuts produced millions of nuts that covered the water and ground and choked other young trees. In this dark, wet place, armies of spiny hellrats—flashing their snouts and sharp claws, they resembled weasels—probed the muck for nuts. Another nut-eating dinosaur, the American harrack, ate the nuts *and* the hellrats.

Centuries later, before the arrival of the white man, the Great Black Swamp remained untouched and covered by water nine months a year. Vegetation grew wildly, becoming by the 1700s the largest deciduous swamp forest in North America. Its soil was a black, oozing muck. An early observer described the swamp as thoroughly impregnated with lime, forming a tough, waxy mud that stuck to wagon wheels.

According to some estimates, the swamp measured 120 miles long and 40 miles wide. The worst part was an area as large as Connecticut, between the Maumee and the Auglaize rivers. It had a split personality; just when it appeared to be all wet, dark, and muddy, a prairie would pop up to tantalize visitors. Some scientists believe the swamp stretched from Lake Erie to New Haven, Indiana. Because nature doesn't provide boundaries like fences, no one knows for certain where the swamp began and ended. Most people agree that it consisted of eight contiguous counties, including Lucas, Wood, Paulding, Hancock, Defiance, and Putnam. Neighboring counties were swampy enough for many people to consider them Black Swamp territory. They included parts of Van Wert, Seneca, Ottawa, Fulton, Sandusky, Erie, and Henry counties. (I call these places the swamp suburbs.)

Pioneers did not draw much distinction between areas inside and outside the swamp. By more liberal estimates, its mucky fingers extended as far south as Allen and Mercer counties, north to Williams and Lucas, east to Hardin, and west to Indiana. (An old surveyor's wall map, which hangs in the study of the Sherman House in Lancaster, shows the Great Black Swamp covering Ohio's entire northwest quarter, all the way to the Indiana border in the west and the Darke County line in the south.) "The perfect uniformity of the soil has given the forest a homogeneous character," historian Henry Howe wrote of the swamp in the late 1800s. "The trees are all generally the same height, so that when viewed at a distance through the haze, the forest appears like an immense blue wall stretched across the horizon."

By the time I traveled in the area, everything had changed. I drove for miles without seeing a single tree. Then I'd see clumps of them. I never did find a swamp, and only one marsh. When I visited my wife's family in Van Wert County, I was surprised to learn that their farm—started by her German immigrant grandfather in the late 1800s—once stood on the swamp's edge. Nowadays, few people know that a big swamp once existed there, or that their ancestors stripped primeval forests, set up logging and tile-making industries, and later established the former swamp as one of the nation's richest farming areas. They transformed the land, created an agrarian culture, and in the process eliminated the songbirds, panthers, bears, and wolves.

Pioneers saw the forests as a challenge to their collective ax. They chopped, sawed, smashed, bumped, banged, and pulled down as many trees as possible. Or they held "burning bees," competitions to burn down the forests. The earliest settlers found 95 percent of Ohio filled with trees—twenty-five million acres of virgin forest. (Today, naturalists identify only about seven hundred Ohio forested acres as virgin.)

Because of wet conditions, Ohio's nine northwestern counties developed last, from 1850 to 1900. By 1930, they were the most heavily farmed counties in the state. Probably the largest forest left in northwest Ohio is in Paulding County—three hundred acres of old-growth ash, walnut, basswood, red maple, oak, and hickory.

Seemingly obsessed, the whole state considered tree-cutting its patriotic duty. And in the swamp, where trees were overly abundant, the cutting took on the fervor of a religious ritual.

Soldiers called the swamp their personal hell. Its bad reputation spread throughout the West. Simon Girty, the hated white renegade who led the Indian attack on Fort Henry in 1777, hid in the Black Swamp, thus adding to his—and its—sinister image. (Today he would be called a terrorist.) There in the mud, Mother Nature joined forces with the enemy. When General Anthony Wayne signed the Treaty of Greenville with the Indians in 1795, he generously gave them some of the Black Swamp.

Wayne had found and burned Ottawa cornfields on lowlands of the Maumee and Auglaize. Later, he wrote that he had never "beheld such immense fields of corn, in any part of America, from Canada to Florida."

While standing in the swamp's woods, people couldn't see the sun. This unnerved them. Dark shadows covered everything. The Indians refused to live there; they entered only the river bottoms to hunt and trap. In the early 1800s, the pioneers settled on its edges. Only the fearless chopped down trees and built cabins in the swamp. It was so dense that a hunter got lost only a short distance from Fort Meigs; for three days he wandered among the trees and wolves, until he accidentally walked into the fort's walls, at which point he did not recognize his wife or children or even know his name. A blacksmith named Jacob Nofziger wasn't so lucky: He tried to go from the Tiffin River to the Maumee and was never seen again. Neither were his oxen, wagon, and belongings. Another settler, Christian Lauber, tried to cross a creek, but his exhausted oxen stopped in the middle and refused to move. Returning the next morning, he and a neighbor found the team frozen in the water. They broke the ice, freed the animals, and slid the provisions across the icy creek. When traveler William Woodbridge arrived at Fort Meigs on January 18, 1815, he wrote: "My great terrour, the Black swamp, is passed. No part of this road seems so very bad as has been represented, but the evil in it is in its perfect sameness; in a moderately wet season it will be generally covered by two or three inches of water and mud nearly a foot, with a few exceptions of dry spots."

Such conditions—and fear of the unknown—convinced many travelers to bypass the swamp on their way west, although the new route required them to travel hundreds of additional miles by wagon. Most travelers never regretted the inconvenience. Experienced frontiersman William Henry Harrison, who fought at the Battle of Fallen Timbers, said a couple of trips across the Black Swamp could kill a brigade of packhorses. American army scouts feared the swamp, but troops at Fort Meigs were awed by its dark wonders. They saw fish so plentiful that their jumping frightened horses on Maumee fords. In keeping with the swamp's larger-than-life reputation, a soldier in Wayne's cavalry company at Fort Defiance once claimed he caught a fish so large that his entire unit feasted on it.

In late winter, mud and water often stood three feet deep, making passage impossible. The swamp had little natural drainage. Two-thirds of it was under water. As late as 1870, brave people ice-skated the thirty-five miles from Paulding to Van Wert. In summer, water stood in big pools, breeding black clouds of gnats. The wet, low environment encouraged hundreds of flora species, including basswood, elm, ironwood, oak, cottonwood, ash, maple, sycamore, poplar, hickory, beech, and black walnut. An early surveyor wrote in his journal: "Water! Water! Water! tall timber! deep water! Not a blade of grass growing or a bird to be seen." Added Williams County pioneer George W. Perky: "We read that God divided the land from the water, but here is a place He forgot."

During the War of 1812, American and British generals knew the swamp cut off the western United States from Michigan. If the Canadians fortified western Lake Erie, they could use the swamp as a buffer and the British navy could control the lake. American scout Robert Lucas, who would become an Ohio governor, realized the swamp's strategic value, so he traveled from the Maumee to the advancing American army to make reports. His journal contained the first reference to the Black Swamp: "Traveled about twenty-five miles, a very rainy day and then encamped in what is called the Black Swamp, had a disagreeable night of wet and Musketoes."

Disagreeable? Travelers saw dark mists heading toward them—mosquitoes! They grabbed their napes, and saw blood all over their hands.

Animals were bitten so many times, they almost went mad. Malaria, then called swamp fever, was common; some people contracted it so often that they became immune. Newcomers died from it. It turned the skin yellow, caused violent chills and high fever, and left the lucky ones exhausted. Only quinine helped relieve the symptoms. When immigrants dug the canal in the early 1840s, they lived in shanties and practically lived on whiskey and quinine. They breathed air polluted with malarial effluvia from the swamps, and as a result they caught the fever and ague. On the Maumee River, "the fever spared no one," the Black Swamp pioneer Louis Simonis wrote in 1835. The area was a "forsaken, desolate, ague-smitten, tangled, and inhospitable wilderness where diseases spread with rapidity and with relentless mortality." Strangely, the Indians did not seem to come down with malaria and other fevers as often as whites, perhaps because they had developed immunity.

Ague—a malarial fever with chills—was so widespread in the swamp that families kept salt, pepper, and quinine on their kitchen tables. Cholera and typhoid struck, too. Pioneers disagreed about the fever's transmission; some said the fever came from eating swamp fish; others said it came from air poisoned by decaying vegetation. Apparently they did not consider the blood-lusting mosquitoes that attacked in squadrons.

In 1910, Wood County historian C. W. Evers explained the agony of ague:

All had it. It was no respecter of persons. It was a singular complication or combination of attacks on the human system. The victim begun the ordeal with a feeling of extreme chilliness; lips and fingernails turned blue as if the blood were stagnant. Then greater chilliness followed by shivering and chattering of teeth. By this time the victim, feeling as if every bone in his body would break, had crawled into bed if he was fortunate enough to have one, and called for more cover, shaking meanwhile as if just out of an icy river in a bleak day. This chilly period lasted from three-quarters of an hour to one hour or more, and was followed by a raging fever in which the patient constantly called for more water, which he gulped down by the quart, and still the thirst was unquenched and unquenchable. The fever in turn would be followed by a relaxation of the system and the most profuse and exhausting perspiration until the sheets and clothing would be wringing wet, leaving in the clothes a disagreeable odor hard to describe, but always the same. There was no mistaking an "ague sweat" by its odor. The only antidote, quinine, could not be obtained regularly.

To discourage mosquitoes, the pioneers burned smudge pots that produced clouds of black smoke to drive insects away. They worked, to a degree, during the day. People burned them constantly. Surprisingly, new people arrived to settle the land. Soon they suffered from violent malarial fevers that struck as often as every four hours, followed by chills that were called the shakes. They didn't understand that malaria was caused by a parasite, but they knew that mosquitoes were involved in transmission of the disease.

Fever struck James Riley Sr., one of the swamp's main scouts and pioneers, in the late 1820s. He helped lay out towns such as Lima; Celina; Coldwater; Delphos; Van Wert (his son, James Watson Riley, would become a cofounder of Van Wert in 1835); and New Rochester, the first seat of Paulding County. Riley became so ill with fever that he had to move to New York. In camp, travelers kept horseflies, gnats, mosquitoes, and other annoying insects away after dark by burning big fires. Because of the fever threat, many pioneers turned back to Michigan and Indiana. Those who moved into the swamp wore heavy clothes and buckskin mittens—even in warm weather—to protect their health. To discourage threatening insects, pioneers covered their horses in blankets and wrapped cloth around their own heads. In humid summer, life was unbearable.

Other diseases arrived with travelers. By the late 1840s, a cholera epidemic spread across the swamp and frightened travelers coming across Ohio from the east. The feared disease raged for years. It hit hard and fast. A person could wake up feeling sick to his stomach and having diarrhea, and by night he could be dead; some people fell dead in the streets. When a family member took sick, some people simply ran away from home instead of staying to care for him, because they knew the disease was extremely contagious. Even some local newspapers closed. In Perrysburg in Lucas County in 1854, cholera killed two hundred people in a town of fifteen hundred. Panicked people fled town. Businesses closed. Two girls orphaned by the disease survived outdoors by eating scraps of food that a kindly neighbor threw to them from her back door. In Eagle Township in Hancock County, one whole cemetery was devoted to cholera victims. Delphos, a Miami and Erie Canal town that straddles the Allen and Van Wert County line, was nearly wiped out by cholera in 1854.

Neither disease nor discomfort could stop people from entering the swamp. As early as 1827, when more travelers started arriving on their way west, Congress built the Western Reserve Road on the spongy ground. The problem was, the land was so flat and clay-filled that it would not drain. Previously, the only "major" swamp routes were a skimpy trail cut from Fort Adams to Fort Defiance by General Wayne's troops in 1794 and then a road that the state expanded from Greenville to Defiance in 1824. Wayne's soldiers simply followed an old Indian trail, the Black Swamp Trail, which they would later build from Upper Sandusky to Findlay. In 1812, General William Henry Harrison used it on his trek to Fort Meigs.

Because of the poor weather, stagecoaches could travel in and around the swamp from only July to September. Travelers said the state road wasn't much better than Wayne's. An early editor called it "a strip 120 feet wide cleared through the woods with a ridge of loose dirt about forty feet wide between the ditches along the side." The more the road was traveled, the worse it became; it was known as one of North America's worst. More roads, all of them bad, opened in the 1830s.

(Frustrated by their lack of success with roads, engineers tried to build an elevated railroad across the soggy land in 1840. The track was to be mounted on wooden poles, installed by two big steam-powered machines. One started at Toledo, the other at Lower Sandusky. Wood-cutters worked ahead. Every time the machines stuck the poles in the wet ground, however, they fell over in the mud. The two machines never did meet as planned in the middle of the swamp. The rail line never started running.)

Settlers walked and rode only a few miles at a time because the roads contained deep ruts that cracked wagon wheels and broke spirits. Between Fremont and Perrysburg, thirty-one taverns—one per difficult mile—opened to serve weary travelers, who sometimes rode all morning, only to return, beaten down, to the tavern where they had stayed the previous night. Tree stumps blocked wagons. Drivers tried to steer around them, creating ruts deep enough to bury a horse. Mud holes sucked down victims like quicksand. Entrepreneurial frontiersmen claimed certain big mud holes as their own; for a fee, they would pull stranded travelers from the mud and help them on their way. Even so, riders sank into mud up to their saddlebags. One man drove a wagon home at night and the next morning discovered he had lost his rear wheels in the mud somewhere down the bumpy road.

In the spring of 1838, John S. Butler, a fourteen-year-old Pony Express rider, and another young man traveled from Sylvania, Ohio, to Indiana, going through the Black Swamp. They carried no guns. When attacked by wolves, the two cut tree limbs for clubs and pushed their tired horses faster, but the howling surrounded them. At a big tree they fought the attacking wolves for thirty minutes. Butler said, "Finally, they retreated, and we knew that one of them had fallen a victim to our clubs, and that it was now our chance to push on. It was only a short time before we could hear those wolves coming on again, and I knew that this fight would be harder than the other, for the taste of blood had added to the fury of those wild beasts. When we were almost exhausted and overpowered, I heard a gun, and knew that the tavern keeper had heard our shouts and was coming to our relief."

On the road one night, wolves approached lone traveler Daniel Sauder, who scared them away by striking six-inch wooden matches all the way home. Stranded travelers overturned their wagons and tried to hide at night, but wolves chewed through the wooden sides. Those lucky enough to evade the packs faced poisonous snakes, bears that could outrun men, lynx, and panthers. One settler heard a noise on top of his isolated cabin, so he tapped the ceiling with a quilt frame. A panther jumped off the roof, growled, and frightened the family. A more serious threat to woodsmen was wild hogs with sharp tusks. They were usually thin and hungry, and when they found a man, they mutilated him. Long bristles stood up on their backs when the hogs were angry. They were so fast and ferocious that they often ripped rattlesnakes and copperheads apart before the snakes could strike. The only way to escape a hog in the swamp was to climb a tree.

The whole place was malevolent. Wood County farmer Amos Dewese lost 8 horses, 21 cows, and 260 hogs to disease during the winter of 1842. His neighbors, wearing rags and starving, fled to the city, leaving empty cabins. The stress of living in such a hostile countryside provoked people to extreme actions. One woman killed her husband because he would not agree to leave the swamp. A man killed his wife and buried her in a tree stump. When neighbors discovered her skeleton several years later, they remembered that her husband had said his wife "went away to Michigan."

Engineering reports said the swamp was uninhabitable, but Middle European laborers couldn't read English and probably wouldn't have believed such reports anyway. They had come in the 1820s to build a canal system in northern Indiana and western Ohio. When they finished their work in the 1830s, they decided to stay. After all, the land was cheap. Nobody wanted it. Europeans accepted the swampy conditions better than most Americans, perhaps because they were used to wet land at home. Where most people saw death and misery, the immigrants saw opportunity. One young man, a native of Dresden, Germany, told writer John Peyton that northwestern Ohio was El Dorado. "You will not find precious metals here," he said while shaking with malarial fever, "but innumerable dangers, discomforts, and toil; but these are inseparable from a new country, and if surmounted by industry, a man can accumulate a fortune." An American pioneer, anonymous and maybe apocryphal, offered a different view: "The white man came and took possession of the Black Swamp before the Creator had it ready."

Despite the hardships, more settlements grew slowly. Immigrants were intrigued because the Indians had left by federal orders, the most dangerous animals were being driven away, and the forests were slowly shrinking. Although area newspapers were filled with horrible stories about swamp life, people rarely complained to their neighbors and families in the East. They were too proud. They had heard that the swamp was a great opportunity. Unfortunately, many speculators lied about the region's potential. J. W. Scott, who later started the *Toledo Blade*, published guides to attract pioneers. He claimed the area would contain the world's largest cities by the year 2000. Thousands of people believed him—until they saw the water rats.

In the 1840s, Methodists came to build churches in and near the swamp. After experiencing Toledo, preacher Joseph Cross told church members in the *Christian Advocate*:

Of all the towns I ever saw, I think it is the most miserable . . . the place is so sickly that few will consent to stay here, except blacklegs and desperadoes, such as can subsist wherever Arabs or alligators can, and seem to feel most at home in such society. A few human shadows, yellow as the autumn forests around them, creep shivering through muddy streets. Our hotel seemed to be the general rendezvous of bedbugs for all the western country, and for breakfast they gave us hash of which I should not dare even to guess the ingredients. Here the philosopher might well light his lamp at noon to find an honest man.

Yet swamp people endured hardship with humor. The *Maumee City Express* published this poem on June 24, 1837:

> On Maumee, On Maumee
> Potatoes they grow small;
> They roast them in the fire
> And eats them—tops and all.
> On Maumee, On Maumee
> It's ague in the fall;
> The fits will shake them so
> It rocks the house and all.
> There's a funeral every day
> Without hearse or pall;
> They tuck them in the ground
> With breeches, coat and all.

In 1859, conditions started to improve when the Ohio legislature passed the first public ditch law, forcing land condemnation and assessment to help drain the swamp. Immigrant farmers renewed their attack against the swamp as though *it* were the intruder. They installed homemade wooden under-drains and, later, clay ones. At first, farmers laughed at the few who installed drainage systems under their farms. To convince farmers of the advantages of under-the-ground drainage systems, the state hired John H. Klippart, a drainage expert, to write land-drainage guides for farmers.

From 1870 to 1920, farmers dug fifteen thousand miles of drainage ditches. The 1870s and 1880s were northwestern Ohio's busiest years, with more than seven thousand miles of ditches dug in more than two million acres. If the region were to become farmland, ditches would be necessary to drain fields. At first, ditches were cut by hand from the heavy clay. Ditchers received $1.50 a day. Later, steam- and gas-powered machines did the heavy work. The soil that piled up was used to build roads.

Machinist James B. Hill of Wood County patented and built a steam-powered ditching machine in 1893. The big metal wheel on a wooden frame could do the work of fifty men. Hill called his invention the

Buckeye Ditcher. In 1902, he sold his company to the Van Buren, Heck, and Marvin Company of Findlay, which became the Buckeye Traction Ditcher Company. Because of Hill's invention, drains were installed all over the Black Swamp and digging ditches became easier. The new company was the largest ditching and trenching company in the world for half a century, and its ditchers helped drain the Everglades.

As farmers dug more ditches in the Black Swamp, whole economies flourished and died. Stave and barrel-hoop factories depleted elm and hickory forests. Black Swamp woodchoppers could clear an acre of big trees in three to four weeks. They lived in shacks in the same woods they were cutting. They called themselves "specialists" and rejected other forest jobs; they said the title gave them the luxury of working when they wanted. To hurry the cutting, they devised a method called tree slashing: they cut deep notches in trees, sometimes halfway through the trunks, with the deeper notches in trees at the front of the woods. Wind knocked over the forests like a table of dominoes.

By 1870, more than four hundred sawmills were operating in the Black Swamp. Wood County alone had nearly one hundred. Sawmill equipment was made in nearby Allen County and sent in by railroad. The sawmill manufacturer evolved into the Lima Locomotive Works. As late as 1880, thirty-four stave factories were operating in Paulding County, making staves for wooden barrels. Even smaller towns had sawmills, to make 12 x 12–foot frames for barns. At the time, timberland sold for five dollars an acre. Settlers arrived, methodically cut the trees, and thus destroyed their financial base. When the logging industry faded in the 1880s, many sawmill operators started making drainage tiles. The companies also became mini-banks, loaning money to farmers and small-business people at rates lower than what the banks could offer. By 1880 the Black Swamp had eighty-one brick and tile mills, most of them powered by horses and, later, steam and gasoline engines. When demand for tile declined in the early 1900s, most northwest Ohio tile makers went out of business. Beneath the ancient swamp were buried millions of clay tiles, enough to surround the Earth eleven times. Today, only a couple of major tile makers still operate there.

Paulding County's last pocket of virgin timber — forty acres in Brown Township — wasn't cut down until 1953, and, because of the immensity of the trees, the job took three years to complete. One elm measured 30 feet around and 150 feet high. The Ohio Department of Natural Resources estimated its age at 450 years, making it one of Ohio's older trees. Woodcutters were so effective that by 1940, Ohio's wooded land represented only 14 percent of the state. Woodcutters chopped themselves right out of their specialty work as the land turned to farms. (In 2003, Ohio was nearly 28 percent forested, the highest percentage since 1880.) In the swamp, most trees were cleared from 1860 to 1885, when the sawmills peaked.

Dwight R. Canfield, a Perrysburg physician who grew up in the swamp at the turn of the century, looked over the treeless horizon in 1949 and wondered if his people had made a mistake: "Were the giant forests that were here when we came destroyed unduly? Is man like an insect that passes over and attacks our fruit trees and destroys them? What is man but another animal? Will he some day and some time be destroyed off the face of the Earth that it may return to its former state as it was before the creation? Deep in the silences of the forests I am constrained to wonder!" His view is modern environmentalism. Another opinion, probably the prevailing one, came from the writers of the Ohio travel guide (the Federal Writers Project) during the Depression: "Today the only reminders of the blight that once infested the region are the parallel rows of drainage ditches running across the fields like strings on a harp." One man's blight is another man's beauty.

By the Depression, the logging towns—places named Timberville, Sophia, Arena, and Toronto—were gone or declining. They had depended on the canal and the timber industry to stay alive. During the timber boom years, 1840–1900, Paulding County's population increased from 1,035 to 27,528, still an all-time high. Supported by sawmills, towns like Worstville started in weeks but dried up when the trees were cut. The Black Swamp was tamed, like a wild animal is domesticated. Instead of killing people, the swamp now served them.

Worstville appeared to me like a mirage on the horizon. All that remained when I visited were rows of used tires, two old mobile homes, and five small houses separated by railroad tracks. A retired factory worker named Henry Wheeler invited me to sit with him in his front yard. He said Worstville was named in honor of the Worst family, prominent merchants.

"The school bus don't stop here. Nobody does," he said. "Not long ago, the oldest man in Worstville—a good friend of mine in his nineties—died at home. He couldn't bear to think of dying no place else.

One day he got to feeling bad. I went over to visit him and he said, 'I'll have to go into a rest home. How can I? I ain't never left Worstville.' I told him he could hire somebody to take care of him. The next day, he went to Paulding to draw up his will. He came home, stuck a shotgun in his mouth, and blew his head off. They tore his house down the other day. I said, 'This town is dead too, only it's waiting for some kind of pronouncement.'"

Paul Huebner, an eighty-seven-year-old farmer whose homestead is marked by the Stars and Stripes, said he has watched Worstville and other old towns lose their reasons to exist. "You can always go by this rule: when a town's elevator goes out, the town goes," he said. "When my dad brought us to Worstville from Germany in 1916, the town was the place you took your grain to and bought your staples at. It was a regular little community, with local families who knew their neighbors. The farmers used to drink whiskey to get them going for the day; one guy always got drunk and threw oranges at the clerk in the general store."

Nowadays, towns can grow if they're closer to larger cities or within commuting range. The more remote ones in the old swamp are declining. In southern Wood County, where an oil boom created new towns practically overnight in the early 1890s, West Millgrove has lost its gas stations, hotel, restaurants, schools, and churches. The population decreased from 171 in 1990 to 78 in 2000; it had peaked in 1900 with 236 people. West Millgrove's downtown died years ago. In 1998, the community sunk into $27,000 of red ink. It sold its park and village hall to get out of debt. As interest in the community declined, local elected officials felt helpless. When a Toledo newspaper reporter asked Mayor James Carr to explain why council meetings attracted so few spectators, he replied, "We used to [attract somebody], but he died."

In Henry County's Napoleon Township, Dogtown once attracted travelers to the intersection of U.S. Route 6 and County Road 17. Church services were held in the local tavern. After the members finished praying, they draped a sheet over the altar and opened the bar. The community was also known as Halfway House and Bostelman's Corners, but was more often called Dogtown. This was possibly because a tavern there once used the symbol of a dog. Or, according to researcher Walter Shockey, a local tavern was a "doggery," the old-fashioned name referring to alcoholic drinks as "the hair of the dog that bit you." When the automobile became common on area roads, fewer people had to stop at Dogtown. It faded.

The swamp consisted of many such tiny towns—a general store and a few houses—because the roads were so poor and useful only in warm weather. Farmers and neighbors had to travel only as far as the nearest crossroads community to buy staples. One such town, Cloverleaf, had a large general store that sold everything from shoestrings to patent medicines to parts for Model T Fords. Across the street, a cheese factory operated until the early 1900s. (The town's nickname, Ratsville, came perhaps from a prank in which some boys nailed rats to a board by their tails.) Now that people can travel long distances by car on good highways in the former swamp, Cloverleaf is farmland and the store is gone.

When the swamp was stripped in the mid- to late-1800s, many towns popped up temporarily to service commerce and industry. The appropriately named Woodville became a timber town. (Its post office was called LeSeuer, in honor of a lumber company owner named Fred LeSeuer.) At its peak, Woodville consisted of thirty houses, a company store (Smiley Higgins managed it), a rooming house, and other company properties. As LeSeuer's stock of timber decreased, the town grew smaller. In July 1894, a fire destroyed the company's operation. The flames spread to fifteen acres around Woodville, where eight inches of bark and up to fourteen inches of sawdust were scattered. Ashes smoldered for more than ten years. Woodville fell into a swift decline.

In Wood County, Galatea was one of about twenty oil towns that boomed in the county from the late 1880s to the early 1900s. The oil business started in Galatea, site of the world's largest strike at the time. The town had a glass factory, a railroad station, a post office, two saloons, a dance hall, a hotel livery stable, a refinery that employed six hundred men, and other businesses. When the oil boom ended suddenly, sending the workers to Texas, Galatea nearly closed. Today, it is a ghost town, haunted by the rumors of ghosts and cults. Some people say the spirits of oil workers float out of the ground at night.

On another trip into the former swamp I found a ghost town called Shunk, on State Route 109 in Defiance County. Shunk started as an Indian town in the 1780s. The Indians took or found American army gold and buried it in the village. According to legend, when soldiers approached a few years later, the Indians left behind a ghost warrior and horse to guard the gold. In the early 1900s, a Shunk boy was lost in the woods. Rescuers found him dazed and talking about a ghostly Indian who tried to ride over him with a horse. A few years later, a frightened treasure hunter told a similar story. Sometimes people still report seeing an Indian on horseback in the woods at night.

My favorite tale is from Munger, a lost town in the heart of the swamp. Writer Charles M. Skinner told the story of an evil man named John Cleves (no relation to John Cleves Symmes), who owned Woodbury House, a mansion two miles south of town. In 1842, he received a visitor who was never seen again. Ten years later, when the house sat abandoned and decaying, two travelers decided to stay the night. As they talked late, a skeleton appeared to them. One of the men, a Major Ward, shot it with a pistol, but the skeleton moved forward, pointed his bony finger, and said: "I, that am dead, live in a sense that mortals do not know. In my earthly life I was James Syms, who was robbed and killed here in my sleep by John Cleves. Cleves cut off my head and buried it under the hearth. My body he cast into his well." Next, Ward heard the voice coming from beneath the floor. It said, "Take up my skull."

Many Black Swamp ghost towns were victims of the dying canal and timber industries. New Rochester, built on the Maumee in 1835, became the county seat. It was the only town in Paulding County with three hotels and two blacksmiths and was a stop on the Fort Wayne-to-Toledo stagecoach route. The town's fortunes changed, however, when in 1840 Benjamin Hollister of Charloe boldly offered a two-story brick courthouse if the county commissioners would make his town the county seat. They agreed. "Both towns depended on the canal traffic," County commissioner Elaine Harp told me. "Now, New Rochester is gone, and Charloe is nearly gone, and Paulding is the county seat. Many of our people have left the county to find work elsewhere." These days, all that remains of New Rochester is a roadside park, a stone marker, and a pioneer cemetery.

Other ghost towns of the Great Black Swamp included farm towns, several of which died during the tornado of March 1920. People still talk about it. On Palm Sunday, strong winds moved across the flat Indiana border and over to Payne, Ohio, where every home was destroyed. Then it struck the small town of Emmett, at State Routes 228 and 115 in Paulding County. The place consisted only of a telegraph office, express office, two general stores, and a hotel. With one mighty blow, the twister blew Emmett off the earth (but not the Ohio map) before moving a few miles northeast to tiny Renollet. Gone—the grain elevator, general store, railroad siding, a few houses, and five people.

Next stop, Brunersburg. The big wind knocked down every building as well as the big bridge. A fleeing family drove their car into a building, which showered them with bricks but left them unhurt. Brunersburg lived but has never regained its momentum. When the tornado entered Lucas County, it struck Raab first, blowing the town into oblivion. In all, the tornado killed twenty people in less than an hour.

In Wood County, an area high point, home to Bowling Green State University (from which my wife graduated), there is a road called Sand Ridge. It is not sandy, and it is only a small ridge, but the settlers built houses on it and rejoiced at finding a dry bedrock hill. Cheryl said she spent four years in Bowling Green and never knew she had lived near a ridge.

At the university library's archive building, we took the elevator to the fifth floor and punched the swamp's name into the computer. Twenty-seven entries came up, many of them unrelated to the swamp, including songs by the singer-songwriter Tony Joe White. In the early 1970s, he recorded songs such as "Black Panther Swamp" and "A Night in the Life of a Swamp Fox." He was a Louisiana native, but his song titles reminded me of the Black Swamp; it was as if he knew the place. In the archives we also looked at books, audio and videotapes, master's theses, newspaper clippings, and a box containing swamp ephemera that was collected by a man named Orin Bernard Workman, who was born October 29, 1908, in Paulding County. The construction company owner founded the Black Swamp Historical Museum, his passion. In a university file I read a list of his museum inventory, which he had handwritten on five pages of company letterhead. His artifacts included old vinegar and wine barrels, newspapers, gaslights, a tapestry, German books, plows, and other farm implements. After he died on December 9, 1971, his museum was closed and a piece of the swamp's past died too.

Also in the archives, we discovered a 1983 note about an elderly woman named Mrs. Gribble of Deshler. She recalled that her grandfather farmed on Jackson Prairie in Wood County in the late 1800s, when the prairie was a little piece of heaven inside swamp hell. By his time, only small pockets of swamp survived in Wood County. She said the prairie's deeply rooted grass burned for weeks after farmers conducted their annual stubble fires to clear out the area. In the archives I also found a yellowed history of the Friendly Neighbor Home Demonstration Club, organized October 23, 1947, and disbanded May 14, 1969, after its two-hundredth meeting. The history explained that the club, in Emerald Township in rural Paulding County, was formed so farm wives could give one another lessons in homemaking. Declining membership caused the group to disband.

Leaving Wood County and heading south, I noticed that from all directions in the former swamp, the horizon is flat. A writer for a 1960s *Ohio Almanac* claimed that "a headlight on a grade in Defiance can be seen in Antwerp, more than twenty miles away."

When mist covers the fields and sunlight reflects on the dew, the landscape unfolds toward the horizon like a green carpet. Ohio's last frontier is now cornfield after cornfield, a place where 4-H clubs and Future Farmers of America are still hip, county fairs are the biggest events of the year, and programs like Farm Focus beckon farmers to sit on the latest tractors and try on red polyester baseball caps with yellow seed emblems.

Roaming farther into northwestern Ohio, I saw narrow country roads crisscross the horizon like grids, intersecting U.S. Route 127 and disappearing into walls of corn. The fields swelled with corn, soybeans, and wheat. Big green and red combines looked like oversized beetles rummaging through rows of cornstalks. When cars turned off the highway, all I could see was their tops moving, as if they were rolling directly through the fields. Out there in the country, I imagined silver-topped silos as missiles poking through the morning fog. I pulled over and parked and watched the sunset. Everything around me was flat and alive. The sun was splashing streaks of orange across a charcoal sky. Sitting there in the Jeep, I imagined the ghosts of ancient trees standing in the swamp world below.

Vanquished now. Forever gone.

12

The Marrying Kind

Aberdeen, Ohio, and Maysville, Kentucky, are linked by a steel bridge and a shaky family tree. The smaller Aberdeen, on U.S. Route 52 in Brown County, never culminated in a typical nineteenth-century business district, as did Maysville and neighboring Ripley, home of Ohio's burley tobacco market. Maysville and Ripley are red brick and Southern in appearance and attitude, but Aberdeen is more informal, all white and sprawling, as if its founders had to keep their options open.

The village of about two thousand people is known for one thing: the Simon Kenton Bridge, built over the Ohio in 1931. It seems a one-way route: Ohioans cross the river to shop, work, and entertain themselves. A century ago, however, generations of Maysville people came to little Aberdeen just to say "I do" because they didn't need a marriage license. All they needed was desire. Ever since, genealogists on both sides of the river have been trying to untangle their conjugal roots.

Aberdeen, meanwhile, has spent the last century trying to live down—or live up to, depending on your family's perspective—its past of lax marriage rules. Some women flowed across the river in yellow velvet gowns; others sneaked across at night in homespun dresses. They all sought temporary relief on Aberdeen's muddy shore, where anybody could be hitched fast and for the right price.

By the time I came along, the marriage paper trail had blown into eternity. It was all a memory, or a retelling of someone else's tale. Yet the Marriage Capital of Ohio lives on in the minds and record books of local people and institutions. The town still celebrates its marital history with a summer festival, which some couples make a nuptial event and where others renew their vows.

Because marriage itself is a gamble, Aberdeen became a rural Las Vegas, and the region's number one marriage market in the 1800s. So many couples married there that neighboring states lost count. The town became a wedding turnstile. As a modern chamber of commerce advertisement points out, the earliest Aberdeen marriage certificate dates to June 11, 1772, "making Las Vegas and Niagara Falls look like modern interlopers to the small river town." Aberdeenians exploited their town's strategic location on the Ohio (fifty miles west of Portsmouth; forty-five miles east of Cincinnati) by bringing in boatloads of couples and offering low-cost witness service. Weddings were Aberdeen's cash crop. Some local men made a living by witnessing.

Today, Route 52 zigzags along the Ohio like a strip of gingerbread, touching rusty trailers and lonely campsites that slowly come to life in spring. In Aberdeen, small businesses—car wash, fast-food restaurant, motel, antique shop—give the village a measure of activity. I felt I was in the country when I saw a sign for Sissy's Restaurant. Directly across the river, a busier Maysville was hunched on the banks, like a collection of Victorian dollhouses. Spires and steeples rose from the hills, which appeared to fall into the misty river below.

On a fine spring day I went to Aberdeen looking for a wedding. I couldn't find one, not even in the mayor's office. These days, few transient couples rush here to be married by public officials, and shotgun-toting fathers rarely charge into town (well, at least not *too* often) from the hills.

In Margaret's Kitchen, a little white restaurant on the highway, the old counter and knotty-pine seats looked comfortable enough to hold a dozen eloping couples, but the place was quiet by early afternoon. I asked where a guy could marry quickly in this town, and people stared as though I were an undercover cop. Two waitresses looked me over from head to foot, possibly considering me marriage material or a molester, then informed me that Aberdeen—and its scenic river vantage point—is the most romantic place in Ohio for a wedding. I had to tell them the bad news: I'm already married.

No matter. As if I should know it, one woman said, "Aberdeen was the home of the marryin' squires."

Another waitress said, "People stop in here all the time to ask about the old boys, who must have hitched everybody's ancestors. We hear about that stuff all the time from genealogists. Yeah, Squire Beasley— oh, gracious, he married *a lot* of couples."

An old man seated at the counter looked up from his serving of apple pie and said, "Uh, yeah—thousands."

His buddy turned to me and added, "Naw, man. *Tens* of thousands."

He was not exaggerating. In the 1800s, Aberdeen was called "America's Gretna Green," referring to a village in Dumfries, Scotland, once known as a runaway lovers' haven. (Aberdeen is also the name of a city in Scotland.)

Aberdeen has no anvils left, but its Greta Green nickname came honestly enough in the form of Thomas Shelton, a Huntington Township justice of the peace who elevated the holy bonds of matrimony to cottage-industry status. His successor, Massie Beasley, took the tradition to new heights. At one point in the late 1800s, it seemed the town would forever serve the impetuous lover. If a couple wanted to elope, all they had to do was go to Aberdeen, where nobody worried about marriage's minute details—license included. Steamboat companies and, later, the railroads, made Aberdeen a regular stop on the Cincinnati-to-Pittsburgh route. Shelton's pockets bulged. Keeping his effort at a minimum, he stood before each couple and said loudly: "Marriage is a solemn ordinance, instituted by an all-wise Jehovah. Jine yer right hands. Do you take this woman to nourish and cherish, to keep her in sickness and health? I hope you live long and do well together. Take your seats."

Beasley's ceremony lasted a bit longer, and he married, by his estimates, twenty thousand paying couples over twenty-two years. Some women complained that the ceremonies joined the man only to the woman, and not the woman to the man, but the squires didn't care.

I drove around Aberdeen's few streets for a while and on Market Street saw Massie Beasley's two-story brick house, which was being renovated. I was told to ask about the squires at the village hall. The white concrete-block building on Route 52 is equipped with a clock that shows only military time. ("All I know," a secretary said, "is when it's time to go home.")

Village manager Graham Ruggles, a ninth-generation Aberdeenian, said he's used to people inquiring about the squires—letters, personal visits, telephone calls. "Beasley," Ruggles said, "married two or three of my relatives. His deputy, Jesse Ellis, was my great-great-grandfather, the mayor, and the best man or witness in many marriages. My wife's side of the family was all married by the squires, who made a mint because the State of Ohio was pretty lax about marriage licenses in the early days. So the village issued its own marriage license. Finally, the state set new regulations governing such things, but personally I don't see the big deal. Is there really a difference between what the squires did and what the mayor does now? A while back, he married a couple on Friday. On Monday they were back in here, wanting him to take it back."

Ruggles said Aberdeen was poised to become a major community in the early 1800s, but industry never arrived and Aberdeen remained small. A tannery, hotel, tavern, and lumberyard were all it had to offer, and then the marriage game started. Out-of-town couples provided local merchants and residents with money. When marriage became big business, well, who could turn it down?

"Now, I think we're finally going to grow," he said, "and it's not because of marriage. We've got another bridge and a $10 million high school to serve four townships. We were going to call it Southern Brown High School, but somebody noticed that the kids would be running around with SB on their jackets."

In the squires' time, townships were powerful local governments that controlled the schools, taxed, built roads, and kept the peace. There were no real "squires," but local people used the term endearingly to refer to their justices of the peace—influential country magistrates elected by the townships. They not only married people, but served as court officers and worked with township constables to prevent breaches of the law.

Shelton did all these things—and more. He was born in 1776 in Stafford County, Virginia, and migrated to Brown County, Ohio, as a young man. Shortly after his appointment as township justice of the peace in 1822, he determined that marrying couples could be a lucrative sideline to politics. From then on, the good squire concentrated on matrimony. He'd marry anybody who could pay—and do it with or without a license. Beasley was worse. He falsely told grooms he could face a long prison sentence for marrying couples without a license, but, for a fee commensurate to the risk, he'd cooperate. The squire invested his considerable earnings in gold and bank notes.

As word of easy marriage spread in the 1820s, Shelton married couples from all over the South and from Pennsylvania, Ohio, Indiana, Illinois, Missouri, New York, and other states. Thousands flocked to Aberdeen. Each morning, Shelton followed a ritual: He'd walk down to the wharf to watch for steamboats bringing other happy—and sometimes desperate—couples. Shelton used to say, "The early squire gets the wedding." He preferred payment in cash, of course, usually twenty dollars, but, if that wasn't possible, he'd take a pocketknife or anything he considered valuable. Twenty dollars was a large fee in those days, but Shelton knew his customers had few options. If they were poor, he'd accept payment in pork, potatoes, apples, turnips, and other vegetables to stock a large produce house that he operated as another sideline.

He was an entrepreneurial wedding machine. He even married slaves escaping on the Underground Railroad. He accepted whatever payment they could offer. "In thousands of cases, the squires didn't bother to record the marriages," said Dorothy Helton, a member of Brown County's genealogical and historical societies. "They married couples under the table, you might say. Other times, the squires intended to file marriage certificates in the courthouse, but they didn't go over to Georgetown, the county seat, too often. When they finally went, they forgot to take the certificates. Most of the 'lost marriages' involved Kentuckians, who came to Aberdeen to avoid an 1800s Kentucky law requiring couples to produce a bondsman—usually a family member with cattle or some other form of security—to assure the marriage's longevity. The funny thing is, Ohio at one time made people wait three days before they could marry. That's why during World War II a lot of Ohioans went to Kentucky to be married fast."

The squires' casual attitude and forgetfulness have caused much trouble across the river ever since the 1800s. "Some families wonder if their ancestors ever did bother to marry," said Molly Kendall of the Mason County Museum in Maysville. "In my own family, the squires married a number of people, so I can tell you from experience that this is a tough genealogical pursuit. Shelton turned in some of his marriages to the courthouse, but Beasley didn't bother much. He was so eager to marry people, though, that he'd row out into the middle of the river, if necessary, and marry them right there in rowboats."

Oddly enough, few villagers complained about his multiple business practices. He operated by popular demand. Years of ignoring the law finally caused trouble, however, when the Civil War ended in 1865. Seeking pensions for themselves and their children, widows of veterans applied to the state of Kentucky, only to be told that their marriages were invalid and their children illegitimate. After thousands of widows complained, Molly Kendall told me, the Kentucky legislature was forced to recognize marriages performed in Aberdeen before the war. Despite the criticism, Shelton did not slow down. In fact, after the controversy his marriage business increased. More eager couples arrived in Aberdeen, many wearing fancy clothes and riding in carriages. Some married while sitting on horses, in case they needed to make a quick escape.

By the time Shelton died on February 15, 1870, it was apparent that Aberdeen's business of matrimony had become too big—and necessary—to be stopped cold. Shelton estimated, conservatively, that he had married ten thousand to fifteen thousand couples in forty-seven years. This amazes me. I am also amazed that the man lived to brag about it—and to be ninety-six years old! But his death did not stop Aberdeen. Beasley, who served as justice of the peace from 1870 to 1892, was even *more* prolific. He refused to accept alternate payment plans (no credit cards then). His business card read: "No money, no marry." He also interpreted the marriage laws more liberally than Shelton, if that was possible. To Beasley, marrying couples was a business, regardless of the circumstances. His son, Thomas, took over as pilot of a riverboat, the aptly named *Gretna Green*, which ran up and down the Ohio picking up eloping couples.

When Squire Beasley left town on business every so often, some local rascal would bet his drinking companions that he could convince a gullible couple that he was the one and only Squire Massie Beasley. Over the years, hundreds of couples left Aberdeen under the assumption that they were married. Probably Beasley himself couldn't determine if he had actually married them. After performing so many marriages, some without licenses, he was as ignorant of couples' names as he was of the fakers. But he honestly believed he was performing a valuable service to society. In his lackadaisical way, Beasley defied church and state, but always with a smile.

Enraged parents in Maysville were powerless to stop him, as they had been Shelton. Dorothy Richardson, a Maysville resident and a writer for the *Louisville Courier-Journal* in the 1890s, determined that illegal marriages ran through three generations of families. "The question naturally arises as to why these men were never prosecuted, and why the people of the town stood by and suffered their laws to be ignored," she wrote in a newspaper story in 1897. "The apparently perplexing query is readily explained by the old adage, 'A kind heart covers a multitude of sins.' A more popular man than either of these rollicking, careless old squires never trod the earth, and if they made money easily and in a questionable way, they in turn spent it just as freely among their neighbors. The only people who ever said harm of

Massie Beasley, or who ever tried to do him serious injury, were the local members of the clerical profession on both sides of the river, who openly denounced him from their pulpits. But in spite of all their preaching and teaching against him, when any members of their congregations wanted to get married, it was often Massie Beasley, and not the minister, who was favored with the job."

Beasley's only known competitor was a preacher who called the squire "this evil crying in our midst." Most eloping couples ignored the preacher, so he quit his church to enter the marriage business full time. Pressed by the competition, Beasley had to temporarily decrease his rates. His agents actually bragged that Squire Beasley was the only official authorized to marry without benefit of marriage license. The preacher, in exasperation, gave up and left town.

"When an agitated and breathless couple came hurrying down to the ferry," Richardson wrote, "with an infuriated father or guardian following close at their heels, it was Massie Beasley who calmed their fears by the assurance that he would see them safely over, and that he would not give their followers an opportunity of boarding the boat. And he was always true to his promise. Nor were any threats or prayers on the part of gesticulating parties in pursuit strong enough to deter him from his purpose of landing his passengers on the borders of the land of promise."

If the pursuers followed in skiffs, the Beasleys were prepared. When the *Gretna Green* whistle blew six times, everybody in Aberdeen ran to the wharf to gather around the squire to offer protection. Beasley usually watched the river through a powerful spyglass, which he carried at all times in his coat pocket. In such emergencies, he shouted his brief ceremony to the eloping couple as they docked and ran from the boat, with irate family in pursuit.

Most couples, especially those whose parents opposed their wedding, eloped at night. They didn't have to worry, for the Aberdeen marriage machine worked around the clock. The *Gretna Green* was so busy at night, in fact, that Beasley's dock supervisor earned additional income by renting skiffs to desperate people who couldn't fit into the boat. Townspeople helped by assisting with the marriages, sewing wedding clothes, furnishing special wedding items, and rowing boats across the river. The town's boys held the reins of wedding party horses. The local printer called his newspaper the *Gretna Green* and promoted the squire's cause at every opportunity.

Steamboat elopements brought Aberdeen many of its large, fancy weddings. Every few days large coaches rolled into town, pulled by teams of expensive horses. The people of Aberdeen left their workstations and homes to watch the bride and her bridesmaids. For those customers, Beasley reserved much respect, offering the bride his arm and walking her to the doorway of his home. But they paid for the honor—$150 for an elaborate wedding. Sometimes, groups of ten couples married at the same time.

Unfortunately for Beasley's neighbors, all was not quiet on the marriage front. They complained when grooms on horseback fired pistols to waken the squire at night. One time, a young Kentucky man and his future bride rode for days to get to Aberdeen. "There had been a feud between the families for generations," Richardson wrote, "and the father of the bride vowed that he would kill the lover rather than permit him to marry his daughter. The pursuers were so near that the noise of their horses' hooves could be heard distinctly when the Squire poked his head out of his window in answer to a volley of shots. . . . The Squire was then in his seventy-eighth year and was too stiff in the joints to dress himself quickly, so he appeared before the excited couple wrapped in a long quilt and shod only in his socks. The Squire mumbled over a hasty marriage ritual at the conclusion of which the new husband flung him a well-stuffed wallet and dashed away toward the hills . . . just as their pursuers came up the street to find they had been foiled."

Another time, a young man paid somebody ten dollars to row him and his girl across the Ohio to Aberdeen. Her father, who was close behind, hired another skiff for twenty dollars. In the middle of the Ohio, the young man stood up in the boat, waved his hat in the air in jubilation, and promptly fell overboard. The father plucked his daughter from her boat.

Such events continued until Beasley's death. His body was barely cold when several greedy men, assuming that tradition would continue, started marrying couples in Aberdeen. But the state decided to enforce its marriage-certificate rules, and the Brown County sheriff chased away the offenders.

Jesse Ellis, Beasley's deputy, became the next justice of the peace, but he didn't try to continue the marriage racket. He had kept the previous squire's files, Molly Kendall said, but nobody knew what they contained. In 1992, fired destroyed them and the home of an Ellis descendant. Dorothy Richardson wrote that she reviewed the surviving files briefly in 1897 and concluded they were a potential hotbed of campaign scandals. Apparently Shelton and Beasley kept enough names—Richardson counted five current and thirty-four former congressmen, even former senators and a retired foreign minister, among the grooms, not to mention the squires' exorbitant fees charged for over seventy years.

No wonder Squire Massie Beasley died with a smile on his face.

13

The King of Ashville

The past of Pickaway County—and the past of small-town America—
is hidden in a little building at 34 Long Street in Ashville. That's the
address of the Ohio Small Town Museum, a tribute to every old town
in an unofficial network of rural communities that ruled America in the
nineteenth and early twentieth centuries.

Ashville is a good place for such a museum because the town could
have ended up like Confederate Crossroads or Hole-in-the-Ground or
any other Ohio ghost town. But it didn't; it had geography going for
it as well as town spirit and luck. People refused to let their town die.
Founded in 1882 on Walnut Creek, off the Scioto River, Ashville got a
late start. It was just another slow-growing community in rural central
Ohio until suburban Columbus started spilling over into neighboring
counties in the 1980s. Suddenly little Ashville received a second look
from people who didn't mind driving forty-five minutes to jobs in the
city. As a new commuter town, Ashville has advantages: nearness to
U.S. Route 23, State Route 316, and the Rickenbacker International
Airport, southeast of Columbus.

Yet Ashville does not aspire to be a city filled with chain stores and
the typical suburban life. That's why the town appeals to people. It
is small enough (population about 2,500) to lack the sophistication
and panache of the larger communities, yet it is conveniently located.
Even the town's Web site is like a letter from home. It features the logo
of Ashville's old-fashioned traffic signal—locally made, one of the nation's first, and an icon known by everyone in town. When I found the
Web site in 2004, it featured tributes to three local soldiers: Sergeant
Joel McDaniel, crew chief on a Black Hawk helicopter; Staff Sergeant

Michael R. Gloyd, instructor for crew chiefs at the New River Air Station in Jacksonville, North Carolina; and Second Lieutenant John Reber Scott, a pilot-training candidate in Oklahoma. Mayor Chuck Wise wrote his homey "A Word from the Mayor" column, and town resident Rose Jamison wrote her regular "Ashville News." Like the town, the Web site reflects a friendliness and pleasantness.

Driving around the tree-lined side streets, I felt at home. I remembered Oxford historian Andrew Cayton's line about Ohio: "Place somehow molds human beings as much as human beings mold place."

I found the Ohio Small Town Museum, a time machine of rural life, in a small building. Older volunteers remember many of the events depicted in their displays, and they enjoy talking about the years when small towns were big deals in America.

Visitors can relive American history through the Ashville visits of General John J. "Black Jack" Pershing, the supreme commander in Europe during World War I; Ohio governor James Cox, the Democrats' 1920 presidential candidate from Dayton and founder of the Cox newspaper chain; and Williams Jennings Bryan, the Democrats' champion of free silver and a presidential nominee in 1896, 1900, and 1908. Other exhibits feature Ashville's connections—both strong and tenuous—to nationally famous people who may have visited briefly, drove near the town, or actually lived near it. They include Billy Carter, Tecumseh, Elvis Presley, actress Sally Kellerman, Roy Rogers (locals maintain that Roy was fired from his job at the town's canning factory when he was caught playing guitar on company time), and Yankees owner George Steinbrenner (a museum guide claimed that the Boss once served at the area's old Air Force base).

Down another aisle are display cases containing personal items owned by a local dwarf who played a munchkin in *The Wizard of Oz* and puppets made by Vivian Michael, one of the earliest puppeteers to use hand-moving rods in traditional hand-in-body puppets.

"The museum has never been what I'd call an attraction museum," volunteer Bob Hines said. "We didn't start the thing to bring in tourists. It's a museum for the local people. After we were up and running, though, we found that people were coming into town just to visit the museum. They enjoy it because our history is universal. It the story of every small town."

Hines assembles the displays and operates the museum with several cocurators, including Jack Lemmon ("I'm not the actor; he had the hair and the moves and I had neither"), Charlie Morrison, Annabelle Ward-Hines, and Charles Cordle.

"We started our museum to reconnect people to our community and its past," Hines said. "We recognized that in order to have a vital community, people that live here must have a strong sense of community, and one of the ways to do that is to reinforce local pride. That is what our museum is all about. We are recapturing and honoring past achievements of a rural community. We are preserving artifacts that are the physical manifestations of these achievements. We are using these items to challenge our children to follow their own dreams. We do not want old buildings to just be objects for vandalism; we want kids to know what older buildings represent and why they exist. We want them to honor and respect the past. We want them to be excited by national and world history when they learn about their connections to that history."

In the nation's first 125 years, rural towns—including and especially Ohio's—dominated national politics and economics. Life was not idyllic then. It was harsh, lonely, and filled with physical labor. Ohio had remarkably self-sufficient towns, supported by local pride that bordered on boosterism. After World War I, however, the towns changed. People started losing their faith in what was possible for them to achieve.

Ohio had its solid small towns and also places so tiny that they could hardly be considered towns: Bacon, Bagdad, Cacklers Corners, Candy Town, Confederate Crossroads, Deep Cut, Halfway House, Happy Hollow, Hardscrabble (the name tells it all), Henpeck (it makes some sort of statement about early Buckeye matrimony), Hole-in-the-Ground, Lick Town (it should have been next to Dogtown), Mysticville, Needful, Nice, Pattytown, Pincher, Pointopolis, Scrub, Skulltown, Slick, Smarts Spur (ouch), Sodom (surprisingly, Victorian Ohio had at least two Sodoms), Spunky Puddle, Striptown (why wasn't it next to Sodom?), Sweet Wine, Rag Town, Rowdy Ville, Wahoo, Whiskeyville, White Woman's Town (so politically incorrect), Zeal, and Zebra.

They popped up and vanished when people realized they had moved to nowhere. Yet rural Ohio is an intriguing place filled with whimsy, drama, humor, pristine countryside, the world's largest Amish population, small college towns—even forgotten towns named Wally and Beaver. (I'm still looking for Ward and June.)

While on the road, I talked to small-town people and tried to imagine what their Main Streets looked like a century ago. Some towns were totally changed; few businesses remained. Sometimes on my trips I'd meet young people and wonder: Why do they stay? So little is left for them to do. Schools are closing. People are moving away. Businesses are shutting down. Between 1990 and 2000, 59 percent of Ohio's 264 incorporated villages (with populations of lower than 500) lost population. In northwest Ohio, 75 percent of the towns lost population.

By 1975, people had started calling Ashville a dying community. A study by University of Cincinnati researchers concluded that Ashville had one of the state's lowest community identity scores; people didn't know much about their town's history, and did not care to preserve it. By 1982, however, Ashville had one of the highest ratings in the state. "What happened?" Hines asked. "Our museum happened. The train station restoration happened."

On a budget of less than $10,000 a year, Ashville volunteers operate a museum that has received national attention. In addition, they have helped the town build a modern library, a home for the elderly, new schools, and a fire station, and they have granted university scholarships.

Improvements began in 1975, when Hines and Morrison collected local historical artifacts, organized the Ashville Area Historical Society, and considered using the old Norfolk and Western Railroad station as a meeting place. When the owner suggested tearing the building down, historians discovered and rescued artifacts from the attic. "We had no idea they were in there," Hines said. "We also didn't know it was one of the original Scioto Valley Railroad system stations. We found old handbills, flags, dated spikes, receipts, lanterns, and even old shoes from the Scioto Valley Railroad that made the building eligible for a National Register of Historic Places designation."

About this time, two local families donated the old refrigerated Zero Locker building (formerly the Dreamland Theater) to the village. The volunteers took it over, set up their exhibits, and invited a television reporter from Columbus. The reporter referred to it as Ohio's small-town museum, and a few years later the society officially adopted that name.

When it opened in 1978, nobody paid much attention. Even today, it remains obscure to Ohioans. Visitors can find an eclectic blend of the routine and the weird. What I like about it is its local nature: You'll see a baseball glove used by a member of the high school's 1950s championship baseball team, and a display of related newspaper clippings.

Thanks to the museum, Ohio now has a rare seventeen-star United States flag. After its discovery in an attic in town in 2001, the flag was donated to the society. Group officers sent it to Textile Preservation Associates of Keedysville, Maryland, to be analyzed. The company reported that the flag is authentic—made with materials consistent with its age. The seventeen-star flag was never an official American flag; it is thought to be a transitional flag made to celebrate Ohio's acceptance into the Union. A record of the flag does exist, however, in an 1837 political cartoon. Sixteen white stars form a circle around one star in the center. The Historical Society has ordered a custom display case made of buckeye "to further signify the flag's symbolic tribute to Ohio." For the 2003 bicentennial, the flag was displayed at the Adena Education Center in Chillicothe.

The flag and other unusual items have given the museum cult status among the people who appreciate such things. They particularly enjoy the old traffic signal, which hangs in the museum now and features a hand that slowly rotates across each bulb, to show how much time is left before the light changes. The signal is the museum's main attraction. Editors of the *New Roadside America* list the museum among their top twenty-five American museums and call it "a cocktail of Americana that's just plain fun to drink in."

This delights Lemmon. He knows all the artifacts and stories and saves them as a part of the town's fading folklore. He said the town used to be the home of characters—people who dared to be different without being rude. Call them eccentrics, but they were respected years ago. In today's homogenized society, we either ignore such people or make them television stars. Lemmon's mission is to preserve their memories, and in the process the history of Ohio. But Ashville has had its share of nonhuman characters, too, and they are honored equally.

"Chic-Chic the rooster was a tough old bird," Lemmon said. "He was one aggressive little guy. If he'd meet you walking down the street in Ashville, you'd better move out of the way. He'd peck you. He'd walk straight up to you and stick you good. Well, Chic-Chic was a smart bird, too. His owner, Mrs. A. B. Cooper, would send him down to the store. She'd say in a high-pitched voice, [Lemmon imitates an older woman], 'Now, Chic-Chic, honey, are you *hungry?* Do you want a *snack?*' Oh, man, that got old Chic-Chic riled. He'd cock his head to the side and crow real loud. Sure, he was hungry! He was *always* hungry. He had it made with Mrs. Cooper. So she'd pull out a dime and lay it on the kitchen floor. Old Chic-Chic, he'd reach down there with his beak and pick up that dime every time."

Hines snickered. "Yeah, Chic-Chic didn't have a degree, but he was the world's smartest rooster."

"Old Mrs. Cooper," Lemmon said, "why, she'd open the screen door and out he'd prance, walking as big as you please right down to Brinkers' Confectionary store on Long Street. The owner, Clyde Brinkers, knew Chic-Chic, see, so when he saw that rooster coming, he'd open the door for him and put out his special bowl of favorite corn feed. Chic-Chic would drop the dime and start eating. When he'd finish, he'd strut over to the bus stop and cockadoodle-doo up a storm to all the travelers. Oh, they loved him. Everybody did. This went on for years. Pretty soon, Chic-Chic became a local celebrity. People came to town just to see that rooster. It's a wonder Mrs. Cooper didn't charge them for the show. People called him the King of Ashville. When old Chic-Chic died back in 1955, his story didn't die. No, sir. His legend grew even bigger. Now, every visitor to our museum hears about Chic-Chic. We even have the famous Chic-Chic display."

He pointed to a little shrine with a taxidermied rooster and a newspaper story about Chic-Chic. (The fowl on display is not Chic-Chic, but some other unfortunate bird.)

"Now, one of my other favorite stories is Buster the dog," Lemmon continued. "Buster was one of them terrier dogs—hey, Jim, what kind of terrier was Buster? A fox terrier?"

"Naw. A *Boston* terrier."

"No, no. Wasn't he a fox terrier? Or a what-do-you-call-it . . . ?"

"No!"

"Okay, okay. Anyway, he was a Boston terrier who had never been to Boston, an athletic little dog. Clyde Brinkers owned him. Clyde and Mrs. Cooper, they owned the two strangest animals this town has never known. Buster'd jump through hoops and up into his master's arms and jump on his back and run through his legs. Words can't do him justice. He was well liked, too."

According to local legend, Buster would bark approvingly every time somebody spoke the name Herbert Hoover. Whenever somebody said Al Smith, the New York Democrat who opposed Hoover in 1928, Buster would growl.

That year, Brinkers thought he might as well take the politically astute dog into the voting booth, and put his paws up on the voting lever. Soon everyone in town was talking about it. When the Depression hit in 1929, however, some people blamed the dog because he voted for Hoover.

"It's all true," Lemmon said. "One day Clyde took Buster with him to vote, as a joke. Clyde somehow put that dog's footprint on the ballot when they was in the voting booth. What he did was, he allowed that darn dog to vote Republican! The next day, the whole town had heard about it. Now, some people weren't upset at all about a dog votin'. It wasn't considered sacrilegious or anything. The problem they had was that the dog had voted Republican."

"Tell him about the movie," Charlie said.

"Oh, yeah! Buster is in our town movie, made in 1937. A. B. Cooper, the man whose wife owned Chic-Chic, owned a Pure Oil Station. He hired a guy to come to town to take movies on 35mm film. Even though times were hard at the end of the Depression, A. B. wanted a permanent record of life in Ashville. So he hired the movie man to shoot all kinds of things that people did. Of course, Buster was one of the stars, doing his tricks and all. Say, fellows, when did old Buster die?"

No response.

"We sell the movie on videocassette for fifteen dollars," he said. "We have to be careful with that original negative of film, though, because if that nitrate becomes unstable, it'll blow up."

"It's quite an explosive movie," somebody said.

Another popular attraction at the museum, Lemmon said, is its moon-dust sifter, invented by a man who grew up near Ashville and later worked for NASA.

Lemmon explained: "We had a guy named Teddy Boor who invented a lot of things, including a corn shocker. It would do the job, too. The only trouble was, the local corn pickers didn't like being replaced by a machine. So they destroyed it—at least they went through the motions. They stacked corn all around the machine and set the whole thing on fire. They burned the corn-shocking machine, but Teddy rescued it, rebuilt it, and kept it going on the sly. Now, Teddy was something else. He also invented our local traffic light. It's one of a kind, the oldest working traffic light in America, and you see it hanging right in the middle of our museum. People say it looks like it come from a flying saucer."

I stood under the cone-shaped aluminum object, watched it carefully as it blinked, and thought that it looked like a prop from a 1930s Flash Gordon film. When I stared at it at just the right angle, I thought I was looking into the angular face of an alien space traveler with bulbous eyes and thick eyelashes (the covers on top of the lights).

"It's worth the trip to town just to see it," Charlie Morrison said. "I'd drive a hundred thousand miles to see it because it's the only one of its kind in the world. It's even been mentioned on *Oprah*."

"Brother, that's *big*," Lemmon said.

"Oh, yeah," another guy said in a monotone that hinted toward the sarcastic.

Apparently her show is the modern index of fame, even in Ashville.

"The Ohio Department of Transportation people liked that darn signal so much," Lemmon said, "that they asked us to bring it up to Columbus so they could examine it. They hanged it up in their building, and called it an ingenious contraption. For fifty years, up until 1982, it hung right here in Ashville, at Long and Main streets. People got used to it. We never had an accident there either. People knew its rhythm, and how it worked. Come to think of it, that's sort of how this whole town works—a rhythm to it."

And the beat goes on.

Vanishing Ohio

Now most people live only on the horizontal, and our time is space: miles and numbers, quantities and travel. The enduring present lives at the point where these lines cross.

—*Donald Hall*

14

A Little Good News

By noon on any Wednesday, Dale Schlabach, the Amish blacksmith of Sugarcreek, puts down his hammer and walks up Main Street to buy a copy of the *Budget*. Then he returns to his little red shop to find out who died, who married, who was born, who traveled, and who planted the most corn. This qualifies as breaking news around Sugarcreek.

Schlabach and his neighbors all enjoy the *Budget*, Sugarcreek's local paper combined with an international Amish journal. Newspaper owners in Sugarcreek distribute the separate Amish edition throughout the world; at home, they wrap it inside the local news section. As most of the world sees it, the Amish paper is a weekly anachronism defying convention in favor of a deeper tradition. No news of wars, movies, business, or fashion stocks the pages; no comics or horoscopes appear. In fact, the *Budget* should have died a long time ago, according to most publishing odds. Yet it continues, a newspaper hopelessly and contentedly out of touch with the times and a ghost of newspapering's past. In that way it's like the Amish. Rejecting the electric cord, they use battery-powered alarm clocks but they also milk cows by hand and use buggies and shun the world's modern ways.

The *Budget* is strong in northeast Ohio, the home of the world's largest Amish population. Their ancestors began in Europe as a part of the Anabaptist movement that started in Switzerland in 1525. One of the Anabaptist leaders, Jacob Amman, left the main group because he believed it was too liberal; he preferred plain dress and old customs. His followers became known as the Amish. A similar group, led by Menno Simons, became known as the Mennonites. The Amish came to America in the late 1700s and early 1800s and settled in Pennsylvania. By the

1970s, they had arrived in large numbers in northeast Ohio farm country, especially in western Tuscarawas and eastern Holmes counties. The area now claims fifteen thousand to eighteen thousand Amish people.

At the news office, I met Don Sprankle, editor, general manager, Lutheran. He laughed at my observation. From a small brown frame building with yellow trim and alpine photographs inside, he directs a newspaper with a circulation of twenty thousand. "Not bad for a town of about two thousand people," he said.

Reading the Amish paper is an unusual experience for a reporter who has worked at modern daily newspapers. There is plenty of essential "news," yet no stories about politicians' broken promises, war, terrorism, bank robberies, and murders. In this way, perhaps, the *Budget* serves as the ultimate modern paper by fulfilling the fantasy of every suburban soccer mom who pleads with newspaper publishers, "No more bad news, please."

On publication day, Sprankle sat back in his office and looked over the crowded, dense pages of the freshly printed eighteen-page national, or Amish, edition. It could be mistaken for a museum piece, or for any small-town paper of 1910, at least until the reader finds the unusual Amish and Mennonite news stories. Six hundred correspondents, called scribes, write about their communities from all over the world. They jointly or individually write about 450 dispatches a week. In exchange, they receive pens, paper, postage, and envelopes—but no money. "It's an amazing workforce," explained Keith Rathbun, the assistant publisher. "We have a bigger staff than the *New York Times*." Whether in Paraguay or Canada or the United States, a scribe usually starts his or her report with the date it was written and a description of the weather conditions. Scribes avoid controversy. Their stories are like short letters from home. Reports fall under bold, unusual datelines: Carbon Hill, Ohio; Punxsutawney, Pennsylvania; Gonzales, Texas. Paragraphs are lean: "It feels like autumn now. Silos are mostly filled. Some fourth crop hay has been put away." And: "May 20—rain again today. Somebody said this was the fourteenth Sunday we had rain. Farmers are starting to make hay, but not much hay weather so far."

Reports from scribes are glimpses into Ohio's and America's past and a little of the present. "I haven't heard the coyotes howl once this month," wrote David Mast of Mondovi, Wisconsin. "I always loved to hear that lonesome, eerie howl during the night."

Another scribe from Aylmer, Ontario, Canada, discussed an important social problem: "At the same meeting at Elmos, another topic was presented for us to think about, and that is the long-range effects of the computer age on our [Amish] churches, and what we ought to be doing to steer clear of the dangers. The question was raised as to how an earlier generation was able to sense the profound effect the automobile would have on society and on the churches, so that it was decided not to allow the ownership of cars. Are we in the same point today in the computer revolution, having already accepted their forerunner, the calculators?"

Wrapped around scribes' reports are advertisements for flycatchers, hand-cranked bread kneaders, kerosene-powered refrigerators, steel wagon wheels, cook stoves, and treadle sewing machines—in short, things that the rest of us see in antiques shops and museums. With its reports from Amish settlements all over the world, the *Budget* is a communications link between a separated people, who are as scattered as the November leaves. They read columns called "Our Suffering Brethren," about people who are still persecuted for their religious beliefs. Another column, "Es Pennsilfaanisch Deitsch Eck," discusses everything from Amish recipes to quilting. And where else but the *Budget* could a reader ask where to buy Cornell Horse Liniment, or what to use for poison ivy? One reader advised another: "For the ivy use homemade lye soap. Make wet and rub on affected area. This is also good for chiggers and other itching. We have found it very effective."

Contrast this old-time approach with the *Budget*'s desire to stay in the public eye. (Some things change slowly, while others, like the *Budget*, evolve in ultra-slow motion.) Although the newspaper is still firmly connected to the turn of the twentieth century, its owners understand that they must serve all of their readers. So they have started a company Web site—www.thebudgetnewspaper.com. It will serve local readers as well as any Mennonites (and any renegade Amish) who don't mind using the World Wide Web to get information. When I looked up the paper's new site in 2004, it told me that I was visitor number 663.

Progress and technology notwithstanding, the newspaper cannot be fully explained or appreciated without first knowing Sugarcreek, a town fiercely proud of its past. The town has proclaimed itself the Little Switzerland of Ohio (one third of its people are of Swiss descent, said historian George R. Smith, associate editor of the newspaper). "Of course," he said, "our Amish brothers came from Switzerland too, but they wandered around all over Europe first. So we really don't really count them as Swiss."

Sugarcreek is a prosperous country town that is preoccupied with all things Swiss. Every September, more than a hundred thousand tourists converge on the town for its Swiss Festival. People expect to see black Amish buggies, an old Amish newspaper, and yellow Swiss cheese. They are not disappointed. These trappings of rural Ohio enable the *Budget* to exist as an independent enigma. The newspaper and its readers fill their own small nooks in this world, a place in love with technology. But in Sugarcreek, the story is a little different. Everyone knows that horsepower still means *horse* power and a newspaper still means long columns of small black type. No color pages, no fancy graphics. No gimmicks clutter the paper.

As I walked around the town, I thought of Sugarcreek as a fort on the edge of the future. The town is a piece of the old Ohio. Here all the refugees—those who want to hold back tomorrow and keep life as it has been for centuries—have gathered for the final stand because there is no other place to run. I wondered how long the fort would hold, for development will surely arrive in time and money will change Sugarcreek into just another modern and homogenous town.

A focal point of the old life is still in the downtown, where the Amish and "the English" work together and coexist nicely. The town has turned its heritage—Switzerland—into a communitywide theme. At first glance, the small downtown is disconcerting, with Swiss music being piped through loud speakers. The whole town seems curiously still and colorful, like a timeless town in a snow globe, dressed brightly in gingerbread with blue mountain paintings and long Alp horns adorning the fronts of shops. Even the town library looks like a ski resort, and the entire business district looks imaginary, a shimmering prism of mad colors amid a wide patch of green.

Life has been this way since 1953, when the town fathers encouraged a growing tourist business in the area's cheese factories. So that year they started the Ohio Swiss Festival and changed their storefronts to look like a little piece of Switzerland. Businessman Ranson Andreas donated a building to start the Alpine Hills Museum. "He decorated his own building like Swiss and then dared the rest of the town to do it too," said Claude Zimmerman, a grandson of the town's founder. "The only problem is, when July comes with its ninety-degree heat and high humidity, visitors can have a little trouble imagining they are in the Alps."

Sugarcreek has been a bastion of the Old World since the 1800s. In 1920, Smith's father, Samuel A. Smith, bought the newspaper. The younger Smith worked there after school and later edited the scribes' handwritten reports. Even after he became the editor, he continued to tend to about three hundred of their letters each week. He sold the paper in 1969 but continued to edit reports from the people who had become his friends. On a more recent visit, I read that ninety-three-year-old George Smith died in the fall of 2000, after working at the *Budget* for eighty years. That figure—eighty—staggered me. In today's flighty workplace, it is unusual to find a forty-year company veteran. After Smith's death, the paper's first photograph—at least the first one that anyone can remember—finally appeared on page one of the Amish edition. If any subscribers cringed, they kept their feelings to themselves.

Smith and the scribes had a close relationship. They trusted him, even though he was not one of their faith. They knew he would not make them look silly. Smith got something out of the relationship, too; he simply enjoyed it.

"Once," he told me on an earlier visit, "a scribe wrote that a woman was going to have her *third consecutive* set of twins—in two years. I know the Amish have large families, but three sets? Another time, we had a person write: 'A farm family had a chimney fire Tuesday night, but, with the aid of the local volunteer fire department, the blaze was soon out of control.' And then every so often we get the stories in which somebody is 'fatally murdered.' I like that style. I won't change the writing much because I don't want to lose the Amish flavor."

That flavor has helped sell the *Budget* since it was founded in 1890, the year Sugarcreek started to grow economically. A local printer, John C. Miller, decided the bustling town needed a newspaper, so he printed one with four 9 x 12–inch pages and mailed copies to six hundred prospective subscribers. From the start, the paper was destined to ignore conventional publishing rules. On October 15, 1891, Miller wrote: "The reason for the delay is that on Tuesday of last week, while returning from Farmerstown on a buggy, behind a kicking horse, we thought it safer to jump out of the buggy, and in so doing we had our right arm broken near the wrist, which will keep us from work for several weeks." In a month, when he was well enough to resume publishing, Miller had already received dozens of letters from Amish friends who had moved to other states. Without thinking much about editorial policy, he decided to include their letters in the next edition. Readers enjoyed them, so he continued to publish them and the Amish continued to write. By December 1892, Miller was sending the *Budget* to 18 states and 463 post offices. Circulation increased to five thousand by 1906, and the newspaper earned a name as an important Amish journal.

Except for a few years during the Depression, the newspaper has been healthy. Sprankle said he does not want to change it or conduct market research or to offer advertising. Lately he has turned his efforts toward expanding the Sugarcreek section of the newspaper, which, in keeping with tradition, is also offbeat. After all, Sprankle dislikes hard news. He looks instead for positive stories when he can find them, and to get them he doesn't mind posing as he milks cows at the county fair. "Next month, I think I'll enter a dress-a-calf contest," he said. He prefers a front page uncluttered with terrible happenings. "I'm probably the only editor of a worldwide paper who devoted only two inches of copy to the shooting of President Reagan. But I did put the story on the front page."

Like Smith, Sprankle can't seem to run from the magnetic pull of the *Budget*. He worked there in high school and quit to enlist in the Air Force after his graduation. When he returned, he decided to buy a part of the business, but he later sold it. "I had quit again, but the owners asked me to come back to run the paper," he said. "I thought, what the heck, I'll buy forty percent of it. Now, I own it with my partner, a Jewish businessman. So you've got an Amish paper owned by a Lutheran and a Jew. Kind of odd, huh?"

Not when you consider the paper's policy. "We like to run only *good* news," Sprankle said. "Of course, out of necessity there are some things we have to get across to our public. For instance, the other week in our local section we ran a picture of a man's front yard here in town. That might not sound newsworthy, but his grass was too long. It looked horrible. The picture fixed that, though. We put it on page one for everybody to see. By the next day, the grass was mowed. A good thing, too, because we were ready to put a goat on his lawn and take a picture for the next issue."

Tired of walking, I stopped at an old building, the blacksmith shop. I looked inside a murky room with two light bulbs dangling from the rafters. A bearded man held an ice cream cone in one hand and a hammer in the other. He looked annoyed.

"If you're closing, it's all right," I said.

"No, no—wait! Do come in, please, but you've got to excuse me. By five o'clock I smell like a horse myself."

He motioned to step closer on a floor littered with the pieces of his life: twisted nails, leather collars, rusty horseshoes, harnesses, and copies of the *Budget*. "It connects us," he said. Without blinking, he picked up the hammer and slammed it upon the anvil. The sound resonated off the walls and died in the street.

Dale Schlabach, Amish, was thirty-four years old at that time, with red hair, a stiff white shirt, and dark work pants. His hands were those of a worker—rough and dirty and thick. The grin was that of a boy. He was loud and warm, a man in whom life's meaning seemed revealed. The center of his universe was the shop. It was low, faded red, and rickety, like something on the set of *Gunsmoke*. He said he came to it every day, early.

The village, which owned the building, kept the rent low so Sugarcreek could show a working blacksmith to the tourists who came to town each year to see how Swiss cheese was made. The arrangement was really subsidized industry. The large Amish population, with a horse-drawn lifestyle, assured the blacksmith of much work.

For some reason, visitors always ended up in front of Schlabach's door, their eyes probing every inch of the dusty shop. "Other day," he said, "a fellow come in and said he heard that blacksmithing was being taught at a college. Can you imagine that? I never went to college, just to the eighth grade. I wonder if they teach you how to milk a cow out at that school?"

Schlabach opened the shop because he has a reverence for hammer and horseflesh. The job forced him to rise at 3 A.M. and, after doing the chores on the farm, to drive his buggy ("My van, man") to the shop in town, about five miles away. Visitors usually gathered around as he opened up the shop each day.

"People come to see a blacksmith," he said with a shrug. "Aren't many of us left these days. Sometimes they stand in long rows in front of my building. About noon I walk over to 'em and say, 'How many of you folks have ever held the foot of a horse?' They don't say anything, so I open up my hand to show 'em something—an old yellow horse's hoof that I keep here on a shelf. They groan pretty loud at that. At least once a week somebody will come up and touch a red-hot shoe. I'll say, 'Was it hot?' The guy'll say, 'Uh, no, I just don't like to hold a horseshoe too long.'"

Visitors look at Schlabach and see a breathing anachronism, somebody foreign. Sometimes he invites people like me out to his farm for a meal and a chance to watch him milk his cows. His family roots are planted as firmly as an oak in this rolling countryside. But, like all Amish, he has maintained a detached sense of citizenship. His people belong first to the earth.

"The old town stays about the same," he said. "Only the storefronts change. Other day a fellow come in here and said he was a missionary in Africa. I said, 'But where are you *from?*' He thought about that for a minute and said, 'I'm from nowhere, really.' Well, being from someplace is kind of like putting on a necktie. You don't have to do it, but it sure helps."

Dale Schlabach lives somewhere: "On a little farm, fourteen acres, where the wife and I are trying to bring up seven kids and fifteen Belgian horses. No electricity, no telephone, no car—just fun. I mean, you ever see seven kids at six in the morning? Ah-ha! Oh, well, I guess the only guy who has no troubles is the guy who has nothing."

15

The Riders of Bentonville

State Route 41 follows the original direction of Zane's Trace in Adams County, still passing through flinty hamlets in a land seemingly lost. Much of it is as densely wooded as it was in 1798 when Ebenezer Zane poked his way south to Maysville, Kentucky, to open the first road. The county is so rural, in fact, that only in the late 1980s did McDonald's golden arches intrude on West Union, the seat of county government.

In the early 1800s, the trace was a popular route linking the Mid-South and Washington, D.C., so Adams County hosted politicians on their way to and from the capital. Andrew Jackson and venerable Tennessee senator Thomas Hart Benton visited frequently, and today two towns on Route 41 bear their names.

I hadn't expected to stop on the road, but then I saw a rectangular monument in the middle of town, dedicated to the Bentonville Anti-Horse Thief Society of Adams County. My curiosity made me stop. An Ohio historical marker also commemorates Bentonville's most long-lived and only horse-thief-catching organization. (Coincidentally, on one of my visits to town, I read a story in a local paper about a pair of chestnut Arabian horses being stolen from a pasture in Clermont County, about forty-five miles west of Bentonville. Rustling is alive in rural America.)

Bentonville is the kind of town that only momentarily distracts travelers' weary eyes and makes them wonder why anyone would live in such a place. No neatly painted signs hang from businesses to attract customers. No public relations campaigns lure tourists. There is no chamber of commerce, no council, no mayor. And as city dwellers quickly notice, there isn't even a restaurant. Needs of the area's two hundred residents are met by a locally owned convenience store, beauty shop, feed store, service station, and two small churches.

Actually, I drove through Bentonville several times in the 1970s and 1980s, and this time I noticed that the place hadn't changed much in appearance or pace. It was still slow. Friendly, outgoing people who had greeted me were etched in my memory. Although some of the older ones have died since my earliest trips, the younger people have carried on the town's traditions—including the Anti-Horse Thief Society—and sought to continue the town in the new century.

After looking around town, I realized that the only worldly diversion was Joe Devore's service station, which featured a pool hall and video game parlor in front. The floor still carried traces of motor oil. Fan belts, hoses, and tires hung upon the high concrete walls. The clicking of pool balls mingled with the steady beeping of video games, which had invaded even this small town. Devore served the pool players with a self-made contraption that suspended from the ceiling—tiny chalks on cord. When somebody pulled down a chalk, a system of pulleys brought it smoothly to the cue stick of the player, and then lifted the chalk back up and away. In the rear, Devore himself repaired automobiles, a more serious sport that separated the men from the pool boys.

On that early spring afternoon, four elderly men sat on park benches inside the station. They watched the younger men shoot pool.

"Tobacca crop has come near fourth of the way up," one farmer said slowly as he chewed in a steady rhythm.

"Well, that's good," said another, after an interminable pause.

Then Grafton Parker, a tan, lean, leathered tobacco farmer, stood up and spit into a metal garbage can lined with a plastic bag. He returned to the bench, and another man repeated the ritual and sat down. As if on cue, the four men stood silently, walked over to the trash can, and spat in unison.

"In the winter," said Leo Tumbleson, "there's a lot of gathering in here. Anybody who's religious doesn't call this place the poolroom, though. He just says, 'I'm going to the *garage*.'"

And so it goes on, day after day, until another year passes.

Later, I found my way to the international headquarters of the Bentonville Anti-Horse Thief Society. That isn't difficult. Everything happens in the local post office. In thirty minutes, I was made an honorary member and given a membership card, a membership certificate (suitable for framing, of course), a little wooden plaque hanging with a miniature horseshoe on it, and assorted memorabilia from the group. I was told that I am now one of several thousand people across the world to hold honorary membership, and it requires no dues or any other stipulations, other than enjoyment.

World crises notwithstanding, the people in the sitting room adjoining the post office in Verna Naylor's house were mostly concerned with who would speak at the annual dinner of the Anti-Horse Thief Society in a few weeks. The deadline stared them down like a stallion in heat.

"It's kind of hard to get somebody to come here to speak," said Verna, the postmaster at the time. "After all, we pay only fifty dollars, and everybody says that won't even take care of the gas money."

"Did you try that Nick Clooney fellow?" a man asked, referring to the former Cincinnati television anchorman and brother of singer Rosemary Clooney.

"Aw, I've known Nick from way back," she snorted. "He's from Augusta, Kentucky, not too far away, but he said he's too busy to come. Too busy!"

Verna thought about the problem as she sat in a thick chair, and then smiled. "Say, Little Jimmy Dickens, the country music singer, is from Blue Creek, down the road," she said, "but I don't think he'd come all the way back to Adams County just to talk to us."

"No, he ain't Dickens," somebody said. "It was Cowboy Copas who was from Blue Creek, but he's been dead for years."

"Oh, yes," she said. "Well, I guess we can't count on him, either."

"Yeah, sure," said Jim Naylor, her son, "but you'd think *some* public person somewhere would like to get the publicity. . . ."

As they collectively hit on the same idea, every head in the room turned toward me. I felt as if they had trained pistols on my head.

"Do you think you could—"

"No," I said. "Thank you, but I live too far away and I know nothing about horses, let alone horse thieves."

"But you don't have to know anything," Verna protested. "All you have to do is *show up*."

When she realized I was serious, Verna looked over the friends and family in the sitting room and reminded them: "Well, we don't have much going on in this town. We can't even get the reporter interested."

Everyone laughed. Things will work out, they said, as the last Saturday in April approaches. That day is traditionally reserved for the annual dinner. The society usually finds area people to speak, such as the newspaper editor from Portsmouth who accepted their invitation last year. This year, however, Verna's daughter, Harriet Naylor, is more concerned because she is the group's president, the first woman elected to the post. "I never went to a meeting of the society in my life," she said. "So one night I went and got elected president."

Neither Harriet nor her mother knows which is older—the society or the post office. The society was established in 1853, and the post office has been around a long time, too, possibly since Bentonville's founding in 1839. In 1949, the post office was opened in the little first-floor room of the Naylor house on Route 41, the town's main street. Verna greets customers from behind old barred windows, a worn metal counter, and brass post office boxes. They have been in use in town since 1909, and Verna has steadfastly refused suggestions from postal officials to go modern. People are accustomed to the Bentonville Post Office, she said, and it will stay as it is as long as she's in control.

Often people step into the adjoining sitting room, the unofficial gathering place for residents who want to discuss anything or nothing in particular. Verna said it's unusual to find such a tiny post office—no more than ten feet wide—next to a sitting room that's four times as large, but her customers applaud the logic. They like to come into the sitting room to talk. Sometimes they read the newspaper and, on frosted winter days when the world becomes a snowy drift, they warm themselves by the old gas stove. The room is an odd collection of old but comfortable chairs, six key-wound clocks that chime irregularly, knickknacks, and a sign on the wall that reads: "You can't hide in a small town. Too many people are watching."

In a town where time is elusive, history is what you make it. To Verna, it seems only a short time ago that her late husband, Harry, the former postmaster, was putting on his colorful uniform and preparing for another concert with the local brass band. A photograph of him in uniform sits on her television, and the thought of him is always on her mind. When he died in 1968, she took over as the town's postmaster. She likes the work, and, besides, it's a job. Work has always been easy to find in Bentonville, but not a job.

Harry spent most of his life driving a huckster wagon through the farm country and working in the town cemetery. Then he got the post office. Other than farmers and self-employed businesspeople, few residents have had the luxury of a job in Bentonville. They work in West Union, about five miles to the north; in Portsmouth, twenty-five miles to the east; and in Cincinnati, about sixty-five miles to the west. The unemployed—roughly 20 percent of the county's twenty-five thousand people when I was there—have little hope of finding a job in neighboring small towns. Not enough business is there, either.

On this afternoon, Verna's son Jim returned home early from his job in a West Union funeral home to do some planting. The funeral home gives him additional income when he's not farming, and he feels fortunate. He knows that in 1982 Harriet was laid off from her job at the old Hercules trouser factory in the village of Manchester, where she had worked for twenty-two years. She was lucky to find a job as a cafeteria worker in the county school system.

A lack of jobs has caused many young people to leave Bentonville. Verna said she is fortunate that three of her five children—Jim, Harriet, and Linda Sue, a schoolteacher—decided to stay in town.

"Harriet is now the second oldest Bentonville-born resident," Jim said proudly.

"Oh, Jim!" Harriet said, trying to get him to stop talking.

"No, really, I'm third oldest," he said. "If Nate Pence were to die, Harriet would be *first*."

Of all the jobs in town, the most prestigious was that of teacher at the Bentonville Elementary School. Everyone respected the teachers for doing a good job despite a low budget. The original inscription on the yellow brick school building—Bentonville Rural School—reminded many people of the day when life was less complex, even in this relaxed town.

Linda Sue was Bentonville's only reading teacher, instructing all eight grades in the school that she attended as a child. "My friend, Ethel Beam, always told me that if I wanted to be a teacher, she would retire and let me have her job," she said. "I owe it all to Ethel, really. She got me a job as a teacher's aide and then she retired so I could teach."

When the yellow brick school closed in the spring of 1989, Linda Sue was transferred. Knowing how much it meant to Bentonville, she was sad to see the old school close, but at least she kept her job. Many of her childhood friends had grown up and left town but she never seriously considered following their paths. "I guess I stayed because I used to be a bashful momma's kid. I don't know, I just stayed. One reason, I suppose, is that I wanted to go to college and I didn't have the money. I stayed home and worked and went to night school. It took years to finish, but I made it."

To Linda Sue, Bentonville is more than a few old houses and businesses. It is where she has lived. It is Aunt Jessie, a kindly old woman who befriended local children; the post office; and the old Bentonville Fair at harvest time. She would like to see the town grow, of course, but that doesn't seem likely. Besides, growth might mean complexity. "Years ago the town considered it," she said of inviting development, "but then we decided that some people would get mad because everybody would have to have bathrooms. There are still a few residents who don't have inside bathrooms. And, oh, yes, we'd have to get a mayor, too."

Near Bentonville, Sherman O. Beam, senior member of the Anti-Horse Thief Society, sat in the parlor of his white farmhouse, trying to remember the last time a horse was stolen in Adams County. "I do not recall when the last horse was taken," he said. "In fact, I don't think there was ever but one or two horses stolen since I can remember, and that goes back a ways."

At eighty-three, Beam was tall and silky-voiced. His distinct pronunciation came, no doubt, from teaching more than forty years in the classrooms of small country towns. Sherman Beam had an old history teacher's sharp recall of dates and events, but he couldn't even remember the first time he attended a meeting of the society. "I'd say it was around nineteen hundred and twenty," he said, shuffling through the memories. "In those days, my parents and grandparents were in it, as were many of my other relatives, the Beams and the Roushes." He stopped talking and lovingly ran his long, thin fingers across the group's faded incorporation papers, signed by his great-grandfather, William Roush, and Beam's uncle, Frank Roush, in 1880.

The theft of horses was the most common major crime in Adams County and all across Ohio from the late 1700s until the mid-to-late-1800s. To counteract it, nearly every county or town in Ohio organized its own anti–horse thief group. "The country was infested with horse thieves," the editor of *A History of Warren County, Ohio* wrote in 1882.

The unsettled condition of the country made the recovery of stolen horses very difficult. The horse-stealing proclivity of the Indians was one of the chief causes of the hatred of the early settlers toward the red men; but, after all depredations by the Indians had ceased, the farmers continued to suffer much from horse thieves, who were believed to be often organized into gangs. The great value of the horse and the difficulty of recovering one when run away, caused the pioneer to look with malignant hatred upon the horse thief. The early legislatures were composed almost entirely of farmers, and they endeavored to break up this kind of larceny by laws inflicting severe penalties—corporal punishment, fines, imprisonment, and even mutilation.

As early as 1809, the Ohio General Assembly set punishment for stealing horses. On the first offense, the thief was ordered whipped with no more than one hundred and no less than fifty stripes on his naked back. On succeeding offenses, the thief received no more than two hundred and no less than one hundred lashes. On the third offense, the thief received a tougher penalty—both ears were cropped, he was sent to prison for two years, fined no more than a thousand dollars, and ordered to return the horses he stole or repay the owner in cash. After one conviction, a horse thief could no longer hold public office, serve on a jury, or even give testimony in a court case. Fortunately, the ear-cropping penalty was used seldom if at all (potential horse thieves received the message).

Like many other rural counties in Ohio, Warren County formed its own anti–horse thief group, the Horse Rangers, described as "among the most noted orders." It was organized in 1849; by the time the county history was written four decades later, the group still had 164 rangers on patrol. "More than twenty horses have been stolen from its members," the editor wrote, "but, by its quick work and detective force, they have never lost a horse, and, in most cases, have captured the thieves. Sometimes the expenses of recovering a stolen horse would amount to $500 (which is always borne by the company) when the horse stolen probably was not worth fifty dollars."

Of all the other anti–horse thief societies that operated around the state and nation, most no longer exist. But one still patrols the wealthy Hamilton County city of Indian Hill, which organized the Indian Hill Horse Rangers in 1903 to "discourage horse thieves, chicken thieves, and other pilferers of farm and home property." The volunteers patrolled forty square miles, on foot or on horseback. By 1910, the group's charter was changed, granting broader powers. Not long after, the force—now the Indian Hill Rangers—became the local police. Meanwhile, a Kansas group, the Anti-Horse Thief Association, operated chapters in Ohio and in seven other states to help protect residents from gangs of horse thieves and thugs who threatened anyone who crossed their paths. The group developed a large network of sources and allied groups, which were called upon to help after a horse was stolen from one of the group's thirty thousand members. In 1906, the group wrote: "An individual could not spend $50 to $100 to recover a $25 horse and capture the thief. The A.T.H.A. would, because of the effect it would have in the future. Thieves have learned these facts and do less stealing from our members, hence the preventative protection . . . [but] the A.H.T.A. is in no sense a vigilance committee, and the organization has never found it necessary to adopt the mysterious methods of [the] 'Regulators' and 'White Caps' or kindred organizations. Its deeds are done in the broad open light of the day."

Other groups took more drastic measures to correct horse thievery. In Butler County in 1805, the pioneer Jeremiah Butterfield's area near the Great Miami River became so infested with horse thieves and other unsavory people that he took action. A nineteenth-century editor observed: "There was no law that could be carried into execution effectually but lynch-law, which was resorted to successfully."

In the 1800s, one of the worst names a man could be called was a horse thief. Naturally, Ohio farmers dubbed John Hunt Morgan, the raiding Confederate general, the King of the Horse Thieves. Morgan's cavalry stole an estimated two thousand horses on its long journey across Ohio. In Mercer County in western Ohio, a man named Marvin Kuhn became known widely as the number one horse thief in the region. Then Fred Hutt was elected county sheriff. Hutt killed Kuhn in a gunfight, and his death nearly stopped the theft of horses in that area. As late as 1890, citizens of Springdale in Hamilton County incorporated as the Springdale Mutual Protective Company, to catch horse thieves and other felons. In 1885, the Ohio legislature granted such groups the authority to pursue and arrest, without a warrant, anybody believed to be guilty of stealing a horse. Local historians don't know how many thieves the group caught. In the passion of the moment, when they were charging around the countryside looking for horse thieves, members of the Mutual Protective Company forgot all about civil liberties.

No wonder. The public backed this cavalier attitude. In Marion County in 1842, commissioners built a two-story stone jail. According to the author of a 1907 county history, the "principal occupants of this jail were horse thieves, who in an early day did quite a thriving business throughout Ohio. The prisoners frequently escaped by picking their way out through the wall."

In the Hocking Hills region, another band of horse thieves (and bootleggers, robbers, and murderers) lived in the sandstone Rock House, a cave with a tunnel type of corridor that ran up a 150-foot cliff. The thieves gave the place its nickname: Robbers' Roost.

Before 1820 in southern Fairfield County, near Lancaster, a group of particularly successful thieves met regularly in a rural area called Sleepy Hollow. They stole horses in the region until a brave prosecuting attorney hired a private detective and formed a posse to catch the gang. The posse discovered the gang's ten members one night, meeting in a house in the country. The posse captured most of them, and a jury sent them to prison.

How seriously did people take horse thievery? On May 11, 1893, the *Williamstown Courier*, just across the Ohio River in Grant County, Kentucky, reported succinctly: "Lynching: mob lynches Jim Collins (alias Clark), horse thief, at Sherman last Wednesday, within 300 yards of the spot where he was born."

Period.

The railroad and the telegraph helped end horse stealing by allowing better detection of criminals and recovery of stolen horses. But before the railroads came into widespread use in Ohio, farmers decided to search for thieves on their own. The Bentonville Anti-Horse Thief Society was formed in March 1853, to operate as a vigilante group. A few years later it incorporated, making it official and legitimate. By the 1920s, when horses were losing to gas-powered vehicles their importance in the rural community, area farmers started losing interest in the society. "There weren't many horses being stolen by then," Beam said. "And horses were beginning to fade out of farm work, so there wasn't much left for us to do. Earlier, though, when horses were stolen, the society would put off its members, called the Riders, into the countryside to inquire if anyone had seen the stolen horses or the thieves. Trustees appointed a captain to lead the group. If the horses were found, the member who located them was rewarded with ten dollars. That was a lot of money then."

By the mid-1920s, Bentonville had an anti–horse thief society and no horse thieves. "I guess we scared them off pretty good," Beam said. "The group had quite a bit of money, too, so it bought the first set of electric lights for Bentonville, and a movie outfit for the school. We also organized annual dinners for the society, and we'd eat, eat, eat. There just wasn't much left for us to do." Membership began to rise again in the mid-1950s, when the centennial of the society revived interest. The group's yearly banquet became the biggest and most popular event in town. The number of guests almost equaled Bentonville's population. In 1961, the society thought it was time to erect its monument in the middle of Bentonville. In 2001, the Ohio Bicentennial Commission and the society erected a historical marker on Ohio 41 to commemorate the group. Someday, the group might move the monument to that spot, too. "Oh, but that will take some years to do, because we take our time around here doing things," Harriet said. "We move at our own pace."

Nowadays, the group is a novelty. From all over the nation, people write to ask for membership. She obliges them by sending membership cards. The group boasts of several hundred card-carrying horse–thief catchers. Group officers purchase cards, plaques, key rings, bumper stickers, and fancy certificates for fellow members.

"We don't do much now, except to get together to eat," Sherman Beam said. "A hundred years ago, they'd give you a necktie party if they caught you stealing a horse. But we haven't had any horses stolen lately. Come to think of it, we haven't had much of *anything* happen lately."

He smiled mischievously, then winked.

And I wondered.

Back in "downtown" Bentonville, I parked on the main street and looked at the nineteenth-century buildings. I watched Leo Tumbleson walk slowly from Devore's to meet Nathaniel Pence—the oldest person in town—across the street. Nate stood as straight as a cornstalk in August, his arms folded tightly across his chest. He looked up toward a ruddy sky, his eyes shaded by a green-gold cap pushed far down on his forehead. Leo, a retired farmer, spoke reverently of Pence, as if to imply that Nate were some local guru or the sole survivor of an ancient race. At sixty-seven, Leo had lived within two miles of town most of his life. But his friend had done better. Nate had lived *in* town. That is the distinction. And Nate, a retired carpenter, wasn't shy about his tenure: "I'm the oldest person living in this town who was born here. I'm seventy-three. There used to be a lot of Pences here, but there ain't anymore."

Leo and Nate see change in a seemingly changeless place. Take the long, wooden house up the street, for example. To most people, it must look the same as it has for years. But to Leo and Nate, it becomes more historic every year. "Old George Clinger hauled that house up here by oxen," Leo said. "It sat on the Ohio River as a wharf boat in the early 1900s. George used four teams of mules to get ahold of it."

Nate nodded, to approve. His house is dubiously historic itself. In the late 1860s, a drunk with a lustful agenda visited a seventeen-year-old girl who lived there, and she chopped his head off with an ax. The killing is now a part of Bentonville folklore. Some people just come by to stare at the house.

Leo said he prefers history that he remembers personally. He knew, for instance, that Bentonville's high point—the accumulation of nearly a dozen businesses—occurred in the 1920s, only to waste away in the Depression. "A hotel sat where I live," he said, "and there was a restaurant with it, too. One day I was walkin' to school, and Mrs. Brooks, the owner, called to me from the porch and said she had some new candy. That night the place burned. I remember the kids were all a-carryin' off things. But I can't remember what day of the week it was."

"Tuesday," Nate said matter-of-factly.

"Oh, all right!" Leo said.

Nate is known for his ability to recall dates and events, and he further demonstrated his process to Leo: "There was five stores left by then. The flour mill had went out in '27. At the hotel, they was heatin' water to shave with and the stove blowed 'em all up."

"Doggone right, Nathaniel!"

By the 1920s, Bentonville had progressed from having a one-room school to a two-story wooden school that stood where the empty Bentonville Elementary is today. In those days, young Nate was a real stinker.

"Every time me and another boy would come to school," he said, "we'd have skunk on us." He drew a line down his body. "You see, trappin' was the only way we could make any extra money. So one day me and ol' Elwood Scott looked at our traps before we went to school, and when we got there the superintendent sent us home because we smelled. We got tired of that happenin' all the time. Heck, we had to trap. So the next time we went to school, we pooshed a stink bag under the big potbellied stove and taped it up underneath. Pretty soon, it smelled. Whew! That's the *last* time they ever sent us home, by gosh."

"Remember old Joe?" Leo asked.

"Old Joe was a rooster that belonged to Bill Naylor," Nate said. "Bill would talk to that rooster and make it crow. One night, some boys had a chicken roast and invited Old Joe. Bill came along later to do some fiddlin' and at the roast he kept sayin', 'Boy, that's the best chicken I ever ate.' Three days later, Bill was still goin' around town sayin', 'I wonder whatever happened to my Old Joe?'"

The laughter of Leo Tumbleson and Nate Pence floated out over Bentonville, as they stared northward. Toward the flour mill, the restaurant, and the hotel that existed, vividly and securely, in their minds.

16

Satisfying an Agrarian Myth

On a drive through Owensville in Clermont County, I stopped to buy a soda in a drab old drugstore. The steaming heat of late summer dropped from villagers' brows and swirled, almost visibly, around the front door of Woodruff's Pharmacy. Inside, the talk was of the heat. Too hot for the county fair. When will the heat break?

Heat was always a harbinger of good business at the country drugstore, a 32 x 50–foot room on the first floor of Charles Woodruff's house on Main Street. The wooden floors were rough and dark. Color advertising signs were lined and faded. Woodruff's was among the last of the independents in the rolling countryside, a throwback to an older time and place—rural America.

Woodruff was sixty-seven years old, with gray hair, an easy smile, and a rather wide midsection. He had worked behind the fountain since he was nine. From this lofty vantage point, he had seen all manner of things, and he had seen many country stores come and go.

"One morning," he recalled, "I guess it was in the 1930s, old Doc Haas was sittin' here at the counter. Somebody came runnin' in asking for a doctor, and I said, 'Well, we got one right here.' The fellow said there'd been a wreck out on U.S. Route 50, and the victim's ear had been cut half off. Doc turned around and said, 'Oh, we can take care of it right here. We don't need to go to the hospital. Just bring him on in.' I said, 'But Doc, you ain't really gonna do that in *here*, are you?' He said, 'Sure, son, we'll just get a little Lysol and my needles and sew it on.' So we went right to the back room and did the job. And I went from fixin' sodas to being a physician's assistant in one day."

The story made his wife, Ruth, moan in mock disgust from the rear of the store. Then he finished: "Well, the funny thing was, that man who was in the wreck stopped in the store about a year later. He said, 'I bet you don't remember me, do you?' I just looked at him and said, 'Oh, yeah, I helped sew your ear back on.'"

The tale brought hearty laughter from the customers sitting on the stools that face the scratched fountain counter. Woodruff smiled and gently dipped some more ice cream. Many of his customers came here out of habit, as they had for years. They enter, greet Woodruff, and sit in a room crammed with an unusual assortment of bottles, amber jars, a red penny scale, oak and cherry cabinets, hand-lettered signs, and kites.

"We used to have chickens out back when I was a boy," Woodruff said. "Some of the fellows would come by about one in the morning when they came home from dates. They'd stand out front and yell to me upstairs, 'Get up, Chuck! We got some chickens for you to fry.' At the time, of course, there were no all-night sandwich places around here. So those boys would come by the store and bother me. I'd come downstairs and fry chicken for them at one in the morning. Oh, we'd have a great time sittin' around eating all that chicken."

"Tell it all," Ruth said.

"Well, the next day, I'd come out back to find that I had fried my own chickens. Even Red Boy, my prize pet rooster. Yeah, those old boys had gotten into our henhouse. And Red Boy was the worst for it."

The villagers probably had their own impressions of Woodruff's confectionary anachronism, and so do city people. Local people mostly thought of his store in connection with some childhood idyll. City people, however, looked at the store and saw what they wanted to see: The myth of agrarian life, small-town happiness, and a place where everything moves as slow as seasonal change and is as simple as a chocolate soda. Woodruff knew these things weren't necessarily true, but why should he be the one to tell them?

"Yeah, the good old days," he said. "Oh, I guess the '30s and '40s were good days for this town; people was workin'. But that wasn't always good times, either, with the war comin'. There was a lot of hard work then, and before. When I first started workin' in here as a kid in the '20s, I had to pack everything in ice every day. Now that's hard work. Put a little salt around it, and keep it good and *cold*. Ev'ry mornin' you had to draw the water off and pack it again. There was a lot of *work* around here. Old Bob Jones, the ice man, he used to drive up here every other day from Batavia in a Model T Ford. We had to have a three-hundred pound block of ice every other day."

The drugstore had been a part of Owensville longer than even Woodruff could remember. His father, Roy, bought the store in 1924 from the brother of a Mount Orab physician, and it was renamed Woodruff's. Chuck Woodruff had an old photograph, the kind with a hard backing, lying on a shelf above the fountain. Taken around 1927, the photograph shows Roy and Chuck standing stiffly behind the cherry counter and its marble top. The soda men look proudly across the room, toward small round tables and chairs with tiny wire legs. A metal sign for Bruck's Near Beer hangs on the wall.

When the infrequent someone would ask about near beer, Woodruff would pause in disbelief. "Why, it's *near* beer," he told me. "Looked like beer, tasted like beer, but it had to be less than one percent alcohol. Same as a soft drink, really. I hated it then, I hate it now. In them days, of course, there was no Seven-Up. You had your orange, sarsaparilla, root beer, lemon-lime, and your Co'-Cola. During Prohibition, we sold Bruck's Near Beer—you see, they weren't allowed to call it *beer*—and old Bruck's kept right on goin'. It was the only brewery in Cincinnati that worked, that I know of."

When the Depression hit in late 1929, things toughened in Owensville. Woodruff was in high school, the old Owensville High School, where all grades were in one building. He continued to help his father in the store, and played guard on the championship basketball team of 1930. One of his teammates, a farm boy, rode a mule to every practice that year.

The Depression was momentarily set aside in the early 1930s when gold was discovered in Brushy Fork Creek. "It all started when some flakes of gold were found in the water," Woodruff said. "Pretty soon, people were comin' down here pannin' for gold, and one fellow brought a good-sized little hunk into the store for us to see. A farmer used his land for a little strip-mining, and he brought a gold mining company in. But they never did make much money out of it. I even panned a little myself. Probably washed it all away."

The gold-mining farmer had a daughter who was an actress in Hollywood. She brought her husband, a songwriter for Hollywood musicals, to Owensville on a vacation about this time. The next time they came, they brought some friends: Alice Faye, George Gobel, and George Jessel. "They all came into the store pretty near every day when they were in town," Woodruff said. "I wouldn't have even recognized 'em, but I had heard they were in town. Alice was in here twice. She didn't try to show off or anything."

In those times, Roy Woodruff kept a good supply of horse liniment, mineral tonics, and veterinary Absorbine, which the older people liked to use as a liniment. Woodruff also stocked things such as Dr. Lyon's Tooth Powder and Sozodont, "the timely, delicate tooth wash." Chuck Woodruff still carries it too, because one man in town uses it. As a pharmacist, Woodruff also keeps a lot of things that his customers find difficult to find in convenience stores and supermarkets. His version of the store, however, has moved ahead, if ever so slightly. The nickel ice cream cones were twenty-five cents—inexpensive by 1980s' standards. Sodas cost sixty-five cents. But the wooden floors were still gritty, and the whole store looked liked something out of a faded color postcard. Woodruff's groped to find its way in the modern world.

"I haven't changed things much since I moved to this location in 1948," Woodruff said. "I guess I'd lose my identity if I changed it. I don't know, maybe I'm looking at it the wrong way, but you'd be surprised at the number of people who like to come in here just to remember."

Perhaps Woodruff's ways were good for business. Shopping was a circumspect matter to many small-town residents. Newcomers, of which Owensville has had a liberal share, didn't seem to care as much about buying tradition. Maybe that's why the subdivision dwellers outside of town preferred to stop at the new discount drugstore so frequently.

"Oh, I hear they've got nearly everything in that store and not much of anything," Woodruff said nonchalantly. "You see, I've never actually been in it, but that's what I'm told. The other day a man said that the place looks like a hardware store that got stunted in growth."

They do things differently at the chain store. The police scanner doesn't blare and, unlike Woodruff, the chain's operators don't close whenever there's a fire in town. Woodruff, the only charter member of the Owensville Fire Department, will leave the store if the department needs him. Some things, he said, are more important than business.

He extends that philosophy to public service, too. He served three terms on the Clermont Northeastern Local School District's board of education. He enjoyed it; it had purpose. Whatever his reasons, Woodruff served, time moved on, and his three children grew up and took their own old-town memories with them. One son became a physician, and the other children made it known that they wanted no part of ever operating a country drugstore. Woodruff respected their decisions, without being upset.

Ruth looked sternly at him. "I told the kids I'd kill them if they ever went into this business. It's a lot of long hours and hard work." The look on her face showed she meant it. To avoid her stare, Woodruff turned toward the end of the fountain and observed a curly-haired young man sitting on a stool, sucking down a chocolate soda. He had overheard a part of Woodruff's old school tales. "Yeah," he said with a straight face, "they sure upgraded the board of education when you left it, Woody."

Chuck Woodruff shook his head, his contagious laughter shaking the store. "And they sure upgraded the school when you left, Squeaky. Now, what else will you have, anyway?"

Ruth walked over to her husband and gently took his arm. She smiled at him. It was the smile of a wife who was proud of her husband and their life together.

Woodruff sat down on a stool and stared at the scuffed soda fountain counter. "Well, I'll just work as long as I can," he said. "What else you going to do? Oh, I haven't made a lot of money, but I do feel that I've made a lot of friends in this town. I've made a small contribution. And I'm happy. You have to be *happy*."

And the myth goes on.

17

Harry and the Midway

On a steamy July morning in 1917, at some long-forgotten fairground in rural Ohio, the cane man escorted his son to a well-worn place behind a midway tent. The boy quivered. He could not recall his mischief that day. Finally, his father said, "Boy, somebody has to be the entertainer. Make folks laugh, make them forget their troubles."

That afternoon, little Harry C. Dearwester had his debut on an apple box, next to a brass scale. To guess people's weight. For the next thirty years, he accomplished the impossible: he guessed correctly 90 percent of the time—and amazed everyone. They didn't mind a dose of weighty realism. After all, they had come to the fair to have some fun. Besides, that Harry had a knack. When he grinned, the people responded—even when he informed them that they weighed 250 pounds. That's why he never left the fair. Where else could a man tell people they were corn-fed and not get punched in the mouth?

Harry's life paralleled the heyday of the county fair in Ohio; he spent a lifetime walking through dusty midways at fairs from Lake Erie to the Ohio River. Kids bragged that they could beat him at his own game, but they were wrong. He won every time when he saw them smile.

Once, long ago, a kid played Harry's cane-rack game at the Butler County Fair in Hamilton on a hot July night. His father fed him quarters until he reached the two-dollar limit. The kid couldn't win. He tossed the rings, but they bounced off the tops of the canes. Then, he ran out of money. Seeing the boy's disappointment, the cane-rack man tapped the last ring with his fancy cane, and the ring fell over the top of a pretty red cane. The boy took the cane home and displayed it prominently in his small room. Every year after, for years, he returned to see the cane-rack man. Time passed and the boy turned into a teenager, and his thoughts turned to more complicated matters. Eventually, he stopped going to the fair with his parents.

Then one hot day, while on assignment for a magazine in Findlay, the adult "boy" saw Harry Dearwester at the Hancock County Fair. To the boy, it seemed that only a few months had passed since he saw Harry, who was still pleasing crowds of children. The visitor decided to stop and talk.

Harry's world was inside a wooden orange rectangle, among hundreds of canes stacked vertically and in front of eager kids, who tried to toss lightweight wooden rings over them. Some kids couldn't throw a ringer if they were standing a foot away from the target. The visitor watched as Harry tried to tip the rings in the kids' favor, and most of the young ones left with flimsy but fascinating and brightly colored canes. Harry always saw to that. Some, the prized ones, had unusual handles, in the shapes of animal heads.

Ohio's county fairs were Harry Dearwester's personal neon world, circumscribed by the midway and a web of cotton candy. But his world changed. As more farms melted into suburbs in the 1980s and 1990s, the county fairs in more populated areas became the ghosts of our agrarian past. The number of Ohio farms declined from 215,000 in 1947 to 78,000 in 2001. The trend continues as farmers encounter low prices and high interest in developing their land.

Not losing sight of their agricultural roots, the fairs keep trying to attract younger people with nonagricultural programs. Some fair boards book heavy metal bands, offer competitions for the best Web designs, and display creative writing. Since 1980, the fairs in Ohio have been transformed as metropolitan areas have changed from rural to suburban. Even in agriculturally predominant counties, the fair is a slicker product these days. And in the many urban and suburban counties, fairs are a slim reason to get together and show off a dwindling number of large vegetables and animals.

The old fair days are lost now in the twilight of our rural past. Harry knew this, yet persevered. He no longer needed the paycheck, but he needed the fair.

He looked older and smaller than I had remembered. I envisioned a strong, large man, but on this day Harry was anything but large. He wore a cheap polyester blue ball cap with the words "Harry's Cane Rack" on the front, a denim shirt, and plaid pants. White stubble stood out on his leathered, tanned face. When he laughed, deep wrinkles appeared and his smoky voice boomed deeply.

Relaxing with a can of Coca-Cola and a cigarette, Harry sat under a tree and recalled a life on the road, all fifty-eight years of it, mostly at Ohio's county fairs. He knew he was growing old and that his time was short.

"I've had experiences," he said. "Could write a book and then do another and never tell the same story twice." He thought of himself as a relic on a now-flashy midway. The kids enjoyed the thrills and lights. His game was a simple one from another time. He looked around—now nothing but electronic games and booths with big stuffed animals and even a device to gauge how fast a person can throw a hardball. This was not Harry's kind of place, but it was the only place left for him.

"My father spent fifty-five years in the games," he said. "He was a big man, six feet eight inches and 247 pounds in his shirtsleeves. People listened to him. You understand why. He started out as a bartender in Findlay. Then I became a bartender. He hit the road with the games and so did I, following in his footsteps. He always said, 'If you can't swim, stay out of deep water.' So I did. I stayed with him. The cane rack is the only game I love and the fairest game around. I hate to say it, but I'm the oldest concessionaire in the state—seventy-five years old. Now, *I'm* the old-timer. There ain't any others like me. I remember it all. We used to have great crowds when the fairs had the buckin' bulls. What happened? Humane Society ruled them out. These days, we got the demolition derby. Aw!

"I've seen too many changes. You used to be able to sell the American people anything. They're greedy. That's no secret. But what they saw and what they got were two different things. All we had to do was give somethin' a fancy name and the people would flow into the tents to see it. I've enjoyed every bit of the fairs, though. I've met a lot of interesting people. They say, 'Here comes the cane-rack man.' I don't remember their names, but I remember their faces. When I'm gone I don't know who'll get all this junk. I just hope it's somebody with some sense."

For thirty years, Harry operated a scale at the fairs. He guessed people's weight. He learned to read minds by watching the movement of the eyes. He used to say anything to get the people to step up to the scale. "I'd tell them their daddy owned a butcher shop. People would stand and watch me forever. They'd come up in overcoats in September, with pockets filled with heavy stones. I'd just add on a few more pounds and guess right again. I'd say, 'Lady, I'll weigh you—horse and all.'"

As people moved closer, he walked among them with the assurance of a beekeeper. Maybe his luck was some genetic inheritance. "To show you what respect my mother had for me," he said, puffing hard on a cigarette, "she bore and reared me on a fairground."

Fairs were mainly daylight events then. Farmers rode in on buggies and ate something called Hokey-Pokey ice cream and waffles. Harry paid six dollars to set up his cane rack. If a fair spilled over into the evening, Coleman lanterns had to be strung up along the dusty walkways. Then the fair people left as quietly as they had come. They could pack everything they owned, jump on an express train in Greenville at eight, and disembark in Van Wert by midnight: daredevils, medicine men, cowboys and their bucking bulls. They all climbed aboard the train.

Harry's father crisscrossed Ohio by rail, just to open his cane rack. He started it in 1892, and for fifty-five years he made it a fixture at Ohio's county fairs. He refused to take it outside the state. He said he was born in Ohio and he would die in Ohio. Harry took over the game in 1947. He loved the rapid-fire ballyhoo: "Hey, folks, welovetoseeya hook'emandhang'em! Hey, yeah. We got dog heads, eagle claws, rat feet—all canes from old Japan. Try it, three rings for a quarter, ten for a dollar. Hey! Who else and how many . . . ?"

He saw things unimaginable. A menagerie of animals, hoaxes, freaks. "Once," he remembered, "a fellow put up a colorful banner at the Montgomery County Fair in Dayton: 'See the Hairless Dog in a Barrel! Only Ten Cents.' Well, I overheard an old farmer say, 'Mother, you wanna go in and see it?' She said, 'No, Daddy dear, you go in and look.' A few minutes later, the old fella walked out, all red-faced and cussin' up a blue streak. 'Mother,' he said, 'there ain't nothin' in that barrel but a damn hot dog on four toothpicks!' By '43, we had to clean it all up. The do-gooders wouldn't have any of it. A guy used to sell nickel hamburgers. He'd put so much meal in them that the burgers would turn white as Styrofoam. He'd have to color them red. Some people complained that they was gettin' a gyppin', but the owner didn't care.

"Then there was the guy who had a tent with a big sign: 'Little People . . . Alive and in Action!' People stood in long lines to get in there. They even brought cookies to feed the 'little people.' When they got inside, though, they got a surprise: the little ones was all mechanical, see—shoe cobblers and farmers, all doin' something, going around a track. Oh, there was all kinds of gimmicks then to turn a dollar."

Harry's laughter boomed across the midway.

"In those days, people wanted something more," he said. "So they came to the midway at the county fair. Like to try your luck? They could buy the same old thing downtown for fifty cents, but they wanted to *beat ya*. Now, all we got is a lot of nonsense."

Except, of course, for the cane rack game. It is the only game Harry will work. He said, "My game is the only one on the midway that will give the kids a fair shuffle. I can't take money from the kids and not give them something to take home. Maybe it's nothing but a memory, but it is something they won't forget about growing up in Ohio and in this time. They seem to have no childhood; they grow up so fast anymore. The game, though, it is the one thing that keeps them like the kids of my day. It's a simple game, and it is rewarding. I sum up my working philosophy this way: When a millionaire over in Troy died years ago, a reporter went to the mansion to write a story about all the man's possessions. The guy had nearly everything. The reporter came back to his news office, wrote up the man's story, and told the editor, 'Here's a hot piece.' The editor frowned and said, 'Hell, son, this ain't news. What did the man take *with* him?'"

Harry always reminded his young workers that honesty mattered. They looked around the midway and chuckled. It wasn't exactly a paragon of truth. Next door, a man named Pitcher John sold lemonade and reclaimed the ice. "He'd put a little chain on each pitcher so you couldn't walk away with it," Harry said. "After you drank your lemonade and left, he'd gather up the ice and hose it off and use it again. He had a sign: 'All you can drink for a nickel.' But he saved money on the ice. One hot September day, a boy drank five pitchers. Pitcher John said, 'You got any more boys like you at home?' The boy said, 'Give me another one!'" Pitcher John, all the wiser, just smirked.

A man named Foxy claimed he had an animal that looked like a groundhog and shrieked horribly. Then, a big wind blew open a tent flap to reveal an old man pulling furiously on a long rosined string to produce the shrieking sound. Never mind, Harry told his boys. They won't stay in business for long. And most of them didn't.

Yet, they were all Harry's friends, every last showman and con artist. When the sheriff closed Red's striptease show in Marion one night,

Harry thought of a plan to save his friend from certain bankruptcy. "I told Red to go into town and get himself two dummies, a man and a woman, and bring them back to the fair and put up a big sign. He should call his show 'The Ruination of Temptation: Why Young Girls Leave Home.' Yeah, that would do it up right, I told old Red. Well, he took my advice and folks lined up for two hundred feet. Men tried to ditch their wives and sneak into the show. Oh, it was wonderful until the sheriff came. He thought he'd close up Red again. The sheriff paid his quarter, but all the old buzzard found was two mannequins holding cigarettes and glasses of Co'-Cola."

As Harry sipped his drink, a plump boy of twelve walked up and said, "Need any help, Mister?" Harry stared at him and said nothing. Then the boy said, "What do you pay, anyway?"

"Now, I'm going to tell you somethin', young man," Harry said. "When I was a kid your age, I never asked how much money was involved. I worked for a man and then collected my pay and was satisfied with it. How much do you think you're worth an hour to pick up them rings and put 'em on a stick?"

The boy's eyes darted. "Uh . . ."

"Well?"

"Uh, I'm just askin' for a friend."

"Well, come on!"

"Uh—six dollars?"

"Six dollars! An hour?"

"Uh, yeah."

Harry wiped his forehead and said: "Son, for six bucks an hour, I'll pick up my *own* rings. In fact, I'll go to work for you for six an hour."

He has picked up his own rings, too, and considered it all in a good day's work. The traveling was the hardest part. It had been lonely, too, despite the characters who surrounded him. Then Harry met Pauline in 1945. One day she pitched the rings and smiled. They started talking and soon began dating. They went everywhere together around their hometown, Findlay, until the warm weather came again and, one day, a new stock of canes arrived. Harry felt the uncomfortable feeling of wanting to head out on the road. It was an itch that he could not stop. "Well, kid," he told her straight, "I got to leave you. Fair time, you know. Time for me to go." Pauline smiled sadly and said she'd try to understand. She felt crushed, and her feelings showed. As Harry started to walk away, he felt the magnetic attraction of Pauline's affection. He turned to her and stammered, "Well, uh, I . . . let's get married. I guess you could go with me. I got a nice mobile home."

For thirty-nine years they ran the cane rack as partners, driving to county fairs in Ohio and returning to their house on Kibby Street in Findlay for the autumn and winter. When Pauline died, Harry cried. It was as though his life had ended; he did not know how to react. Two weeks later, he set up the cane rack as usual at the Butler County Fair in Hamilton. What else could he do? He said he felt as if somebody had just cut him in half, but he had to go on with the game. He knew no other way. The work gave him purpose.

"This is the place for me to be, at the cane rack," he said. "There will always be another fair for me, somewhere."

He picked out a red cane and handed it to me. "A souvenir," he said, breaking into a familiar grin. "But this time, kid, you don't have to toss no rings. It's yours."

As I walked away, I turned to look back at Harry Dearwester one last time. He had stepped into his little wooden rectangle again and started hustling canes. For a moment, time failed to move. Harry seemed perfectly timeless.

His voice grew softer as I walked farther: "Hey, folks! We got dog heads, eagle claws, rat feet, and some canes from old Japan. Hey! Who else and how many? Who else and how many . . . ?"

At that instant I heard the fading echo of a forgotten Ohio.

18

By Any Other Name:
Ghost Towns and Other Fabled Obscurities

The river of time takes the hard rock of a real life, moves it along
through history, scraping off the rough edges as it goes, and deposits it on a distant bank as a smooth stone of myth for all to
admire. Free to choose what we believe, Americans choose myth
over reality ever time.

— *Dayton Duncan*

Alpha

Alpha is a mirage of history, overcome by time and Dayton sprawl, a
ghost town. Historians disagree on how the community received its
Greek name. Some say it came from the town's proximity to the area's
first settlement. Others say the founders borrowed the name from a
local mill, which stamped the name Alpha on its first barrel of flour in
1798. Because the mill was important to the town's economy, the name
stuck. Located near busy U.S. Route 35 in Greene County's city of Beavercreek, Alpha lies near a large shopping mall. Few remnants of the
past remain. While preservationists restore some log buildings, visitors
wonder whether Alpha still exists. It has been absorbed by the invad-
ing city, which is expanding like a fresh ink spot. Once, Beavercreek
Township was the seat of local county government. The Xenia, Dayton
and Belpre Railroad arrived in town in 1853. Then, small places were
important in Greene County: New Germany, Knollwood, Zimmerman,
and, of course, Alpha, which started in the earliest days of Ohio statehood, in 1803. The town grew slowly around an early courthouse. A
post office opened in 1850 and a school in 1882. The population finally

reached one hundred. The community had high expectations for itself; people realized that it was a natural commercial center. Unfortunately, the town had already peaked. It was divided into three parts: Upper Alpha, Middle Alpha, and Lower Alpha. Lower Alpha was the industrial section, which included a woolen mill, a five-story flour mill with five water wheels, a three-story distillery with a hundred-foot-long corn house, a lime house and sawmill, and a toll gate house. In Middle Alpha, the Pennsylvania Railroad shipped the town's whiskey, grain, and lumber. Upper Alpha had several blacksmiths, wagon manufacturers, and general stores. In 1888, Alpha's future changed abruptly one night when most of the town's men were attending a political rally in Cincinnati. A fire started in a hay shed and spread to the mills and distillery. All the buildings burned, anguishing Alpha and dooming its future.

Ash

In the late 1800s, Ash existed in Jersey Township in west Licking County. Little is known about the town today. "Licking County has a lot of these kinds of places—ghost towns that were once postal drops," said Martha Tykodi, president of the West Licking Historical Society. "Ash was just up the road from us. There were a lot of little settlements here and there in those days, when people couldn't travel too far and they needed a lot of post offices for the convenience factor. Ash had a post office, a general store, and a few other businesses. The town really wasn't significant—only a crossroads. What happened is what is happening and will continue to happen to a lot of small towns: they lose their post offices, then their schools, and then themselves. Nothing is left. It's the way things go. It's not necessarily the better way, but it is reality."

Bear's Mill

Bear's Mill, 6540 Arcanum–Bear's Mill Road, Greenville, is one of only a few gristmills still operating in Ohio. The four-story building was listed on the National Register of Historic Places in 1977. It features a store that sells handmade pottery and other items. Major George Adams bought the land and built a sawmill on Greenville Creek in 1832. Eventually, the sawmill gave way to the flour mill, which is still covered with its original black walnut siding. The wood is in such excellent condition that I thought it had been replaced in the last twenty-five years. Today, the mill still grinds cornmeal, whole-wheat flour, and rye flour. The property is privately owned by the Friends of Bear Mill. Its mission is to preserve and maintain the mill for public touring and education. The group's most successful month is December, a time when visitors stop to buy Ohio products. The group sponsors its Candlelight Open House, which includes an illuminated millrace path through the woods and a roaring bonfire. In 1849, founder Gabriel Baer (Bear's Mill is a corruption of his last name) paid local schoolchildren fifty cents a day—a good wage then—to dig the eight-hundred-foot millrace. He opened the mill the next year. The second owner operated it only a couple of years, then closed it in fear that Confederates would strike Ohio and burn the mill. On a late-fall visit, I bought a jar of raspberry jam and a loaf of cherry bread and wandered around the place. I enjoyed seeing a collection of old Darke County Fair posters from the early 1900s and other ephemera. I asked a volunteer about the story that the mill is haunted. She acknowledged that some people claim to see a ghost who looks like a farmer from the late 1800s. But, she added, "I have never seen him, and personally I believe the story is an old wives' tale." Yet other people say they have seen the farmer coming up and down the wooden stairs.

Bear's Oil Village

In the 1790s, the Massasauga tribe inhabited the area near Conneaut in Ashtabula County. Led by a chief named Macqua Medah, also known as Bear's Oil, the tribe consisted of older people who could not resist the pioneers' invasion. One day a traveler accused a tribe member of stealing his gun. A fight led to the shooting death of the traveler. When other settlers heard of the incident, they sent a party to the Indian village to arrest the offender. But Bear's Oil refused to give him up. When the whites returned with a larger group, they found the village deserted. The chief had fled with his people, but before he left, he made sure they understood one thing: if they trespassed on sacred land, where a ten-foot red pole marked the grave of his mother, he would scalp every settler he could find. Unimpressed by his threat, the settlers took over the tribe's cabins (all fifteen feet high with bark roofs) and the chief's palace, which they promptly turned into a barn. Bear's Oil never returned.

Bear Swamp

In northwest Tully Township in Van Wert County, bears roamed freely in a wide area aptly named Bear Swamp. Covered by willows, tall prairie grass, and brush, the swamp was a good place for bears to hide. The area, including Union Township, was known as bear country in the middle of the nineteenth century. Around the swamp, farmers lost corn and hogs to hungry bears that were bold enough to raid barns. As late as 1858, farmers killed a dozen bears in one year in or near the swamp. But they couldn't drain the land easily because it had no natural outlets. The county gave the swamp to the state, and the state condemned it and offered it to anyone who could drain it and remove the bears. A group stepped in and spent a considerable amount of money digging ditches in the swamp. When that didn't work, they dug a small canal in a wooded area to the north of the swamp. Finally, they were able to drain it and transform it into a rich agricultural area. The bears left when their habitat disappeared. By the late 1800s, once unwanted swampland was selling for a hundred dollars an acre—good money in those days.

Big Bottom

In 1790, in the southeast part of the Northwest Territory, thirty-six settlers from the Ohio Company founded a community called Big Bottom. They built a wooden blockhouse and several cabins. The company, based in Marietta in 1788, was one of Ohio's early settlements. It sponsored Big Bottom and named it for the flood plain. On January 2, 1791, a group of Delaware and Wyandot warriors attacked Big Bottom, killing twelve people (including one woman and two children) and burning its blockhouse and cabins. This incident enraged the Americans and triggered a four-year war that the army referred to as the Miami campaign. It finally ended in 1794, when General Anthony Wayne defeated an Indian coalition at Fallen Timbers in what is now Lucas County. The Big Bottom massacre resulted in the signing of the Treaty of Greenville, which opened the Ohio country to settlement. In 1970, the massacre site was added to the National Register of Historic Places. Today, a twelve-foot marble obelisk marks the site, about one mile southeast of Stockport, in Morgan County's Windsor Township. Families now play at the Big Bottom State Park, where frontier families once died.

Chattanooga

Chattanooga is a ghost town on State Route 49 in northeast Mercer County. From 1895 to 1910, it was booming—the center of an oil strike in Liberty Township. Before the strike, about sixty people lived in town. Fast money attracted hundreds of men who fought, drank, and worked, in that order. "Those were wild days and women were afraid to be away from home alone, after dark," Mrs. Roy Pifer was quoted as saying in a 1961 county history. "My father exercised his own special kind of Christianity. Often a noisy, lost drunk would stagger into our yard. Father would quiet him and fix him a place on the porch to sleep off his drunkenness." By 1889, the town was growing so fast that it could employ a full-time undertaker, John Allmandinger. His first client was Jacob Baker, a sawmill operator who cut himself in half in a factory accident. A one-room school, appropriately named Wildcat School, met the needs of oil workers' children. One teacher taught ninety students, some of whom were eighteen years old and still in the seventh grade. With the oil workers came crime: A widow named Mrs. Emerick sold the oil rights to her farm and kept the money in her house; somebody broke in and murdered her, but no arrests were ever made. By 1900, Chattanooga's oil was nearly sucked dry and the wildcatters were moving over to Wood County and other areas with rich deposits. Chattanooga has not reawakened.

Christian Republic

In the 1850s, several socialistic or free love societies operated around Berlin Heights. The final one, the Christian Republic (also known as the Berlin Community), was founded in 1865 with a dozen adult members and six children. All but one member came from out of state. Officially, the Republic lasted one year, but a "Christian communist" group of some kind operated on the same grounds for a number of years. Members founded propaganda journals such as *Social Revolutionist, Age of Freedom, Good Time Coming,* the *New Republic,* the *Optimist,* and *Kingdom of Heaven.* They espoused an unusual blending of religion, politics, and socialism. An earlier version of *Age of Freedom* caused turmoil in 1858. According to a nineteenth-century historian, the magazine was "so obnoxious that twenty Berlin women seized the mail sack which Frank Barry, the editor, had brought on his shoulders to the post office, loaded with copies, and [the women] made a bonfire with them in the street."

Columbia Settlement

On November 18, 1788, Columbia became the first settlement in Hamilton County, founded on the Ohio River by Major Benjamin Stites and twenty-six men and women from New Jersey. The major had grand plans. He boasted that he would build a great city, for which he had purchased twenty-thousand acres at the mouth of the Little Miami River. The town consisted of a number of log homes, a stockade, and blockhouses. Settlers planted corn on the east side of the town, in an area called Turkey Bottom. One month after the pioneers arrived, another group landed at Yeatman's Cove. Led by Colonel Robert Patterson, they scrapped their wooden boats and built a settlement called Losantiville, meaning "town opposite the mouth of the Licking River." Losantiville grew into Cincinnati. Columbia Settlement was later known as East Cincinnati.

Compromise

Compromise, a ghost town in Champaign County in central Ohio, received its name literally—through a political compromise. The prairie town, on the Middle Fork of the Vermillion River, was founded by Isaac Moore in a little place of brush and timber called Buck Grove in 1830. He and his neighbors had been squatters there for several years, so they decided to make their residency official and start a town. Parts of two other small towns, Kerr and Rantoul, were absorbed into Compromise. The southwest part of the town was composed of mainly German immigrants. The local post office was called Flatville, reflecting the topography.

Crosswick

Crosswick is known as the home of the Crosswick Monster. In the mid-1800s, developers John and James Jennings created a paper town with twenty lots, at a location about a mile north of Waynesville in northern Warren County. They named the proposed community in honor of their hometown in New Jersey. Crosswick never was laid out, although some people had lived in the area as early as 1821. The most significant event to occur there came in 1885, when two local brothers, Ed and Joe Lynch, eleven and thirteen years old, were fishing in a local creek. They saw a large, scaly creature, thirty to forty feet long and about sixteen inches wide, emerging from a hollow sycamore tree. The monster had fangs and a forked tongue protruding from a big red mouth. The thing grabbed Ed with arms that came out of the bottom of its body. According to a story in the *Miami Gazette,* the monster stood erect and ran with the velocity of a racehorse. A minister, Jacob Horn, and two other men who had been working nearby pursued the thing as it attempted to drag the boy into the hollow place beneath the tree. "They scared the monster momentarily, and the boy got away," said Dennis Dalton, a Warren County historian. "Sixty men went back to hunt it and they chased it into a cave on Mill Run Creek. They dynamited the cave shut. When they went back later to unseal the cave and find the remains, it was empty. I talked to an old woman whose father, a local Quaker, saw the thing slither up an embankment and cross a railroad track on the day the boy was taken. His word is as good as anything to me. The boy was so frightened that he was scarred for life. He remained extremely quiet, and later moved to Indiana to get away from all the questioning."

Dogtown

In Licking County's Newark Township, Dogtown once existed on the north fork of the Licking River. The town never was much of a place. It burned dimly in the first part of the nineteenth century, then faded. The city of Newark now sits on top of old Dogtown. But it is not completely forgotten. According to local historians, the town took its name from a strange legend. The area where the town sat was long ago the home of creatures that were half human and half canine. They could talk *and* bark. For some reason, Ohioans of the 1800s had a fascination with naming their towns for dogs. In my travels I came across at least three other places called Dogtown, including one in Perry County. But only the Licking County community has the legend of the "weredog."

Eclipse

In 1901, a man named Jackson founded the Eclipse Mine in a rural area along State Route 33, near the Plains in Athens County. A company town grew and borrowed its name from the mine, whose nickname was Dog Town. At its peak in the 1920s, four hundred employees worked at the company mine and about twelve hundred people lived in the town. When the mine closed in the early 1940s, a local man named E. A. Cottingham bought the property. Company houses were basic wood-frame buildings—shotgun houses, each with four rooms in line with each other, including a kitchen and two bedrooms. Today, some of the old mine-related buildings still stand. So do thirteen miners' houses now owned by Eclipse Ltd., a business of five area people who operate the ghost town as a tourist colony called Eclipse Company Town. They rent out some of the houses as cabins for hikers on the Hocking-Adena Bike Trail. Other houses are occupied by artists, the Starvin' Wolf and Yellow Moon cafes, a holistic health center, the Buckeye Forest Council, the Eclipse Company Store, and a physician's office. Eclipse is three miles north of Athens.

Erastus

Erastus, a ghost town in Mercer County, is named after the owner of a general store. About 1890 the town was called Murphysboro, after the owner of a sawmill. The town also had a Methodist church, two tile mills, two general stores, a blacksmith shop, and other businesses. The farm town was dry, very dry, at least until a new resident opened a saloon. Farmers' wives strenuously objected; one day their disgust bubbled over and they grabbed axes and came into the saloon looking for trouble. The men ran. Frightened by the women's fervor, the owner left town and never returned. The saloon closed, and Murphysboro remained dry. A few years later, when the town asked the postal service to open a branch in town, the government told the people to select another name. Murphysboro was already being used by another town's post office. When the townspeople failed to decide the matter, the postal service chose a name for them—Erastus, after Erastus Walker, the general store owner who had filed the original application.

Fallsville

Fallsville was named for a falls in the area, and obviously not for John Timberlake, who founded the community in 1848. The town lies about six miles north of Hillsboro, the Highland County seat. Fallsville had three streets, Main, Mill, and Cross; eight houses; a Methodist church; and several businesses. Residents predicted big things for their community. They also spoke of buried treasure left by the Indians and witches who might roam the rural area outside of town. But no treasure was ever discovered, and Fallsville died of natural causes before the turn of the twentieth century.

Fort Rowdy

Fort Rowdy was built in 1793 by General Anthony Wayne's troops as they headed north into Indian country. With them they took some camp followers, including wives, peddlers, and wagon operators. On the east bank of Stillwater River in what is now Miami County, the troops erected an earthworks and log fortification on limestone bluffs overlooking the river. "After the fortification was completed, it was christened Fort Rowdy," historian R. L. Harmon wrote. "Local legend states that the ceremony concluded with the baptism of whiskey poured on the breastworks from the soldiers' canteens and a lively celebration followed. It is said the name Rowdy was derived from the behavior of the troops and camp followers; another less colorful explanation is that the site was named after an officer friend of General Wayne's named Rowdy." When the town was founded, leading citizens considered giving it the name Rowdy, but they decided that rowdy wasn't the proper image. Today, the town of Covington lies near the site of Fort Rowdy. The Fort Rowdy Gathering is held every fall at Covington Community Park on West U.S. Route 36.

Franklinton

On the sunny afternoon when I arrived in Franklinton in urban Columbus, I was surprised to see a black metal sign identifying the community as a historic place. Attractive blue banners hung from light poles, welcoming visitors to Franklinton. Of the nineteen larger Ohio towns of the Northwest Territory, including Cincinnati and Marietta, only Franklinton is a ghost town today. In 1797, Lucas Sullivant laid it out in Franklin Township in Franklin County, near Columbus. He established Gift Street, on which he offered lots to settlers for free if they would come there to live. People predicted great things for Franklinton. Pioneers traveling west stopped here on their long journey, and others stayed and took up farming and laboring. John Huffman set up a distillery on four acres in the area in 1801; he paid one gallon of whiskey for each acre. When Ohio became a state in 1803, Joseph Foos, who would become a general during the War of 1812, opened a brick hotel. Franklinton also had a jail and post office. As Columbus continued to expand, it engulfed Franklinton, which became a victim of early urban sprawl. After its post office closed in late 1834, the town lost its remaining identity.

Funk Bottoms

Funk Bottoms (not Funky Bottoms) is a ghost of pioneer Ohio: old-growth forest scattered across 206 acres. Visitors can see it from a 1.5-mile boardwalk trail; it is as though a slice of the old Ohio were singled out and saved as an outdoor museum piece. The entire Funk Bottoms wildlife area consists of 1,422 acres behind the Mohicanville flood-control dam in Wayne and Ashland counties. The ecosystem includes five-hundred-year-old trees, buttonbush swamps, and a variety of bird species. The place also shelters bald eagles, deer, many kinds of fish, pheasants, migratory birds, and, since 1985 the endangered (in Ohio) sandhill cranes. Ohio never was a good area for sandhills: At least two small flocks lived near Toledo and disappeared in the 1880s. Another flock near Huron disappeared in 1926. At the bottoms, the birds finally reproduced in 1987. The state began purchasing the bottoms to open a wildlife sanctuary in 1991. In 2000, state senator Bill Harris, an Ashland Republican, announced the budgeting of $72,000 to allow the state to purchase another twenty acres of bottoms that will help protect the wetland and wildlife habitat from development.

Grenadier Squaw Town

Grenadier Squaw Town, an old Shawnee community on Scippo Creek, was located between the Pickaway Plains and a heavily wooded area in what is now Pickaway County. The village was named for Nonhelema, a sister of Chief Cornstalk who stood six and a half feet tall. She was strong and intelligent. White people remarked that she carried herself like a grenadier, and the name stuck. After much bloodshed, she helped bring peace to the area in the 1700s. An Ohio historical marker at 4174 Emerson Road, near Circleville, commemorates her village. Her community included a council house and a gauntlet through which white prisoners were condemned to run. On a hill near the town, called the Burning Ground or the Burning Stake, prisoners were burned at the stake. Villagers had full view of its gruesome spectacles. Other small Indian towns in the area could also see the Burning Ground. Across from the creek, Black Mountain was a ridge that rose about 150 feet above the prairie. From this place the Indians could watch their enemies approaching. Another dubious distinction of Grenadier Squaw Town: A man named Slover, who was taken prisoner at Crawford's Defeat in 1782, escaped from his captors. The Indians had stripped him naked and tortured him, but they stopped when the skies suddenly erupted in thunder and lightning. Tribal leaders thought the Great Spirit was trying to send them a message, so they tied up Slover and locked him in a house. They decided to kill him the next day. All night he worked at untying his bonds. A guard taunted him: "How would you like to eat fire?" Later that night, after the Indian guards had fallen asleep, Slover freed himself, stole a horse, and rode off. When the horse gave out, Slover walked through nettles, brush, briars, and thorns. Mosquitoes bit him hundreds of times. When he arrived home, "he had more the appearance of a mass of raw flesh than an animated human being," historian Henry Howe wrote in 1888.

The Harrison Tunnel

The Harrison Tunnel, on South Miami Avenue in Cleves, was filled with silt when I visited, but I did find an Ohio historical marker that explained the tunnel's history. Made of sandstone and brick, the tunnel is a part of the defunct Cincinnati and Whitewater Canal, which opened in the early 1840s to connect the markets of southern Indiana with downtown Cincinnati. City merchants lobbied for the twenty-five mile extension of the Whitewater, which ended in Lawrenceburg, Indiana. They feared that their business would suffer without a connection to the canal. During construction, the project engineer saved money by building a canal tunnel instead of a series of locks. The tunnel ran 1,782 feet from Cleves to North Bend and was 24 feet wide at the waterline. The center arch was 20 feet from the canal bottom. "The tunnel was unusual," said Bob Mueller of the Ohio Canal Society. "Only two canals in Ohio that I know of, both in the northeast, have tunnels anything like this. The Cincinnati and Whitewater Canal didn't last too long—it closed in the 1860s—but it had a lot of business in its heyday in the 1840s and early 1850s." The tunnel is also called the Harrison Tunnel because President William Henry Harrison of North Bend believed in the canal and bought stock in it. He sold a part of his farm for the right-of-way and provided clay to manufacture an estimated two million bricks that were used in construction. On March 31, 1838, the steamer *Moselle* brought passengers from Cincinnati for the groundbreaking ceremony. In 2003 the village of Cleves planned to build a thirteen-acre park around the tunnel.

Hartford

Hartford, on the Auglaize River and the old Defiance Trail, was platted in 1828 on about seventy-two acres in Allen County. It had a tannery, miller, trading post, school, boat yard, and tavern. When word of the Miami and Erie Canal made the rounds of the area, Hartford momentarily boomed. Four doctors moved to town. The population tripled. One hundred and fifty new lots were sold. Founders didn't hide their hopes that the town could be a stop on the canal. To demonstrate their faith, they renamed the community New Hartford and hoped for some good luck. Unfortunately, when the construction dust settled, the canal missed Hartford by two miles. The distance might as well have been two hundred miles, for it was enough to cause the town to fail. Still seeking to change their luck, residents renamed their town Gallatin in 1839, to avoid confusion with another Hartford in Ohio. In 1840, Gallatin had fifty-nine adult residents, but by 1866, most of them had died or moved. Today, all that remains is the Hartford Christian Church, a cemetery, and unfulfilled dreams of wealth and success.

Hemlock

Hemlock is one of my favorite town names. It is in eastern Saltlick Township in Perry County, and it once included a post office, a general store, woolen mill, and a number of houses. When the coal boom declined in the early 1900s, Hemlock started its slow fall. No word on how it was named. I stopped there in 2003 and found a number of closed businesses, a few homes still hanging on, and a small, messy town park. A historic Church of Christ sits on a hill overlooking the town. Hemlock is a ghost town in the making.

Hobson's Choice

From May 9 to October 7, 1793, General Anthony Wayne drilled his troops, prepared for war, and accumulated supplies at a place called Hobson's Choice. The military camp received its name from a seventeenth-century English liveryman who refused to give customers their horse of choice and instead always gave them the horse nearest to the stable door. The site is near Fourth and Mound Streets in Cincinnati. What is today a ghost camp became a small community, in that soldiers and their families lived there for months. (The soldiers couldn't train near Fort Washington because of flooding.) After the men marched north, toward eventual victory at the Battle of Fallen Timbers on August 20, 1794, Hobson's Choice was abandoned, its land absorbed into the city.

Jacksonville

They should have named this town Old Hickoryville, but Jacksonville sufficed. Named after Andrew Jackson, Jacksonville was on the Chillicothe Turnpike on Brush Creek Hill in Adams County. Seaman historian Stephen Kelley said the town received its name because Jackson used to take the road from Tennessee to Washington, D.C., in the years before he became president. His visits made him a popular figure in Adams County. In 1815, William Thomas laid out the town and named it. Jacksonville established a post office, with James Dunbar as postmaster. Jacksonville's fortunes soon declined, and by 1827 the post office was closed. Later, it reopened as the Dunbarton Post Office, but by then fate had already dealt Jacksonville a mortal blow: the railroad selected the new town of Peebles as a stop, leaving Jacksonville in the dust of history.

Miami

Shortly after the pioneer land speculator John Cleves Symmes landed at what would become North Bend on the Ohio River in 1789, he began having bigger dreams for his part of rugged Hamilton County. He predicted that little North Bend would become "the Eygpt of the Miami," referring to the Great Miami River, which flowed into the larger river nearby. To realize his dream, he planned another town, which he called Miami, to link with North Bend on a one-and-a-half-mile strip that led to the Great Miami. But hilly land prevented the founders from fully developing their town. In a few years, all talk of it had died, and Symmes was worried about his personal finances. Miami became a ghost town. Symmes died broke.

Middlebury

Middlebury, a ghost town in Van Wert County's Harrison Township, started as Daisie on November 10, 1850. What's left of it is at the intersection of Willshire–Harrison Center Road and Van Wert–Decatur Road. The town peaked at the turn of the twentieth century, before rural free delivery made Middlebury's—and many other small towns' post offices—obsolete. In 1899, Middlebury was a booming agricultural town with its own doctors, barbers, Grange hall, saloons, growing stores, blacksmiths, and twenty-one houses. But the times conspired against Middlebury and its kind. Prohibition closed the saloon in 1919. As people moved out of town, other businesses closed through the 1940s. Middlebury became just another example of America's fading rural heritage.

Newport

This is the *other* Newport—not Sin City, Kentucky. James Kirkpatrick laid it out in 1819 at the west fork of the Ohio Brush Creek in Adams County. In 1869, a post office named Wilson (honoring Congressman John T. Wilson) opened in Newport. Presumably some people thought that the town might change its name to Wilson; after all, he had been a prominent conductor on the Underground Railroad and a captain in the Union infantry during the Civil War. Later, he opened a children's home in his county. But Newport's name was never changed officially. The railroad arrived and, for a brief time, gave hope for a future. Prosperity didn't last, however, and today Newport is a ghost town.

New Rome

New Rome is Ohio's most hated ghost town. The former village, seven miles west of Columbus, was for years a notorious speed trap. The *Columbus Dispatch* called it "the per-capita corruption capital of Ohio." *Car and Driver* called New Rome "a little police state." Attorney General Jim Petro said, "New Rome made government look bad." As the community was overcome by urban sprawl, 46 percent of its population left in ten years. By 2000, only sixty people remained and the town consisted of about ten homes, three small apartment buildings, and several businesses. But officers continued to write tickets as though the community were a large city. Tickets generated more than $300,000 annually, and the town's sole traffic signal was used to help catch unsuspecting motorists. By then, New Rome had shriveled to a size of only three blocks long and three wide, including the infamous thousand-foot stretch of West Broad Street—the old U.S. 40. Before motorists realized it, the speed limit decreased from 45 mph to 35 mph, and they were busted. The price for driving 42 mph in a 35-mph zone on West Broad was ninety dollars. Naturally, the tickets infuriated commuters who didn't even realize that New Rome existed.

The town didn't have much of a history until its later years. It was founded as Rome in the late 1830s near Alton, another town on the National Road. Alton attracted most of the new people and businesses. *The History of Franklin and Pickaway Counties* said of Rome in the late 1800s: "Its classic name did not draw any considerable number to dwell therein, and whatever glory may have gathered about this point has assuredly departed from it." In 1941, officials changed the name to New Rome and incorporated the community. In 1947, New Rome officials discovered that big money could be made in the ticket business. By 1975, New Rome was known as Ohio's worst speed trap. In 1997, state inspectors condemned the town hall, forcing town officials to move into a trailer. But the police continued to write tickets. Driver Jim Bussey became so upset that he created his own Web site, www. newromesucks.com, to publish unflattering photographs and stories about the village. In November 2001, Jamie Mueller quietly ran for mayor and staged a New Roman coup d'état, winning all six votes that were cast. He tried to eliminate the police department for two years, and then Attorney General Jim Petro filed suit to dissolve the town. In November 2003, a new state law, aimed specifically at New Rome, allowed the state to request dissolution if towns of fewer than 150 residents declare a fiscal emergency for three straight years. When I drove through New Rome on a summer day in 2004, I made sure I didn't exceed the speed limit. By then, though, New Rome police had already stopped writing tickets. The town was finally dissolved on September 8, 2004, when New Rome became a part of Prairie Township. Bussey celebrated that day by writing on his Web site: "New Rome, Traffic Trap, 1947–2004: Rotten for Years, Buried at Last."

Peach Grove

Peach Grove, the epitome of rural life in the early 1900s, was a community on Springdale Road near Blue Rock Road in Hamilton County's Colerain Township. This was before development invaded the area and made Colerain the state's largest township—in size and population. The name Peach Grove lingered into the early 1900s, but today few people know of it, and the area is the antithesis of peach groves—a place filled with shopping strips and subdivisions. The name came from the community's peach orchards, planted by German immigrants in the mid-1800s. When I interviewed an apple farmer in Dearborn County, Indiana, he quickly identified his hometown—Peach Grove. He claimed he was forced to move across the state line to find land suitable for his apple and peach orchards and said the people from Peach Grove had something in their blood that enabled them to successfully grow fruit. Today, all they grow there are traffic jams and soccer matches.

Pine Hill

Pine Hill was a wooded area where some pioneers lived in Saltcreek Township, Wayne County, in 1811. William Searight, an Irish immigrant, lived there in a cabin with his wife, the former Jane Johnson, and their two children. Friends described him as a "monarch of all he surveyed." After the War of 1812 ended, killings resumed in the wilderness, the work of some Indians and pro-British forces. For protection, Searight moved his family into a blockhouse in neighboring Holmes County's Prairie Township. They remained there until the fighting subsided. According to Wayne County history, an elderly Indian chief was visited the blockhouse one day and told Mrs. Searight that he had "cut out the tongues of ninety-nine women, and wanted *hers* to make the even 100." She was not impressed.

Pickleville

In the early 1800s, settlers in Hamilton County founded O'Banionville. James Loveland owned the general store. The town also had two blacksmith shops, an inn, a post office and a wool-carding factory. By 1830, a subdivision was planned, but promoter Colonel William Ramsey heard about a rail line coming through, and changed his mind about houses. He envisioned bigger things for the town. Unfortunately, the arrival of the Marietta (Baltimore and Ohio) Railroad had the opposite effect on O'Banionville. It became a mere flag stop, while Loveland, the subdivision, outgrew its parent town. When the post office was moved to the growing Loveland, O'Banionville started to die. Perhaps to attract better luck, residents started calling it Pickleville, in honor of A. C. Pickleheimer, who operated a local stone quarry and shipping company. By this time, however, fate could not be stopped. Pickleville died by 1920. Today, O'Bannionville is indistinguishable from Loveland. Only a few homes remain.

Post Boy

This tiny community near Newcomerstown was tagged Post Boy after a boy was killed there in the 1820s. For years a wooden sign marked the place, which is gone now but not forgotten. "I remember my father-in-law telling about the spot called Post Boy," said Winona Wherley of Stone Creek. "It seems they were about to hang the wrong man [for the murder] when a spectator saw John Funston in the crowd—and they got him." Funston was hanged at the corner of West High and 6th Street in New Philadelphia on December 30, 1825. For a century, Post Boy retained its macabre name, until it, too, was dead.

Providence

Providence was an ironically named town in Lucas County. (Providence was not kind to Providence.) In the 1840s, when traffic boomed on the Miami and Erie Canal and the Maumee River, Providence had five hotels to accommodate all the travelers. People from Michigan came there to relax. The boom continued when the railroads came and when oil was discovered in the area. In the early 1900s, however, life in Providence slipped into slow motion. When the automobile arrived and the road system improved, travelers no longer needed to go through Providence. My friend Joseph Donnermeyer, a professor of rural sociology at Ohio State University and a fellow back-roads traveler, believes these are the best and the worst of times for modern small towns, depending on their individual situations. Providence is a good example. "Towns tied to urban economies are doing well," he told me. "Those towns that aren't around the urban areas are usually doing poorly. They have no economic base. Towns near growing suburban areas have a chance but the ones farther away have a difficult time. Rural towns in Ohio aren't ever going to be what they used to be. Some are hurting. Kids don't come back. The economy is stagnant. Many towns don't survive."

Richardville Indian Reservation

In the early 1800s, Miami chief Jean Baptiste Richardville, his four wives (Golden Leaf, Little Fan, Little Tree, and Martha), and their family lived on 1,380 acres between Wren and Willshire and the St. Mary's River. The tract ran along the present State Route 49 and extended into Indiana. Richardville, whose Indian name was Pechewa, led the Miami tribe from 1815 until his death in 1841. Supposedly he was a nephew of Little Turtle, the Miami chief who fought General Anthony Wayne in the 1790s. Richardville signed the Treaty of St. Mary's in 1818 and received from the federal government about 12,800 acres for the tribe. His personal land was near Wren; it included a new brick house. The larger tract was divided into sections for Richardville's family and other prominent Indians. About a hundred tribe members lived on the reservation in Van Wert County; it was a good place for hunting. He lived there until his death at age eighty-one, when he was buried in Fort Wayne. Through the years, his descendants lived on the reservation, which eventually was split up and sold and became farm country. A bronze plaque on a large stone marks the site of the reservation, near Route 49.

Rossville

Rossville, named for Senator James Ross of Pennsylvania (1762–1847), developed on the west side of the Great Miami River, across from Hamilton in Butler County. Founders John Sutherland, Henry Brown, Jacob Burnet, James Smith, and William Ruffin planned Rossville as a port from which goods could be shipped down the river to the Ohio, and on to the Mississippi. The community grew steadily, connected to Hamilton by ferries. On September 3, 1841, the town council adopted Rossville's seal, a circular one featuring the image of an eagle. By 1850, Rossville had 1,447 residents. In 1854, voters united both communities into a single town, Hamilton, and Rossville became its western neighborhood—and thus a ghost town. In 1866, a double-lane covered bridge was built to connect the two places. In those days, Rossville's Baptist church gained a reputation for being haunted. According to Butler County historian Jim Blount, "There persisted a story that the place of worship was haunted by the ghost of a headless woman. As late as the 1880s, some people claimed to have seen her frightening form in the church." The church was torn down in the early 1900s. A Rossville branch of the Hamilton Post Office opened in 1879, in a store at the corner of Main and B Streets. For years, the west side movie theater was called the Rossville. A few other reminders of the old name are evident, but these days, most reminders of Rossville are gone. The Rossville Historic District consists of nineteenth-century homes and commercial buildings.

Salem Heights

No witches lived in Salem Heights—at least none who ever admitted to practicing the old black magic. Instead, the lives of its people centered around a Methodist church that was organized in 1805. When I arrived in this ghost town at the intersection of Salem and Sutton Roads in Hamilton County's Anderson Township, I didn't even realize it once existed. Then I read the historical marker that stands in front of the church: "Families of Salem settlement first held services in Francis McCormick's log house. A log church was built here in 1810 on land McCormick gave for religious and educational purposes. A new brick church was constructed in 1825. In 1863, the existing church was built, the bricks from the second church being used for the education building next door."

Today, the settlement is built over by 1940s and 1950s brick and wood ranch homes and Cape Cods. About a dozen newer homes stand behind the church—the Ashton Grove subdivision. The church is striking in its simplicity: wood frame, painted gray, with white trim, but the interior is as new as the latest fad. I peeked inside and saw the sanctuary filled with small round tables; it looked like a restaurant. The altar area contained a set of drums, a piano, and other musical instruments. Clearly, this was a modern United Methodist church, despite the building's age. "It's such a contrast to what you seen on the outside, but the style is really in character with the history of the church," the Reverend

John Larsen told me. "We have a contemporary congregation. We have a big screen, all high-tech. We have a live, big band. Pretty upbeat. Things get moving nicely. Our small, nightclub tables were not put here by design. We had a nonalcoholic Margaritaville night, and we brought the tables in for only that weekend. The moving men decided not to remove them until Monday, so when the congregation showed up for services on Sunday, they had to sit at the tables. That caused quite a stir. Because of the casual nature of the church, the people actually loved the tables—they wouldn't let them be removed. The style is in keeping with the church's founder, who wanted a modern church in those early days."

Judging by the cemetery next door, I wouldn't have guessed that anything modern ever happened here. The old headstones are weathered and oddly shaped. I walked through on a cold February day; my cheap pen froze in the freezing wind. Names on the stones include Hannah Miller, who died in 1837 at age twenty-one; Ralph Thompson, a Kentucky native who died at age fifty in 1844; and Benjamin Thompson, who came from Pennsylvania and died at age twenty-eight in 1819. On the white, wooden front door are two brass plaques, identifying the place as site No. 267 on the National Register of Historic Places. These days, the church is about all that's left of Salem. Over the years the town died, and a neighborhood rose on top of it. I don't think many people even noticed its passing. Now, it is just another forgotten place in a suburban township and a reminder of genealogical roots and religious convictions.

Saltair

With a name like this, you'd think the town would be near the ocean. But it's at State Routes 222 and 232 in Clermont County's Tate Township. Saltair never had anything to do with salt or air: It was named for the founding family, the Salts, whose name originally came from a big estate in England, named Salt Aire. According to county historians, Edward Salt came to the remote area that is now Clermont County in 1796. After fighting for the colonies in the Revolutionary War, he decided to come to the western frontier. A little community took his last name. Today, it is a ghost town, although some homes are scattered around the area.

Shasta

The name of this Van Wert County town sounds more like a 1970s soft drink than a community. Actually, it was named after another town that was named after the Shasta plant. In the 1880s, our Shasta was a town with limited promise in Liberty Township. For a town of fewer than a hundred people when it started, Shasta was well equipped with an express office, rail depot, and a post office. The town was also referred to as Shasta Station, because the trains ran through it. John A. Smith had the vision for Shasta, which he named for a town and county in California. Nobody knows much about Smith. Did he live in California earlier? (Interestingly, Shasta County, California, is today the home of a number of ghost towns, including Cottonwood, French Town, and, my favorite, Bulgin' Gulch.) Smith lived adjacent to his new town and oversaw the development of a sawmill, a post office (it used the Shasta name), and several houses. But when the hardy pioneers of the county cut down the trees and turned the area into farmland, there wasn't a need for a sawmill. Shasta faded into the barely visible place that it is today.

Snaketown

This Shawnee ghost town existed from about 1789 to 1794, when General Anthony Wayne's troops defeated an Indian coalition at the Battle of Fallen Timbers. The Indians abandoned Snaketown when Wayne marched toward their village. The place was named for a chief named Captain Snake, a moniker that conjures up all sorts of negative images of torture and death. Yet little is known about the man. His town later became another town named Florida, in Henry County's Flatrock Township. It is now a ghost town too. A marker stands on the site, recognizing both towns.

Squawtown

Squawtown, a ghost town in Licking County's Washington Township, took its name from a horrifying incident. By the early 1800s, the Indians had moved farther north and west when the pioneers settled in the area. As historian N. N. Hill explained in 1881: "The general feeling between the whites and Indians at that time was one of peace, with an occasional exception among the pioneers of some who had suffered in the earlier Indian wars from their peculiar mode of warfare. There were a few whose deadly hatred could only leave them with their breath [in death]." The Squawtown tragedy is an example. The community, two miles east of Utica, was the scene of a tragic shooting. Three white men played cards to decide which one would shoot a certain Indian woman. Nobody knew why the men wanted to kill her. A Mr. McLean was later convicted of the shooting and received only two years in prison. Some people of the time claimed he was pardoned a short time before his sentence had been served and that he died soon after his pardon. Another account is that when he left prison, a prison official asked him to reveal the name of the man who pulled the trigger. McLean replied, "I am innocent, but I have suffered; one is enough to suffer, and I decline to tell." Soon the town in which the shooting occurred became known as Squawtown. Today it is gone.

Tobasco

Nothing saucy ever happened here—that historians recorded, that is. They believe the name originated in September 1865, when Buckeye generals and Civil War heroes Ulysses S. Grant and William T. Sherman and their wives were traveling east on the Ohio Turnpike (State Route 125) to visit Grant's relatives in Clermont County. When they passed through a small community, admirers approached their carriage and asked Grant to speak. On that hot day, Grant is said to have removed his jacket and remarked, "It is as hot as Tabasco sauce today." The veterans who heard him never forgot the general's words; when the town established a post office in March 1878, they listed the town's name (spelled incorrectly) as Tobasco. These days, nothing remains of Tobasco but a name. It is a part of a large suburban area filled with subdivisions and shopping strips at Route 125 and Interstate 275 in Union Township.

210 Row

This is the only ghost town that I know of with a number in its name, but there could be others. This one was a little town near Peach Ridge in Athens County. Even the local historical society can provide little information on 210 Row, which sounds like a mining-company town.

When I went looking for it, I found no town sign and no indication that the place ever existed. All I noticed were several mobile homes. The town is on some old maps, however, as well as in the modern *Ohio Atlas and Gazetteer*. It is near State Route 550.

Walhonding

In 1841, William K. Johnson, G. W. Sullivan, and T. S. Humrickhouse platted the town of Walhonding in Coshocton County, when it was a new stop on the Walhonding Canal. They founded the community with hope that Walhonding would become the county seat of a proposed Walhonding County, then under consideration by the Ohio legislature. The proposed county was to be carved from parts of Coshocton, Knox, Holmes, Muskingum, and Licking Counties. Unfortunately for Walhonding, the issue failed by one vote. At the time, the town, population eighty, consisted of two stores, two blacksmiths, a foundry, a post office, and a flour mill that turned out eighty barrels of flour a day. One vote meant oblivion.

White Eyes Town

White Eyes Town, a Delaware Indian ghost town from the 1700s, stood about two miles east of West Lafayette in Tuscarawas County. The town consisted of three large houses in 1775. The community leader was a man named Captain White Eyes. A pioneer named Cresswell wrote on August 28, 1775: "Lodged at White-Eye's Town . . . Kindly treated at a Dutch Blacksmith's, who lives with an Indian Squaw. Got a very hearty supper of a sort of Dumplings made of Indian Meal and dried Huckleberries which serves instead of currants. Dirty people, find it impossible to keep myself free from lice. Very disagreeable companions." The community disappeared in the early 1780s, possibly after another—and final—serving of the blacksmith's dirty "currants."

Bibliography

"Adams County History: Meigs Township." www.scioto.org (December 30, 2003).

Aversa, Jeannine. "Manufacturing Falters in December." *Hamilton Journal-News,* January 18, 2003.

Bartels, Steve. "Ohio Continues to Lose Prime Farmland." *Hamilton Journal-News,* November 18, 2002.

Bauer, Cheryl, and Randy McNutt. "Fizzleville, U.S.A." *Ohio Southland* (Spring 1990).

Beavercreek Chronicles: History and Remembrances. Beavercreek, Ohio: Beavercreek Bicentennial Historical Committee, 1976.

Bell, Clayton, and Daniel Bensen. "Perdition Lost: The Great Black Swamp of Eastern North America." www.bowdoin.edu/~dbensen/Spec/Swamp.html (January 9, 2004).

Beller, Janet Brock, and Maxine Elliott Nason. *Loveland: Passages through Time.* Loveland, Ohio: Greater Loveland History Society, 1992.

Blackmar, Frank W. *Kansas: A Cyclopedia of State History.* Chicago: Standard Publishing Company, 1912.

Blount, Jim. "Ross Named for Popular Pennsylvania Senator." *Hamilton Journal-News,* December 18, 2002.

———. *Rossville: Hamilton's West Bank.* Hamilton: Past/Present/Press, 1994.

Cayton, Andrew R. L. *Ohio: The History of a People.* Columbus: Ohio State University Press, 2002.

Centennial Anniversary of the City of Hamilton, Ohio. Privately published, 1891.

Cincinnati in Bronze. Cincinnati, Ohio: Child Health Associates, 1959.

"Civil War Soldiers Trained at Ohio State Reformatory." *Mansfield News-Journal,* May 24, 1970.

Clark, John R. "Hamilton Landmark Returns." *Cincinnati Enquirer,* March 7, 1991.

Collins, Paul. *Banvard's Folly: Thirteen Tales of Renowned Obscurity, Famous Anonymity, and Rotten Luck.* New York: Picador USA, 2001.

Crout, George. "Venice: The Goddess of Love?" *Hamilton Journal-News,* May 22, 1991.

Douglass, Ben. *History of Wayne County, Ohio.* Indianapolis, Ind.: Robert Douglass, 1878.

Elwood, P. H. *Scenic and Historic Ohio.* Columbus: Ohio Archaeological and Historical Society, 1925.

Fleischman, John. "The Heart of Flatness." *Ohio Magazine* (October 1994).

Gilmore, Helen Dehlia. *The History of the John Randolph Freed Slaves Who Settled in Miami and Shelby Counties.* Piqua, Ohio: Rossville-Springcreek Historical Society, 1984.

Gurney, Alan. *The Race to the White Continent: Voyages to the Antarctic.* New York: W. W. Norton, 2000.

Hagedorn, Ann. *Beyond the River: The Untold Story of the Heroes of the Underground Railroad.* New York: Simon & Schuster, 2000.

Hannah, Jim. "Neglect Endangers Many Ohio Sites." *Cincinnati Enquirer,* January 4, 2003.

Harmon, R. L. *Fort Rowdy Gathering.* Brochure. Miami County (Ohio) Visitors and Convention Bureau, 2003.

Helwig, Richard M. *Ohio Ghost Towns No. 11.* Galena: Center for Ghost Town Research in Ohio, 1988.

———. *Ohio Ghost Towns No. 53.* Galena: Center for Ghost Town Research in Ohio, 1988.

——— and Dr. James Nagel. *Ghost Towns of Northwestern Ohio.* Archibald, Ohio: Northwest Technical College, 1976.

Henson, Josiah. *Truth Stranger than Fiction: Father Henson's Story of His Life.* Boston: John P. Jewett, 1858.

Hill, N. N., Jr. *History of Licking County, Ohio.* Newark: A. A. Graham, 1881.

Hinchey, Frank. "Town-Gown Tension Has Long History in Athens County." *Columbus Dispatch,* September 21, 2002.

Historical Collections of the Mahoning Valley. Vol. 1. Youngstown, Ohio: Mahoning Valley Historical Society, 1876.

History and Biographical Cyclopaedia of Butler County, Ohio. Cincinnati: Western Biographical Publishing, 1882.

History of Ashtabula County. Chicago: L. Baskin, 1880.

History of Ross and Highland Counties, Ohio. Cleveland: H. Z. Williams and Brothers, 1882.

History of Springdale, Ohio. www.springdale.org/history/spring7.html (January 6, 2004).

History of Van Wert and Mercer Counties. Wapakoneta: R. Sutton, 1882.

History of Warren County, Ohio. Chicago: W. H. Beers, 1882.

Hoeken, William T. *The Black Swamp and Its Effect on the Development of Northwestern Ohio.* Van Wert, Ohio: Van Wert Public Library, 1962.

"Horse Owners Warned to Watch for Rustlers." *Cincinnati Enquirer,* December 12, 2002.

Horstman, Barry M. "Dr. E. Lucy Braun: She Crusaded for Conservation." *Cincinnati Post,* September 27, 1999.

Howe, Henry. *Historical Collections of Ohio.* Vols. 1 and 2. Columbus: State of Ohio, 1898.

"It Is a Hollow World." *Pittsburgh Dispatch,* February 9, 1896. www.ku-prism.org/hollowworld (February 2, 2003).

Jacoby, Wilbur J. *History of Marion County, Ohio.* Chicago: Standard Publishing Company, 1907.

Jorgensen, Bruce. "Mt. Nebo: Cultists' Crest." *Athens* (Fall 1973).

Katz, Michael Jay. *Buckeye Legends: Folktales and Lore from Ohio.* Ann Arbor: University of Michigan Press, 1994.

Kelley, Stephen. "Fizzleville Remembered." *Ohio Southland* (Spring 1990).

———. *Mineral Springs, Adams County, Ohio.* Seaman, Ohio: Kelley Publications, 1980.

Kinney, Ken. "Black Swamp Once Ruled the Land and People." *Bowling Green Sentinel Tribune,* June 10, 1999.

Kinney, Terry. "Museums Must Fend for Themselves; Rely on Volunteers, Local Donations." *Cincinnati Enquirer,* January 4, 2003.

Knoop, Jeffrey. "At the Edge." *Ohio Southland* (Spring 1989).

Lake County Historical Society. *Here Is Lake County, Ohio.* Cleveland: Howard Allen, 1964.

Landmarks of Historical Montgomery. Montgomery, Ohio: City of Montgomery, 1994.

"Land of the Cross-Tipped Churches." www.Grandlake.net/lctc/ (January 5, 2003).

Leifeit, Drew. "Amish Keep in Touch Through Newspapers." www.truth-news.net/culture/2001-05-amish.html (May 17, 2001).

Let's Explore Ohio. Columbus: Standard Oil Company, 1961.

Maloney, Alicia. "Symmes Monument to Return Soon." *Hamilton Journal-News,* March 5, 1991.

"Many Roadside Attractions in Area: John Cleves Symmes Monument One of Hidden Treasures Offered in Ohio." *Cincinnati Enquirer,* December 12, 1996.

"Marking Milestone." *Hamilton Journal-News,* October 10, 2003.

McBride, James. *Pioneer Biography.* Vol. 2. Hamilton, Ohio: Lane Public Library, 1984.

McNair, James. "Wanted: Innovation." *Cincinnati Enquirer,* January 19, 2003.

McNutt, Randy. "The Dead—Hot on Tour Again." *Cincinnati Enquirer,* October 25, 2000.

———. "Every Ghost Has a Story as Halloween Nears." *Cincinnati Enquirer,* October 28, 2001.

———. *Ghosts: Ohio's Haunted Landscapes, Lost Arts, and Forgotten Places.* Wilmington: Orange Frazer Press, 1996.

———. "Town Boasts of 'Most Haunted Street.'" *Cincinnati Enquirer,* October 31, 1991.

"Mt. Nebo," *Athens Herald,* November 2, 1871.

Mollenkopf, Jim. *The Great Black Swamp: Historical Tales of 19th-Century Northwest Ohio.* Toledo, Ohio: Lake of the Cat, 1999.

Mulford, Robert. "Civil War Episode in Colerain Township." *Venice Graphic,* September 9, 1887.

Ohio Atlas and Gazetteer. Yarmouth, Maine: DeLorme, 1999.

"Ohio Farmland Yielding to Development." *Hamilton Journal-News,* January 30, 2003.

"Ohio's Historic Zoar Village." Brochure, Zoar Community Association, 2003.

"One More Strange Tale." *Athens* (Fall 1973).

Perry, Dick. *Ohio: A Personal Portrait of the Seventeenth State.* New York: Doubleday, 1969.

Perry, Lisa. "Piqua Cemetery Rich in Slave History." *Dayton Daily News,* May 28, 1997.

Peters' Athens County. Athens, Ohio: Athens County Historical Society. Date and publisher unknown.

Phillips, Rob. "State Buying Development Rights." *Cincinnati Enquirer,* January 25, 2003.

Plumber, Elizabeth L. "Glacier Left Black Swamp." *Bowling Green Sentinel Tribune,* September 8, 1977.

Pohlen, Jerome. *Oddball Ohio: A Guide to Some Really Strange Places.* Chicago: Chicago Review Press, 2004.

Price, Don H. *History of Paulding County, Ohio.* Paulding: Privately published, 1975.

Radel, Cliff. "Squeaky-Clean Queen City Once Had 3,000 Speakeasies." *Cincinnati Enquirer,* January 11, 2004.

Rayner, John. *The First Century of Piqua, Ohio.* Piqua: Magee Brothers, 1916.

Reiner, Martha S. *Sesquicentennial Quilt of the Venice Presbyterian Church, 1828–1978.* Ross, Ohio: Venice Presbyterian Church, 1978.

Richardson, Dorothy. "The Marrying Squires of Aberdeen." *Louisville Courier-Journal,* August 4, 1897.

"Roadside Attractions You May Have Missed." *Cincinnati Enquirer,* December 8, 1996.

"Romantic Gretna Green and the Scottish Marriage." www.gretnaweddings. com (February 6, 2003).

Rutledge, Mike. "Legacy Returns to Park." *Hamilton Journal-News,* March 12, 1991.

Sallah, Michael D. "Vanishing Ohio Farmland." *Toledo Blade,* August 17, 1997.

Sandler, Martin. *This Was America.* Boston: Little, Brown & Company, 1980.

"Simzee." www.bonstemps.com/Symmes.Simzee.htm (February 2, 2003).

Speidel, Sandy. "Strange Tales of a Strange Town." *Athens* (Fall 1973).

"Spiritualists Wrong, Mt. Nebo Not Closest to God." *Athens News,* May 17, 1975.

Strafford, Jay. "The Legend of Peach Ridge." *Athens* (Spring 1972).

Stuart, Nancy Rubin. "The Raps Heard Round the World." *American History* (August 2005).

Swickard, Lisa. "When the Mediums Became Large." *Zig Zag* (October 1998).

Switzer, John. "History Books Offer Little on New Rome." *Columbus Dispatch,* February 8, 2002.

Turner, Violet. "From Gangster to Governor: The Ever Popular Story of Highland County's Jesse James." *Ohio Southland* 3 (1991).

"Underground Railroad in Erie County, Ohio." www.sanduskyohiocedarpoint.com/underground/ (October 21, 2003).

"Villages Disolution Final Now." *Hamilton Journal-News,* September 9, 2004.

Volgenau, Gerry. "Castle of Doom: Abandoned Prison Stirs Ghostly Excitement." *Detroit Free Press,* October 13, 2003.

Whitford, Linda. "Descendants of George Shelton." http://www.ssimicro. com/~xlindag/First%20Families%20of%20Brown%20County,%20Ohio %20-Shelton.htm (February 3, 2003).

Wilhelm, Peter. "Draining the Great Black Swamp: Henry and Wood Counties, Ohio; A Case Study in Agricultural Development." M.A. thesis, Bowling Green State University, August 1983.

Williams, William H. *History of Ashtabula County, Ohio.* Philadelphia: Williams Brothers, 1878.

Wilson, James Grant, and John Fiske. *Appleton's Cyclopedia of American Biography.* New York: Appleton, 1887.

Wimberg, Robert J. *Cincinnati Breweries.* Cincinnati: Ohio Book Store, 1997.

Zoar: An Ohio Experiment in Communalism. Columbus: Ohio Historical Society, 1997.

Index

Brunersburg (Paulding County), 126
Brushy Fork Creek, gold in, 169
Budget (newspaper), 147–54
Burnet, Jacob, 196
business, and farmers, 17
Bussey, Jim, 193–94
Buster the dog, 142–43
Butler, Charles, 23
Butler, John S., 118
Butler County, 162; towns of, 27–32,
  196–97
Butterfield, Jeremiah, 28–29
Byrd, Richard E., 63–64

Camp Bartley (later Camp Mansfield), 91
canals, 182; effects on towns, 189–90, 195;
  as industry, 69–70, 72, 125
Canfield, Dwight R., 122
Carpenter, L. B., 23
Carr, James, 123
Cayton, Andrew, 138
Champaign County, 184
Chapman, Gertrude M., 24
Chattanooga (Mercer County), 183
Chic-Chic the rooster, 141–42
cholera, 24
Christian Republic, 183–84
Cincinnati, 60; breweries in, 49–50, 169;
  canal to Indiana from, 189–90; towns
  absorbed by, 184, 191
Cincinnati and Eastern Railroad, 44
Cincinnati and Whitewater Canal,
  189–90
Civil War, 20, 29–30, 91
Clark, Benjamin, 29
Clermont County, 167–71, 198, 200
Cleves, Harrison Tunnel in, 189–90
Cleves, John, 125
Colerain, Oxford & Brookville Turnpike,
  29
Colerain Township (Hamilton County),
  194
Columbia Settlement (Hamilton County),
  184
Columbus, Franklinton and, 187–88
*The Communistic Societies of the United
  States* (Nordhoff), 71–72
Compromise (Champaign County), 184
concentric spheres/hollow earth theory,
  53–64

Connecticut, Western Reserve land of, 35
Cooper, Mr. and Mrs. A. B., 141–43
Cordle, Charles, 139
Coshocton County, 201
Cottingham, E. A., 186
county fairs, 172–78
Covington (Miami County), 187
Cowger, Mary and Ed, 74–78
Cowles, Giles H., 35
Cross, Joseph, 118–19
Crosswick (Warren County), 184–85
culture, small town, 17, 30–31
Curtis, Eli, 86–87

Dalton, Dennis, 104–10, 185
Daniels, Robert M., 97–99
Dearwester, Harry C., 172–78
Defiance County, 124–25
Defiance Trail, 190
Delphos (Allen County), 117
Demyas, Jan, 100–101
Devore, Joe, 156
Dewese, Amos, 118
diseases: cholera, 116–17; Great Black
  Swamp and, 114–17; tuberculosis,
  102–3, 108
Dog Town (Eclipse Mine as), 186
Dogtown (Henry County), 123
Dogtown (Licking County), 185
Donnermeyer, Joseph, 195–96
Dorman, Laura Peck, 37

Eagle Township (Hancock County),
  116–17
Eagleville (Ashtabula County), 36–37
Earhart, Estil, 4
Eclipse (Athens County), 185–86
Eliphalet, Aaron C., 36
Ellis, Jesse, 130, 135
Emerson, Ralph Waldo, 82
Emmett (Paulding County), 125
Erastus (Mercer County), 186
Erie County: Sandusky in, 22–23; Venice
  in, 20, 29–30
Euler, Leonhardt, 57
Everett, J., 83
Evers, C. W., 115–16

Fairfield County, 163
Fallsville (Highland County), 186–87

farmers/farms, 28, 35, 41, 182; decline
of, 17, 173; Great Black Swamp and,
120–21, 126–27; Zoar Separatists as,
69–70
Fiehrer, Paul, 30–31
Figgins, Phil, 6, 8
Fite, Jim, 6
Fizzleville (Hiett), Ohio, 3–9
Foos, Joseph, 188
Footville (Ashtabula County), 37–39
forests, clearing Great Black Swamp's,
112–13, 121–22, 124
Fort Defiance, 114
Fort Meigs, 113–14
Fort Rowdy (Miami County), 187
Fort Sandusky, 21
Fox sisters, 82
Franklin County, 187–88
Franklinton (Franklin County), 187–88
Friendly Neighbor Home Demonstration
Club, 127
Funk Bottoms, 188
Funston, John, 195

Galatea (Wood County), 124
Gallatin (Allen County), 190
ghosts, 80, 181, 197; in Great Black
Swamp, 124–25; at Ohio State Refor-
matory, 91–92, 95, 99–101; in Waynes-
ville, 104–5, 108–10; in Zoar, 76–78
Girty, Simon, 113
Glattke, Arthur and Helen, 95
Gloyd, Michael R., 138
Grant, Ulysses S., 200
Great Black Swamp, 111–27; disappear-
ance of, 120–21, 126–27; diseases from,
114–17; ghost towns in, 123–25; roads
in, 117–18, 120, 124
Great Miami River, 28–29; towns on,
191–92, 196–97
Greene County, 179–80
Grenadier Squaw Town (Pickaway
County), 188–89
Grierson, Walter D., 4

Haldeman, Cyrus Benton "Ditty," 32
Hall, William D., 86–87
Halley, Edmund, 57
Hamilton County: horse stealing in, 161–62;
towns of, 184, 191–92, 194–95, 197–98

Hamilton (Hamilton County): Rossville
and, 196–97; Symmes family and,
53–59, 61–62, 64
Hanson, Melanie, 31
Hardyman, John, 5–6
Harmon, R. L., 187
Harper, R. Kevin, 105
Harris, Bill, 188
Harrison, William Henry, 114, 190
Harrison Tunnel, 189–90
Harsha, Paul, 42
Harshaville (Adams County), 42
Hartford (Allen County), 190
Helton, Dorothy, 132
Hemlock (Perry County), 190
Henry County, 123, 199
Henson, Josiah, 23–24
Heywood, Russell H., 26
Hiett (Fizzleville), Ohio, 3–9
Highland County, 10, 186–87
Hill, James B., 120–21
Hill, N. N., 199–200
Hillsboro (Highland County), 17
Hines, Bob, 138–40, 142
Hobson's Choice, 191
Hocking Hills, Robbers' Roost in, 163
Hollow Earth Convention, 55
Hollow Earth Society, 60
Holmes County, 148
Houdini, Harry, 85
Howe, Henry, 58, 112, 189
Huebner, Paul, 123
Huffman, John, 188
Humrickhouse, T. S., 201
Hutt, Fred, 162
Hyob, Lawrence, 30

Indiana, canal from Cincinnati to, 189–90
Indian Hill (Hamilton County), 161
Indians, 21; Mount Nebo and, 79, 82;
relations with pioneers, 43, 181–82,
194; Richardville Reservation of, 196;
towns of, 181, 188–89, 199–201

Jackson, Andrew, 191
Jacksonville (Adams County), 191
Jamison, Rose, 138
Jefferson (Ashtabula County), 33–34
Jennings, John and James, 184–85
Johnson, William K., 201

Jones, Theo, 5
justices of the peace, 131

Kelley, Stephen, 40–50, 191
Kendall, Molly, 132, 135
Kepler, Johannes, 57
Kirtland, Turhand, 35
Klippart, John H., 120
Koons, Jonathon, 82–86
Kuhn, Marvin, 162

Lake Erie, 24, 33; and Great Black Swamp,
    111–12, 114; ports on, 22–23, 25
Larrick, Louisa Stetson, 102–4, 105–10
Larsen, John, 197–98
Lauber, Christian, 113
Lemmon, Jack, 138–39, 141–44
Licking County, 180, 185, 199–200
Little Miami River, 184
Lorenz, Alma and John, 4, 6
Losantiville (Hamilton County), 184
Loveland, James (Hamilton County),
    194–95
Lucas, Robert, 114
Lucas County, 126, 195–96
Lynch, Ed and Joe, 185

Macmillan, Bruce, 45
Mahoning Valley, 34
Mansfield Reformatory Preservation
    Society, 91–93, 100–101
Mansfield (Richland County), 90–101
Marble Furnace (Adams County), 42–43
Marietta (Baltimore and Ohio) Railroad,
    195
Marion County, 162–63
Marirovits, Susan, 34
marriage, in Aberdeen, 128–36
Mason, William P., 23
Massie, Nathaniel, 43
Mast, David, 148
Matthews, Thomas, 57
Maumee River, 195; Great Black Swamp
    and, 111, 113, 115
Maysville, Kentucky, 128–29, 133, 155
McBride, James, 56, 58
McDaniel, Joel, 137
McIlvaine, Right Reverend Bishop,
    25–26

McKimie, Robert "Little Reddy," 18–19
McMahan, John, 39
Mercer County, 162, 183, 186
Miami and Erie Canal, 190, 195
Miami campaign, against Indians, 182
Miami County, 187
Miami (Hamilton County), 192
Middlebury (Van Wert County), 192
Miller, John C., 151–52
Mineral Springs (Adams County), 43–50
monsters, 185
Moore, Isaac, 184
Morgan, John Hunt, 162
Morning Star Community, 86–88
Morrison, Charlie, 139–40, 144
Mount Nebo (Athens County), 79–89
Mueller, Bob, 189
Mueller, Jamie, 193–94
Murphysboro, 186

Naturalist's Guide to the Americas
    (Braun), 47
Naylor, Harriet, 158–59
Naylor, Jim, 157, 159
Naylor, Linda Sue, 159–60
Naylor, Verna and Harry, 157–59
Newark (Licking County), 185
Newport (Adams County), 192
New Rome, 192–94
Niebel, John W., 98
Nofziger, Jacob, 113
Nonhelema, 188
Nordhoff, Charles, 71–72
North Bend (Hamilton County), 191–92

O'Banionville (Hamilton County), 194–95
Ohio and Erie Canal, 66, 69, 71–72
Ohio Historical Society, Zoar maintained
    by, 67, 74
Ohio River, 128
Ohio Small Town Museum, 137–44
Ohio State Reformatory, 90–101, 97
Ohio University, at Athens, 79–80
oil industry, 124, 183, 195
Owensville (Clermont County), 167–71

Parker, Grafton, 156
Patterson, Robert, 184
Paulding County, 113, 121–22, 125